Linda McGinnis

THE BRIDAL BALL

All rights reserved. No part of this publication may be reproduced, stored in a retrieval system, or transmitted in any form or by any means, electronic, mechanical, recording or otherwise, without the prior written permission of the author. This is a work of fiction. The characters, incidents and dialogues in this book are of the author's imagination and are not to be construed as real. Any resemblance to actual events or persons, living or dead, is completely coincidental.

Copyright © 2015 Linda McGinnis

All rights reserved.

ISBN: 10:0996613714
ISBN-13: 978-0-9966137-1-2

To Marla,
whose wedding gown
was worthy of a princess.

ACKNOWLEDGMENTS

With special thanks to Suzy Somers of
R.S.V.P.
an event coordinator with
extraordinary flair, imagination, and generosity.

CHAPTER 1

Kristi Peyton-Scott balanced a heavily loaded tray of dishes and stooped to pick up one last napkin. Cleaning up after the guests had moved upstairs would have been easy if the hostess had turned on the spotlights. Instead, she'd left the crew to work in near darkness. Catering an event in a four-level home was challenging, even in the daytime. In the dark, it was nearly impossible. That night, the sprawling estate sparkled like a spaceship set in a sea of black.

Kristi checked the pool area as best she could; the eco-friendly solar lights were not catering-friendly. Music from the three-piece-band floated out from the hillside mansion and carried over the pool beside her. After one final look, she headed for the downstairs kitchen—one of two in the massive home.

She didn't see the puddle. If she had, of course she would have slowed down—or walked around it. *Of course.* But it was late, she was tired, and all she wanted was to finish clearing the patio and go home.

When her foot hit the water, her heart hit the panic button. She reached out, dishes flying, grasping desperately for anything that would break her fall. She went down hard.

The plates hit the cement and shattered, scattering shards in every direction—toward the lawn, toward the bushes, and toward the incredible infinity pool.

The client, ever-present during the interminable evening fundraiser, rushed out of the kitchen. "What in the world have you done?" Her voice was a barely controlled shriek.

Kristi scrambled to her feet, pushing back curls that had escaped from her headband. "I'm sorry, Mrs. Abernathy. I didn't realize the patio was wet."

"Didn't realize?" The woman's voice was darker than her scowl. "How stupid can you be?"

Their lead crew member, Lexi Solomon, hurried out of the house, broom and dustpan in hand. "I've got it, Kristi," she said, and began to sweep up the debris.

"Be careful, for heaven's sake," Abernathy said. "You'll get it in the pool."

Lexi looked at Kristi, pausing just long enough to see her nod.

"We'll take care of it," Kristi said.

"Why do caterers always manage to make a mess?"

"It's dark. It was an accident."

"Of course it was an accident. Nobody said you did it on purpose. Do you think *I'm* stupid?"

"No, ma'am." Kristi bent to pick up the largest pieces. "We'll clean up all we can tonight and check for any damage tomorrow." Kristi's back hurt now, and her head pounded.

She wanted to sit.

She wanted to chill.

She wanted to get the heck out of there.

"There's bound to be damage. You've dumped half of the dishes into the swimming pool."

"I don't think any of it went into the pool," she said in her talking-a-crazy-client-down-off-a-ledge voice.

Mrs. Abernathy walked over and looked into the water. "I'm sure there's something down there. It's probably ruined the filter already. I'll have to call my insurance agent."

Guilt grabbed Kristi's gut and wadded it up like a dirty dishrag.

"If there's any damage, *our* insurance will cover it. Please, everything has gone so beautifully tonight. You told me yourself that your guests loved the food, right?"

"Well, yes."

Kristi pressed on. "And they thought the floral arrangements were perfect, right?"

"Yes, but..."

"And we served without a single mishap, right?"

"I guess that's true."

Kristi lowered her voice, pulling the woman closer with her tone. "I'll be here in the morning, and we'll make sure everything is in order. There's nothing else we can do about it tonight. Please, go join your guests, and let me take care of this. I'll see you first thing."

"Well..." the client said.

"Does nine o'clock suit you? Or, I could come later."

"Nine o'clock is fine. Please, don't be late."

"At Current Events, we're never late."

The woman huffed up the stairs, exhaling like an old tea kettle with each step.

The minute she'd disappeared, Lexi stopped sweeping. "Are you really okay?"

"Except for a headache, I'm fine."

"Did you hit your head?"

"No."

"Are you sure?"

"Yes." Kristi leaned close to Lexi. "Dealing with her gives me a pain."

"We're almost done. Go sit down and I'll get you some aspirin. You deserve a couple of minutes."

Kristi decided a five minute break wouldn't hurt. She pointed toward the pergola at the far end of the yard. "I'll be over there if you need me."

Kristi walked toward the pergola. Only then did she

notice a distinguished looking, grey-haired gentleman sitting in the shadows, smoking a cigar.

"Are you okay?" he asked. "You took quite a spill."

She flushed, embarrassed that he had seen her fall. "I'm fine, thank you." She sat in the chair farthest from the man, hoping to avoid a conversation.

"You handled that situation very gracefully."

"It was stupid. I wasn't paying attention."

"Accidents happen."

Kristi's boss, Heather Ames, came down the stairs from the upper deck. "Lexi said you fell. Are you okay?" She handed Kristi a bottle of water and a packet of aspirin.

"I'm fine. Completely my fault. I didn't see the puddle."

"Did you hit your head?"

"No."

Heather leaned close to Kristi and whispered, "If she'd put the lights on, you wouldn't have fallen. Don't worry about it. I've been hoping for an excuse not to work for her again." She saw the man, and stopped. "Mr. Townsend. I didn't realize you were here."

Townsend stood and extended his hand. "Hello, Heather. Nice to see you again. You did a fabulous job tonight. The food, the service, the presentation, all flawless, as usual."

"Thank you. But actually, Kristi was in charge tonight."

Townsend looked at Kristi. "You were brilliant at deflecting the flames when the dragon lady attacked."

Heather looked around, as if the woman might magically materialize.

"Don't worry. She's gone."

"Let me introduce my assistant, Kristi Peyton-Scott. I couldn't manage without her. Between her training and natural instinct, she's a *wunderkind*. She runs more than half our events. Kristi, this is JT Townsend. Mr. Townsend owns the Royal Princess Hotel."

Kristi stood slowly, her back protesting every movement. "I'm glad to meet you, Mr. Townsend. I adore the Princess, especially at Christmas. My grandmother used to take me there every year."

"I like hearing that. We work hard to make Christmas at the Princess memorable." He puffed on his cigar and then said, "Keep a close eye on her, Heather. She took a nasty fall."

"Yes, I will." She turned. "They're almost finished inside. You rest a couple of minutes, and we'll be ready to take off. Nice seeing you, Mr. Townsend."

"Please call me JT. I've told you a hundred times."

"Yes, sir," she said, smiling at him. "I remember."

Kristi eased back into her chair.

JT pulled his chair closer to her. "So Kristi, where did you get your training?"

"In New York, at the Cornell School of Hotel Administration."

"Impressive."

"It's a good program. I believe it's ranked in the top ten Hotel and Hospitality schools in the country."

The cigar bobbled when he chuckled. "I believe it's number one."

"You know it?"

"I do." A puff of smoke appeared and then vanished like a silent ghost. "How long have you worked for Heather?"

"Part time through high school, and full time since college."

"And you like catering?"

"I love it. I love working with our clients." She glanced toward the upper deck where Mrs. Abernathy had disappeared. "Most of the time, anyway."

"Some clients are more challenging than others. But I've always believed that catering would be boring if it weren't for the unexpected surprises."

"An interesting viewpoint." One that probably applied only long after an event ended.

Heather came out to them again. "I think we're set. Are you ready to go, Kristi?"

"Yes." Kristi tried her best not to wince or groan as she stood.

"It was nice meeting you, Kristi. Take care of yourself. Heather, I'll talk to you soon."

"Yes, sir," Heather said. "Good night."

"Good night, sir," Kristi said.

"JT, please," he said again, and Heather laughed.

Tension drained from Kristi's shoulders as she followed Heather out to the wide, circular drive. The further she was from the hostess, the better she felt.

"Mr. Townsend seems nice," Kristi said.

"Very nice. As old fashioned as they come. A real gentleman."

"And he owns the Princess?"

"Townsend's great-grandfather built the Princess after the 1906 earthquake. He studied in France before the turn of the century, and apparently fell in love with Art Nouveau design."

"Hold up, you two," Lexi called from behind them.

The women stopped.

"Want me to take Kristi back?" she asked. "You know, in case she smacked her head, and hasn't realized it yet."

"I'm fine, for the fifth time."

"Where is the rest of the crew?" Heather asked.

"Matthew drove them back to the office."

"Good." She glanced at Kristi. "It's not a bad idea. We probably should get her into the city, anyway."

"It's half an hour, for heaven's sake. And, I didn't hit my head." She could make the drive from the hills of Mill Valley to the city by the Bay without any help, thank you.

"I'll meet you at the office," Heather said. "If she still seems okay, we'll let her drive home."

"I'm right here, you know." Kristi handed Lexi her car keys, then climbed in the passenger side. "I'm really fine."

"Sometimes these things don't show up right away," Lexi said.

"You're such a nurse."

"That I am." Lexi started the car, and then followed Heather down the steep, winding driveway.

"How is Tori doing?"

Lexi was looking for a home in the east bay and had been concerned about how her daughter, Tori, would handle the move.

"She's good. She's looking forward to the move. The truth is, she's an easy kid."

"They all are at that age, aren't they?"

"Some not so much. She's precocious. She's impatient. She loves preschool, but can't wait to start kindergarten next year."

"We've got to get together again before she starts high school. I don't want Tori to forget who I am."

"I agree." Lexi slowed the car on the switchback. "I'll call you. We'll make a plan. I promise."

An hour later, after a steaming shower, Kristi crawled into bed, refreshed, relaxed, and rejoicing that the next day was free, a rare Sunday without an event.

*

On Monday, Kristi arrived at the Current Events office at ten o'clock. She had a dinner to run that night, and Heather had told her to come in late.

"Good morning," she told Heather, who was busy at her desk.

"Hi. How're you feeling?"

"A little stiff, but fine, otherwise."

"Did you check on the Abernathy's swimming pool yesterday?"

"I did. Much ado about absolutely nothing. The pool survived the ordeal without a scratch."

"And Mrs. Much Ado?"

"She apologized. She even managed to ask if I was hurt."

"I hope you told her you spent the night in the hospital."

"No, although I think Lexi was ready for that. Since I was still conscious when we got here, she discharged me."

Kristi put her coat and purse in the closet.

"There's one more thing." Heather's tone said talk, but not trouble. "Come sit for a sec."

Kristi perched on one of the chairs across from Heather's desk. "What's up?"

"JT Townsend called me this morning. He wasn't kidding when he said he'd talk to me soon. He was impressed by the way you handled yourself the other night. He says they're looking for an event coordinator at the Princess. He thinks you might be a good fit."

"Me?"

"Yes. He asked me all about you—your background, your responsibilities, your education, your experience. He was quite thorough. However, I had the impression he'd made up his mind before he even picked up his phone."

Kristi didn't know what to say.

"This would be a wonderful opportunity for you, Kristi. Whether you end up with your own business or not, working in a four star hotel would give you valuable experience you wouldn't get here."

"Are you trying to get rid of me?"

"Of course not. But, I don't want to stand in your way, either. You're talented, Kristi, exceptionally talented. You won't be content here for much longer."

"You're wrong. I love working for you. I don't want to go anywhere."

"You're comfortable here."

"Yes."

Heather gave her a mother's-best-friend-knows-best smile.

"What?"

"Nothing. JT would like to talk to you. Do me a favor. Give it some thought."

"Okay."

She went into her office and switched on her computer. They had a busy week ahead; the last thing she needed was to be distracted by an unsolicited job offer.

Unsolicited and probably unwarranted. What did Townsend even know about her? That she was clumsy? That she wasn't rude to a rude client? Why would he want her based on that? And why would she want to work anywhere but Current Events?

Heather brought the subject up three more times that week, each time more insistent that Kristi consider the idea.

"I don't want to work for him. I told you, I love working for you. Besides, I owe you. You gave me my first job."

"Your only job."

"Right. I owe you."

"You owe yourself the chance to grow professionally. All that education and you're back at the same job you had in high school."

She tried to dodge the dart but she knew Heather was right. "That's not fair. I'm exactly where I wanted to be and I'm perfectly happy. If it's not broke…"

"I'd like to hear what Mr. Townsend's offer is, even if you don't. Do it as a favor to me."

After a week of Heather's constant pressure, Kristi made arrangements for her best friend, Laura Fisher, to meet her for brunch at the hotel. Maybe a fresh look around the Princess would help with her decision.

CHAPTER 2

Kristi pulled open the heavy, arched glass door to the Princess Hotel, and walked back into her childhood. Each time she stepped into The Princess, she felt the same happy anticipation as she had the first time. Her grandmother had made every visit there an adventure.

The Art Nouveau, wrought iron grillwork surrounding the entrance doors, guaranteed guests an unforgettable architectural experience. The spacious lobby always featured an elaborate arrangement of brilliant seasonal flowers, combined with greens and tall grasses. The sweet aroma of fresh lilies welcomed Kristi like a warm embrace.

A quick look around the room confirmed what Kristi expected. Laura was late. Laura was always late. For years, Kristi had wanted to get her a license plate that read: *I M L8*.

Of course, Laura always had an excuse. Lately, the excuse had come in the form of her adorable baby girl, Chloe. Kristi tried to be patient and understand that children changed both your plans and your priorities. But, patience was the weakest link in Kristi's armor, and she found herself pacing the floor of the lobby with increasing annoyance.

"May I help you?"

Kristi turned at the sound of the deep voice, and looked up into impossibly deep blue eyes; extraordinary eyes; eyes that could have won awards. Thick, dark eyelashes swept up when he blinked like tiny brooms.

Eyelashes like those were so wasted on a guy.

She clicked on a professional smile. "I'm waiting for a friend."

"Are you here for brunch?"

"Yes." She hoped he wouldn't say anything else. She wanted to gawk, not talk.

He wasn't just beautiful, he was gorgeous. Like a model staring out of a magazine, all healthy and hunky and horribly fit. She knew exactly what his thick, sandy hair would feel like in her fingers. And those eyes…

"Try the salmon. It came in fresh this morning."

"Good to know. I love salmon."

"Then that settles it. Let me know if there's anything I can do for you."

She could come up with an idea or two. "Thank you, I will."

She watched him walk to the concierge desk and sit down. She dragged her eyes away, not wanting to be caught staring. Not a bad place to work if she had *him* to look at every day.

"Hello?"

Kristi started. Somehow, Laura was standing right next to her.

"Hi." Kristi hugged her, noting the faint smell of baby oil.

"Sorry I'm late. Chloe is cutting a new tooth, and she wasn't happy about me leaving."

"No worries." If she'd been on time, Kristi wouldn't have seen the killer concierge. "Are you hungry?"

"Have you ever known me not to be hungry?"

"Nope. Not once in nineteen years." The words astonished her. Nineteen years. How was that possible?

Shortly after Kristi moved to San Francisco, Laura appeared at the front door, and said she expected Kristi to be her new best friend. She explained that her former bestie had lived in that house, and since Kristi now occupied the girl's bedroom, it was only right.

The two women couldn't have looked more different: Kristi, five foot ten, olive-skinned, with wildly curly chestnut-colored hair and green eyes; Laura, five inches shorter, with stick-straight strawberry blond hair, and fabulous blue eyes; they made a stunning contrast wherever they went.

The hostess greeted them with a practiced smile. "Two?"

"Yes," Kristi said. "I have a reservation for Peyton-Scott."

"Please come with me." The woman led them into the lavish dining room, a huge space, richly appointed in the Art Nouveau style.

A broad corridor wrapped around the entire room, punctuated by wide, open arches. Massive crystal chandeliers hung from the domed ceiling, and sparkled even in broad daylight.

To Kristi, it wasn't just majestic, it was magical.

They sat at a linen-draped table in the center of the room. "May I get you something to drink?" the hostess asked.

"We'll each have a mimosa," Kristi said.

Laura looked up in surprise. "We will?"

"We will."

"Very good. I'll be right back."

"What's up, Ms. Peyton-Scott?"

Kristi folded her hands on top of her menu. "I'm having the salmon. It came in fresh this morning."

"Really? Did it walk by you in the lobby?"

"No. The concierge told me."

"Okay. I'm good with salmon."

"Good. Then we're set." Kristi looked around, remembering the first time she'd been there for brunch. "I love this room. My grandmother used to bring me here before the ballet. It was like *being* a princess."

"I remember. I was so jealous. I was the one taking ballet lessons, and you were the one who got to go."

Kristi leaned toward her. "Let's go to *The Nutcracker* this year. You and me. We'll come here for brunch first."

When the hostess brought their drinks, Kristi lifted the delicate flute toward Laura. "Here's to the ballet."

"You still haven't told me what this is all about. Did you get a big raise or something?"

"No. It isn't that. It's sort of complicated. Let's order first."

After the waitress had taken their order, Kristi took another sip of her mimosa and leaned forward. She lowered her voice even though no one was nearby. "Last Saturday, we did a job in Mill Valley—a fundraiser. I can't mention any names, but if I did, you'd recognize them."

This had been the policy ever since Kristi had gone to work at Current Events; Heather's clients were well-known society scions and dot-com millionaires who valued their privacy as much as their portfolios. Laura would never tell anyone else, but even so, Kristi was expected to keep business confidences.

"At the end of the evening, I was collecting dirty dishes around the patio, and I slipped in a puddle of water." She made a face. "The dishes didn't survive." She took another sip, and told Laura about meeting Townsend and his phone call to Heather.

"He wants you to work here?"

"Shhh. Not so loud."

Laura looked around. "This place is beautiful. What's holding you up?"

"It's a big change. You know how much I love something new."

"When was the last time you changed anything but your underwear?"

Kristi grimaced at Laura's all too accurate observation. It was true: she hated change. The move from Seattle to San Francisco after her father died had nearly killed her. At eleven, Kristi thought nothing could hurt more than losing her father. The move proved just how naïve she was.

"Think about it: you live in the same house where you grew up; you've worked the same job since high school; your hair is the same; your perfume is the same; I'd be surprised if your underwear wasn't the same."

"How do you stand it? I'm a bore."

"That wasn't what I said, and you know it. What does Heather think?"

"She wants me to consider it."

"Told you."

The grilled salmon came with fettuccini Alfredo, and a salad of mixed red, yellow, and orange peppers, with purple onion, and slivers of green zucchini. The plate was as colorful as a toddler's toy box.

Kristi took her first bite of salmon, and moaned. The rich, creamy fish melted in her mouth like butter in a hot skillet. "Oh, Lord. This is orgasmic."

"I see you took my advice."

Kristi looked up into the amused blue eyes and blushed pinker than the salmon. "Yes," she said, managing a smile. "It's delicious."

Was it possible he was even better looking than when she first saw him?

"I'm glad. Enjoy," he said, and continued through the dining room.

Kristi was sure she heard him chuckling.

"And that was...?"

"The concierge. The one I mentioned earlier."

Laura's grin stretched as wide as the Golden Gate Bridge. "Take the job."

*

The next day, Kristi asked Heather about Townsend's request.

"Are you considering it?"

"Sort of. Laura and I went there for brunch yesterday. The dining room is a beautiful place."

"It is. Of course, your office might not be so grand."

"No. Nor would I be a guest there. But, I could walk around it once in a while." She thought of the concierge. "You seemed to know Mr. Townsend fairly well. Why is that?"

"I did several events at the Princess years ago. After Wilhelm Müller was hired as event coordinator, he started running the events himself. He's very territorial—prefers everything done in-house."

"What happened to him?"

"JT says they're reorganizing their management structure. Wilhelm is now the Assistant General Manager."

"How is he to work with?"

"I don't really know. I haven't heard any complaints. But then, our clients don't say much about other event planners."

Kristi was quiet for a bit.

"What are you thinking?"

Kristi scooted forward in the chair to a spot that, after all her years of doing so, should have been worn thin. "I have this idea; sort of a dream; something I've been thinking about for a couple of years."

"What's that?"

"I call it 'The Bridal Ball.' It's a themed event designed to give women a chance to dance with their husbands, in their bridal gowns, without all the pressure and stress that come with a wedding. I've always pictured it in the Crown Ballroom at The Royal Princess."

"Sounds romantic. What prompted this lovely idea?"

"Laura never got to dance in her wedding dress. There was a gas leak in the hotel where they had the reception, and we were evacuated. She cried about it for weeks. All her planning and preparation shot to heck by a hole in a pipe. She still dreams about that dance."

"I see."

"Ever since, I've tried to figure out how to give Laura a re-do. I'm sure lots of women would like to wear their wedding gown again. After all, it's the most expensive dress they've ever bought, they only wore it once, and the day was full of frayed nerves, fussy kids, and a fractious mother-in-law."

"You make a wedding sound like such fun. Remind me to keep you away from our brides in the future."

"You know what I mean."

"I do. It's a stunning idea and I'm amazed no one has thought of it before. You're spot on about wedding dresses. Women love them. The Crown Ballroom would be the perfect setting; that stained glass ceiling is the epitome of elegance. Just walking in makes you feel like royalty. You know, if you worked there, you'd have a good chance of making it happen."

"You think I should consider it?"

"You should certainly talk to Mr. Townsend and see what he's offering."

"Okay. I'll call him and set up an appointment. One thing though, if I decide against taking the job, you'll accept that, right?"

"If you turn it down, maybe I'll take it."

*

Three days later Kristi stood in the spacious foyer of the Royal Princess Hotel, her chest full of excitement and expectation. Her trim grey suit, white silk blouse, and Jimmy

Choo heels said class and style without a word being spoken. She wished she felt as confident as she was sure she looked. She'd be fine as long as there were no unseen puddles.

She was heading toward the front desk when she heard the deep, sexy voice. "May I help you?"

She turned, and he smiled at her—a beautiful smile, the perfect smile to complement the beautiful eyes.

"Well, hello. Back for more salmon?"

She felt blushing pink press against the collar of her blouse. "No. Actually, I'm here to see Mr. Townsend."

The beautiful blues narrowed. "I'm Mr. Townsend."

"Uh, the Mr. Townsend I'm talking about is a bit older."

"Oh. You're thinking of my father, then, JT?"

JT's son was the concierge? "Yes."

His face changed from pleasant to perturbed. He looked like he was going to say something, but instead, turned and walked to the clerk at the front desk. "Have you seen my father?"

"Yes. About ten minutes ago. He said he was going into the dining room."

Josh considered her answer before turning back to Kristi. "Why don't you come with me?"

She followed him down the heavily carpeted hallway to the dining room. Why hadn't Heather mentioned JT had a son—a son who obviously didn't appreciate the fact that she was meeting with his father?

The majesty of the dining room was lost on Kristi as she followed Josh in quick step to his father's table.

"This young lady says she's here to see you?" he said, stopping abruptly next to JT's chair.

JT stood. "Kristi. How nice to see you again. Please, join me."

Tension hung heavy between the two men like thick smoke from a wet fire. Kristi sensed that sitting down with JT would be crossing into the DMZ.

She looked at Josh, hoping for a reassuring sign.

"Go ahead. I'm sure we'll be talking later."

"Thank you." She eased into the chair JT had pulled out for her.

"Coffee?" JT offered as Josh walked away.

"Yes, thank you."

And maybe a shot of bourbon. She had a feeling she might need it before the day was over.

CHAPTER 3

Kristi sat back, doing her best to look relaxed. "I brought you a copy of my resume, and three letters from clients I've worked with the past several months." Kristi handed JT a file folder.

He glanced at them and put them aside. "I've spoken to several of Heather's clients this week. Without exception, they were pleased with your work. They all agreed you have a special talent. It shows. And, it's precisely what we've been looking for at the Princess."

"Heather told me you're reorganizing."

"Yes. Our former Event Coordinator, Wilhelm Müller, is now the Assistant General Manager."

"I'm guessing the majority of events here are weddings."

"Weddings and corporate dinners. If you accept the position, you can say goodbye to your weekends."

"I did that months ago."

"It's not an easy life. It's demanding, and can often be thankless."

"But so worth it when you see the look on a satisfied client's face."

They talked for nearly an hour before JT asked, "Do you have any concerns about accepting the position?"

"It would be a big change for me. I'm not entirely sure I'm ready to leave Current Events."

"I think we can make it worth your while."

"It isn't that…" she began, but faltered. She wasn't ready to tell a stranger her innermost fears. "I do have one conflict. I'm on a panel speaking to the Consortium of Hotel Event Coordinators the last weekend of next month. I can't back out on my commitment. It's been on the calendar for nearly a year."

"Is that the one in Yosemite?"

"Yes, at the Ahwahnee."

"If I'm not mistaken, Wilhelm is registered for that as well. He rarely misses a chance to attend a conference. I think Josh and I can manage one weekend without both of you." He gave her a moment and then asked, "Anything else?"

"Not that I can think of."

"The question is, are you interested? If so, I'll have you spend a little time with Wilhelm."

Anticipation bloomed in her chest and brought an unexpected smile to her lips. "I'm interested."

"Fine. Come with me, and we'll take the next step."

Wilhelm was in his office, and from the look he gave them, not prepared to be interrupted.

"Wilhelm, this is Kristi Peyton-Scott. I believe she's the perfect candidate to fill your former position."

"Oh?" Wilhelm said, the word double-dipped in doubt.

"Here is her resume," JT said, handing Wilhelm the folder. "As you can see, she's been an assistant to Heather Ames for several years."

JT's overstatement did not appear to impress Wilhelm, who was still frowning. He gestured toward a chair for Kristi to sit down.

"When you're done, please bring her to Josh's office."

"It won't be long. I have a tight schedule today."

"You always do," JT said. Kristi couldn't miss the amusement in his voice.

"Yes, well, I'll see you shortly."

Although his accent was thick, Wilhelm wasn't difficult to understand. She thought he had probably been in the United States for some time. He looked back at Kristi. "So, you fancy yourself an event coordinator."

His words left no possibility of misunderstanding. Carefully, she said, "I trained with Heather Ames during high school, graduated from Cornell's School of Hotel Administration, and have worked with Heather ever since."

"There's a big difference between Current Events and the Princess," he said, sounding as though she were trying to parlay a job at a fast food faire into a prime position at the Princess.

"Yes. Heather thought working here would round out my experience." She did her best to sound respectful, but struggled to get past his cold condescension.

"What do you know about the Princess?"

"I know about its history. I studied your website and read what I could find online. My grandmother used to bring me here for brunch before the ballet."

"A limited view. Tell me about the last three events you did with Heather."

She tried every approach she could think of, but after talking for nearly half an hour, Wilhelm was every bit as aloof as he had been when she walked into his office.

"It's been nice meeting you," he said, standing. "I'll take you to Josh's office and get back to work."

She picked up her purse, took a business card from the stand on his desk, and followed him out the door. It would take more than a cute concierge to convince her to take this job.

He led her to a large, airy suite, and introduced her to Josh's administrative assistant, Debby Cunningham.

"At the moment, Josh is in a meeting," Debby said, glancing at the closed door to her left. "Let me get you a cup of coffee while you're waiting."

"That isn't necessary."

"It may be a while. How do you take it?"

"Black is fine."

"I'll be right back," Debby told her.

Kristi glanced at the business card in her hand. She was glad JT had said Wilhelm's name with a V in place of a W. She felt sure his ridicule would be as sour as his face.

Debby had been gone only moments when the door to Josh's office opened, then closed again, though not completely. Tense voices carried out to Kristi.

"You said you were retiring, Dad. If you've changed your mind, I'd like to know. It's only fair. Not only to me, but to all our employees. It's hard to run a business with two heads. No one knows who's in charge. Especially me."

"I did retire, Josh. And, you are in charge. If you aren't impressed with her, don't hire her. But, I've seen her at work, and I'm convinced she's the perfect fit. She'll add a human touch to that department, which we badly need."

"Perhaps. But, she's young. She hasn't had a lot of experience. Can she handle our crew? Will they respect her? Will she be able to get the job done at the level of excellence we maintain at the Princess?"

"From everything I've seen and heard, I'm confident she can."

"Here's the other thing, Dad. Don't quote me on this, or I'm sure I'd find myself in front of the Labor Board. She's good-looking—too good-looking. Some guy is going to come along, sweep her off her Jimmy Choo's, and carry her away."

Kristi looked down at her shoes. He recognized Jimmy Choo?

"That's a chance I'd be willing to take," JT said, and opened the door. "Ah, Kristi. What perfect timing. Josh and I were just now finishing up."

She stood.

"Come on in," he said, swinging the door wide.

Josh came around from behind his desk and extended his hand. "Hi, Kristi. It's nice to see you again."

His deep voice resonated down his arm and tingled in her hand. It was similar to his father's, but had a sexy undertone that reverberated through her entire body.

Or was it her?

"Thank you."

"I'll see you soon, Kristi," JT said. Kristi watched Josh's smile morph into a grimace.

Why did JT want to see her later?

And, why did Josh object?

Josh was right: a creature with two heads was a confusing entity.

Josh sat behind a rich, walnut desk, which said important, but not self-important. His look was a mixture of resignation and anticipation. "You seem to have bewitched my father. Not just anyone could have brought him out of retirement."

"That can't be good," she said, hoping to make him smile.

"No, it certainly isn't."

She had no idea what to do. Try to convince him she could handle the job? Get up and leave?

"You have an impressive resume. Where do you see yourself in five years?"

The classic interview question, but after what she'd just heard, she knew her answer was critical if she wanted this job.

"I see myself having five years of additional experience; of knowing better how to satisfy clients, manage staff, and keep a part of myself *for* myself. I'd like to grow professionally by staying involved in relevant organizations, and taking courses to improve my knowledge base."

He was quiet for a bit, and then said, "My father is convinced you're the ideal person for this job, Kristi, and he's known to be a good judge of character. We'll put a proposal in the mail. Give me a call after you get it, and we'll meet again." He stood. "It was a pleasure to see you."

Kristi popped to her feet, and shook his outstretched hand like a robot, struggling to recover from his abrupt dismissal. She left his office in near shock.

JT was standing at the concierge desk when Kristi reached the lobby. "You weren't in there long. How did it go? I hope you weren't too hard on him."

"He only asked me a few questions, and then he said he'd send me a proposal. Maybe your recommendation was enough."

"I better get back in there and make sure it's a good package. I wouldn't want you to turn us down."

"Thank you, sir."

"What will I have to do to get you to call me JT?"

"That would hardly be appropriate if I'm going to be working here."

His face brightened like one of the chandeliers. "Are you?"

"That depends on the package."

His pat on her arm was paternal but not patronizing. "Then I'd better get to work. I'll see you soon."

Traffic was heavy when Kristi drove out of the hotel garage. The Princess was located on Van Ness Avenue, not far from Fisherman's Wharf. She looked at the hotel in her rear view mirror. The Princess was beautiful, and Josh Townsend was beautiful. But, working there might be ugly. The conflict between Josh and JT could be nasty to navigate.

No matter how appealing the offer, the reality of three men, all with different expectations, was daunting. And that was before the job even started.

Did she want that?

Maybe she should forget the job and ask Josh for a date.

He really was gorgeous.
Was he married? She hadn't seen any pictures in his office; didn't notice a ring on his finger. Surely if there were a woman in his life there'd be some sign of her.
Maybe, like her, he had no time for a relationship.
Maybe she could fix that.
Maybe.
If she didn't take the job.

*

Kristi lived in the converted second story apartment of her mother's Sunset District home, the home where they'd lived since Kristi's father's death.
When Victoria Peyton married Evan Scott, she married the love of her life. After he died, she devoted herself to Kristi and her art. She had paintings hanging in three Bay Area galleries. The only thing that kept her mother from her easel was the arthritis that plagued their family.
Kristi stopped at a neighborhood market to buy fish and fresh vegetables. She had told her mother she would fix dinner that night. On a lark, she grabbed a bottle of champagne. They might be having a celebration soon.
She let herself in and called, "I'm home. I'm going up to change."
She barely heard her mother's voice. "I'm in the studio."
"I'll be back down in five."
She ran up to her apartment, turned on all the lights as she walked through to her bedroom, and stripped down to her underwear. She hung up the suit and blouse, then pulled on a pair of sweats. She put her Jimmy Choo's into the shoe rack, and again wondered how Josh had recognized the brand. Maybe his girlfriend wore Jimmy Choo heels. With those eyes, he must have a girlfriend—or a wife.
Or maybe, just maybe, he was single.

"How did your interview go?" her mother asked when she joined Kristi in the kitchen.

"Really well. They're going to send me a proposal." She pulled out fresh dill to make a sauce for the salmon, and chopped it fine.

"Do you need any help?"

"No, thanks." She put water into a pan and added rice. "What did you work on today, Mom?"

"Nothing important. Tell me more about the interview."

"I talked to Mr. Townsend first, then the former event coordinator, Wilhelm Müller, and finally to Josh, who is Mr. Townsend's son."

"But not the one with the eyes?" her mother asked, getting plates out of the cupboard.

"The son *is* the one with the eyes."

"So, what do you think?"

"Wilhelm was unimpressed, condescending, and dismissive. Josh is pleasant, but he thinks his father should stay retired, and not bring in prospective employees. There's a lot of tension between those two. Other than that, it went beautifully."

"And you think you want to work there?"

"Heather thinks it'd give me valuable experience." She took goblets from an under-counter rack, and poured them each a glass of white wine. "Otherwise, she wouldn't have encouraged me."

"I hate to see you leave a job you love, to take a position where the work atmosphere might be unpleasant."

"Don't you think I can win them over with my happy-face earrings?"

Her mother's laughter was quick and light. "I'd forgotten about those. You're right. That would do the trick. By all means, take the job."

"Let's wait until I get the proposal."

"I see you bought champagne."

Kristi stuck the bottle on the bottom shelf of the

refrigerator. "We'll open it when I get the letter. One way or another, we'll celebrate."

"You think you might not like the offer?"

"I think it depends on who writes it. Wilhelm isn't going to do me any favors; Josh is indifferent; and JT is like a doting godfather."

Kristi's mother raised her glass. "In that case, here's to JT."

*

On Friday night, Kristi met Laura and their friend Nicole Jackson at a sushi restaurant on Chestnut Street, not far from Nicole and her husband's beautiful Victorian home. For years, the three had met once a month for GNO.

Kristi pulled out the chair next to Laura. "I can't believe you got here before I did. We've had Girls' Night Out for ages, and you've *never* made it here first."

"It'll probably never happen again," Laura said. "We should check the stars for alignment. This might call for a lottery ticket."

"Did you order me a glass of wine?"

"Naturally," Laura said.

"What's up, guys?" Kristi asked.

"Same old, same old," Laura told her. "What are you up to, Nicole? Did you ever hear back from Cal Poly about your degree?"

Laura and Nicole had met when they were living in the same dorm at Cal Poly, San Luis Obispo. After Nicole's website business took off, she spent more time on it than she did on classwork. During her senior year, she stopped attending a programming class, but failed to do the paperwork to drop it. The incomplete prevented her from graduating. At the time, she didn't care.

In September, she'd decided to make up the class at San Francisco State, in order to complete her Bachelor's. Her alma mater had not been impressed.

"I'm still arguing with them."

"Why don't you hack into their system and fix your grade?" Kristi asked, her sweet face a pretense of innocence.

"They wouldn't know the difference, and breaking in would certainly prove you could do the work."

Laura nudged her. "That's not funny."

"I think it is," Nicole said.

"You could get in some major trouble." Laura took a drink of wine. "Is it worth it?"

"Chill," Kristi said. "I was kidding."

"I wasn't," Nicole said.

After they ordered dinner, Laura said, "Kristi has news."

Nicole looked at Kristi. "You met someone?"

"Not *that* kind of someone." Kristi told her about JT, the Princess, and the anticipated offer.

"You'll be married to the job." Nicole's voice was tinged with disgust.

"Like she's not already? I think it would be a good move. Different venue, if nothing else."

Kristi ignored the barbs. "Besides the whole change thing, my main concern is Wilhelm. He's so...sour. Dealing with him could be a major pain."

"Too bad JT wouldn't be your boss," Nicole said. "It sounds as if you could wrap him around one of those well-manicured fingers."

Nicole kept her nails clipped short, and had always admired Kristi's nails, which were faithfully manicured.

"I think you should take the job just so you can hang out with the concierge," Laura said. She looked at Nicole. "He's gorgeous. Ghirardelli grade eye candy."

"He isn't the concierge, as it turns out. He's JT's son. And, he's not much happier about the prospect of me working there than Wilhelm."

"Write down the pros and cons," Laura said. "That will

tell you which way to go."

"I'd compare salaries and hours, and then choose the job with the best food." Nicole picked up a piece of sashimi and lifted it to her lips. "This is delicious."

"How can you eat the way you do, and never gain any weight?" Laura asked.

"She has a gym at her house instead of a nursery," Kristi said, "not to mention a workstation on her treadmill."

"It's a necessity. More importantly, it's a write-off." Nicole popped a sesame seed–covered roll into her mouth.

They were quiet for a while, as sushi and wine disappeared from plates and glasses.

"Have either of you heard from Sam?" Kristi asked.

Samantha Colton, who referred to herself as their D'Artagnan, was a travel writer with a penchant for the exotic. She and Laura had met in a scuba-diving class; Laura broke up with the boyfriend who wanted her to learn, and never actually dove. Sam, on the other hand, had written about scuba diving all around the world.

"She's in Belize," Nicole said. "Haven't you seen the post on her web page? She's been diving in the Great Blue Hole. She took some incredible pictures. Just looking at them gave me the creeps. I can't imagine myself swimming into a black hole in the ocean that's four hundred feet deep. She's nuts."

"I think I'd rather do that than paragliding," Laura said. "Imagine jumping off a mountain where the only thing between you and death is a piece of silk."

"It's a parachute," Kristi said, "not a camisole"

"Even so."

"The worst—the very worst," Laura said, "was bungee jumping over that river in Brazil."

"That was full of piranhas!" Kristi shuddered. "Yes. Crazy. She is certifiably insane."

Nicole shook her head, as if understanding were too mysterious to imagine. "She loves the adrenaline rush. It's not normal." She pointed to a piece of dragon roll on Kristi's plate. "Are you going to eat that?"

Kristi pushed the plate toward her. "Go ahead. I'm saving myself for something sweet. We're going to the dessert bar over on California Street, right?"

"That's the plan," Nicole said, finishing the roll.

"Nobody ever answered my question about Sam. Has anyone actually spoken to her?"

"You mean as in a proof of life?" Nicole laughed. "When was the last time she bothered reassuring any of us?"

"No verbal contact," Laura said. "But, as long as she keeps posting, I think we can assume she's safe."

"Why couldn't she get a job for a newspaper like a normal person?" Nicole asked.

"She told me she tried normal once," Kristi said. "Worst two minutes of her life."

"She'll never settle down. Her DNA doesn't have that twist. She'll wander for the rest of her life," Laura agreed.

Kristi leaned back, thinking of Sam. Sam loved the unknown, Kristi loved knowing. Sam loved the unexpected, Kristi loved routine. Sam loved freedom, Kristi loved stability. Yet in many ways, they were just alike. "She'll settle down when she falls in love."

Laura shook her head. "Not going to happen."

"Someday," Kristi said, "the right guy will come along and poof, like magic—she'll be back home."

"Planning a big wedding at the Princess," Nicole hummed the opening notes of the "Wedding March".

"No chance," Laura said. "She'll find some sky diving minister, and say her vows at thirteen thousand feet above the Loire Valley."

"Holding a Go Pro," Kristi said.

Nicole nodded. "It'll be one hell of a reception."

And, Kristi knew that none of them would miss it.

"Well, this bridesmaid will meet her in the drop zone, hand her a bouquet, and a glass of champagne," Laura said.

"And since we'll be in France, it will be *real* champagne."

"If everybody's finished," Nicole said, "let's get the check and get ourselves over to the dessert café."

Kristi nudged her. "Don't you ever get tired of pushing?"

"Nope."

*

The offer from Josh arrived on Monday, and was more generous than Kristi could have anticipated. She took the letter to work on Tuesday and showed it to Heather.

Heather read down the page, then glanced up at Kristi. "Somebody at the Princess wants you, and is willing to pay a princely sum to get you."

"It certainly isn't Wilhelm. I doubt it's Josh. Which only leaves JT. I heard them talking in Josh's office before my interview. I'm sure they didn't realize the door was ajar. If I had to guess, I'd say Josh's idea of retirement is completely different from his father's."

"That could work for you, or it could work against you. The worst thing you could do is play one against the other. Make them be clear about whom you report to, and don't deviate from that. Never go behind anyone's back, or the knife will ultimately end up in yours."

"You think I should take the job?"

"Yes, I do. I certainly would. You don't have to stay there forever."

"You mean I can come back to Current Events?"

Heather leaned across the desk and handed the letter back to Kristi. "Try to think of it as moving forward, not marking time until you can move backward."

"I suppose I should just jump in at the deep end."

"You're a good swimmer, Kristi. Do it."

Kristi found herself nodding in agreement even though she had doubts. Doubts would surely dissipate with experience, wouldn't they? "Okay."

Heather was right. It was time.

"That said, I could use your help for the next couple of weeks while I decide on your replacement. It's going to be tricky. Matthew will be a big help. Lexi, too. I told them you might be leaving, and they said they'd fill in wherever they can. But they can't take your place."

"Matthew's a good guy. And, Lexi is terrific."

"But it's hit and miss with Lexi. She works three days a week at the hospital, and she naturally wants to spend as much time as she can with her little girl."

"I'll insist on two weeks' notice." She paused and then said, "Thank you, Heather. To be honest, I think you're right about this. It's beginning to feel like the right move."

Excitement bubbled in her stomach. Her future held a new job, a new venue, and perhaps best of all, Josh Townsend.

CHAPTER 4

Kristi arrived at Josh's office late that afternoon; Debby buzzed Josh on the intercom, to tell him she was there. Moments later, he appeared in the doorway. "Hi, Kristi. Please, come in."
 She followed him into his office, where he motioned to a chair. "Please, sit. That is, unless you intend to refuse our offer." His laugh was short and sharp and said the possibility was remote. "I think my dad eliminated that option."
 It wasn't so much his laugh; it wasn't so much his look; it wasn't even his semi-smug-smile that made her do it; it was the thought that throwing him off balance would be good sport. "Actually, I don't think the offer is all that impressive."
 If eyebrows had wings, they couldn't have flown up faster. "What?"
 She fought for a straight face, but her years in Children's Theater failed her. Try as she might, she couldn't repress the grin. "I'm kidding. It's a fabulous offer. I'd be crazy not to accept."
 His smile simmered a moment and then spread. "You got me."

"Sorry. I couldn't resist."

"I hope you can keep that sense of humor while you're working with Wilhelm. He takes events at the Princess pretty seriously."

"Yes, I noticed."

"You'll be reporting directly to him."

"Thanks for making that clear. I wondered about the chain of command."

"You and the chef report to Wilhelm; he reports to me."

"If you don't mind me asking, where does your father fit in?"

"I've been asking myself that question for months," he said, and then looked like he wished he hadn't. "Dad retired a year ago. At least that's what it said on the cake. The problem is, he lives here. My great-grandfather built a penthouse for the family on the top floor. Dad has no hobbies—nothing to do whatsoever—except hang around here and…"

He stopped suddenly, and straightened. "Dad's retired. I'm in charge."

It was like watching a soliloquy. Kristi was surprised that he'd divulged so much. "I take it he's in the hotel a lot."

"Every day. This was his office; he has no place to go. He just wanders around and…"

"…confuses people?"

"Pretty much."

"So, I should check with you about a conflict I have at the end of next month."

"You mean the conference in Yosemite?"

"Yes. He said you could manage without Wilhelm and me for one weekend."

"It'll require some planning; schedule changes, at least. We'll figure all that out."

His eyes were, Kristi wasn't sure what. Frustrated, maybe?

"We'll cover your costs, of course."

"That's very generous."

He laughed again, this time with less delight. "Exactly what I told Dad."

She was suspended between the two men, like a lakeside dock with a boat tied on either side, knocking against the mooring. "I don't mind paying."

"It's not a problem. We'll cover it. Anything else?"

"Heather needs time to find a replacement. She was hoping for two weeks. I could be here this Thursday for orientation if you'd like, and one day next week as well. Or, I could wait."

"Let's wait." He looked at his calendar. "Can you start two weeks from today?"

"Yes."

"Good. Let's plan on that."

"Does Wilhelm know you offered me the position?"

"He does."

His tone left no doubt; Wilhelm was not thrilled. Another boat at the dock. "I'm sure he would have preferred more say in the matter."

"We all would," Josh said, and then quickly added, "but I'm sure you are well qualified and will do a fine job."

"I'll do my best."

"We can't ask for more." He picked up a packet from the credenza behind his desk. "This is the Employee Handbook, a copy of the benefit package, and a bushel of paperwork for you to fill out. Debby included a parking pass as well. You'll have your own space in the garage."

She took the packet, which weighed as much as a small town phone book.

"I intended to introduce you to the chef, but he already left for the day. He works longer hours than anyone. We kick him out early whenever we can."

He glanced up when they heard a knock at the door.

"Am I interrupting?" JT asked.

Kristi watched exasperation bloom on Josh's face, then

fold as fast as it appeared.

"Come in, Dad."

"What's the verdict?" JT asked, walking around the desk to stand beside Josh.

"She accepted our offer."

Kristi heard how-could-she-have-refused in his voice.

"Good, good, good," JT said. "When can you start?"

"Two weeks from today," Josh answered before Kristi could respond.

"Wonderful."

Josh stood. "I think that's about everything."

She got up, too, startled by his dismissal.

"If you're finished," JT said, "let me take you for a cup of coffee."

Josh's expression was another knock from the boat.

"I'd love that," she said, "but I'll have to take a rain check. Heather is expecting me to help with an event tonight."

She watched Josh's eyes narrow, appraising her. It had been the right response.

"Another time, then," JT said.

"I'll see you in two weeks," Kristi said, eager to escape.

"We're looking forward to it," JT told her.

He was; the other two, not so much.

She drove away from the hotel, still jarred by the banging of the boats.

Debby called her the next day. "It would be helpful if I could turn in your paperwork to Personnel before your first day. Is there any chance you could get it back to me next week?"

"Sure," Kristi said. She looked at her calendar. "We're not busy on Monday. I could bring it over in the afternoon."

"That would be great. It'll make a smoother day when you start."

And, it would give her another look at the stunning not-concierge.

"See you then."

Kristi had done her best not to think of Josh except as her boss. His eyes made it difficult. They drew her in like the Great Blue Hole in Belize—deep and mysterious, full of the promise of adventure.

She thought of the look he gave her after the salmon remark. She'd love to see that look again. She'd love to hear that laugh again. She'd love to…

Stop, stop, stop.

She should never cross That Line.

Never.

Still, she savored the thought of a trip to his office, just as she would a delicious dessert.

*

She arrived at Josh's office on Monday afternoon, disappointed to find he wasn't even there. She was glad she'd resisted the urge to dress up.

She handed Debby her paperwork. "I think it's complete. Call me if I missed anything."

Debby flipped through the stack. "Looks good to me. I'll pass it on to Personnel. They'll get in touch if they find any problems."

"I'll see you next week."

"Take care," Debby said, already back at her computer.

Kristi looked for the staircase to the garage, a small concession to her need for exercise. Every flight of stairs she took, helped her avoid going to work out. When she finished at the end of her work day, she was finished with a capital F: a twenty-four hour gym was the last place she wanted to go.

That night she called Lexi to thank her for working extra hours for Heather.

"You're welcome, of course. I can use the extra money for the new house. Assuming we get it. These foreclosures take forever."

"I'll keep my fingers crossed."

"Thanks."

"And, as soon as I'm dialed in at work, we'll get together."

"Deal. Good luck, Kristi."

"Thanks."

On Friday, melancholy struck Kristi like a delivery van; leaving Current Events was like leaving the nest. She made one last check in her desk drawers. "I'm really going to miss you, Heather. I sure hope this isn't a mistake."

"Any time you have a free weekend, you're welcome to come visit us at the jobsite. We can always use extra help."

"I imagine I'll have fewer weekends off at the Princess than I've had here."

"I imagine you're right."

"Any last-minute advice?"

"Only what I've always said: a successful event comes from listening; it has to have energy in the room; and most important of all, it's the client's event, not your event."

"How long did it take to figure it out?"

"About six months of mediocre events."

"They'll fire me if it takes that long."

"You'll do fine, Kristi. And you can always call me if you get into a bind."

"Thanks, Heather. You know I've loved every day I've worked for you."

"I'm glad. You may find working for Wilhelm a challenge. Still, I know this experience will be valuable, so even if it gets tough, stick with it. You won't be sorry."

CHAPTER 5

Kristi felt wrapped in the bright Bay sunlight when she arrived on her first day at the Princess. She greeted the garage attendant, making a mental note to remember his name. The cast of characters at the hotel was larger than the one at Current Events, and she intended to learn their names quickly.

Once upstairs, she spoke to the *real* concierge, the desk clerks, and the hostess in the dining room. She found the door to Wilhelm's office closed; there was no response when she knocked.

Debby arrived five minutes later. "I don't know what's wrong; Wilhelm is never late."

Kristi wondered if Wilhelm was sending her a message. The man's rudeness when they met, and now his failure to be there to welcome her on her first day, seemed clear signs that he was not happy to have her at the Princess.

She was sitting in Debby's office when Wilhelm walked in half an hour later. "I didn't expect you so early," he said, as if she were at fault.

Kristi bit her tongue, unwilling to argue or apologize.

"I suppose we'll have to find a place for you to work

until your office is ready."

Kristi looked at Debby for support, but the woman was busy on the phone.

"For the moment, you can use my office. Come along."

She followed him down the hall to his office, where he offered her nowhere to put her purse or her jacket. She sat across from his desk and waited while he made three calls.

Finally, he turned his attention to her. "We'll start you out slowly, Kristi, to give you time to learn our procedures before you run any events."

"I was in charge of at least half of the functions at Current Events."

He cut her off. "The Princess has a reputation for excellence that I'm not willing to jeopardize. When I'm convinced you're sufficiently prepared, I will ask you to help run an event."

If he held the reins any tighter, she'd choke.

"What I'd hoped for in the Event Coordinator was someone with a vision of their own; someone with fresh ideas to offer; someone who could bring expertise to the table, and make every function at the hotel an event unrivaled anywhere else in this city." He gave her a look that said she was not that person.

"I plan to do all I can to…"

"Good. Let's get started." He handed her a file. "This is our packet for new clients. Please familiarize yourself with the forms."

She had expected him to show her the facilities, introduce her to the staff, at the very least welcome her on board. This was the antithesis of being hired by Heather, who had welcomed her with the warmth extended to family.

Was this a mistake?

*

She spent the day in Wilhelm's office, like a recalcitrant

school girl remanded to the principal's custody. Every move, every question, every comment, was met with a rude response.

Wilhelm was in and out of the office, supervising the two events scheduled that day. Kristi looked through the notebook of past events four times. Was she supposed to memorize it?

At five o'clock, JT knocked on the door.

"Come in," Wilhelm said.

"So this is where you've been hiding her," JT said. "How was your first day, Kristi?"

Horrid.

"Fine," she said.

"She has a lot to learn," Wilhelm said.

"She graduated from Cornell, Wilhelm. I doubt there's much she hasn't learned."

Wilhelm looked at Kristi. "That's all for today. We'll pick up at the same place tomorrow."

"I'd like to stay and watch the event tonight."

"I'm afraid you'd be in the way."

"Nonsense," JT said. "She's been in charge of functions five times as big." He looked at Kristi. "Have you been in here all day?"

"Yes."

JT's look said he was not pleased. "No tour?"

"No."

"I thought…" Wilhelm began, but he had no chance to finish.

"Come with me," JT said. "I want you to meet Tony."

Once again, JT was taking her across an invisible line. Kristi was sure Wilhelm would charge her dearly for the trip.

"I'll see you tomorrow, Kristi," Wilhelm said. "Try not to be late."

"No, I'll be here by seven-thirty, just like this morning," she said, unwilling to allow him the last word; another trip that would no doubt cost her.

"Tony Lugano is our Chef," JT told her. "He's a great guy, fabulously talented and easy to work with. He's not a prima donna like some folks around here."

He led her through a labyrinth of hallways to the enormous kitchen, where the tempting aroma of simmering sauces filled the air.

"Tony," JT said, "this is Kristi Peyton-Scott. She's the one I talked to you about."

Kristi had expected a much older man. Tony appeared to be about fourteen, tall and gangly, with a smile he could use to melt butter.

"Glad to meet you, Kristi." Tony shook hands like he was beating eggs. "Real glad. It's great to have some fresh ideas coming into the place."

"It's nice to meet you too. How long have you been at the Princess?"

"Ten years."

He must have started when he was four.

"I came here from the Culinary Institute in New York. JT hired me. He assures me he has a keen eye for talent."

"Most of the time, anyway," JT said, without explanation.

"Let me know if there's any way I can help you," Tony said. "I know how hard it can be to start a new job. It's a big place, and there's a lot to learn. But, there's nobody better than JT for watching your back."

"Thanks, Tony. I appreciate the support."

"We'll let you get back to work," JT told him.

Kristi followed him to the service elevator. "This will take you down to the garage."

"Thank you," Kristi said.

"Don't worry about Wilhelm. He'll come around. I won't let him keep you cooped up. Your office will be ready by the end of the week." The elevator opened. "See you tomorrow."

"Yes. I'll be here."

*

When Kristi arrived at work the next morning, Wilhelm was already in his office.

"I'd hoped to see you before this," he said by way of a greeting.

"I understood I was to start at eight," she said. "It's seven-thirty."

"With as much as there is for you to learn, I would have expected you to get here early. No matter. We'll make do."

"I was hoping I could get a look at my office."

"We don't have time for that now. We're meeting with Tony about the events this weekend. Did you get a chance to look over the schedule?"

"What schedule?"

"The one I gave you yesterday."

"I don't believe I got a schedule yesterday."

"It was in the packet. No matter. Let's get to the meeting. He's waited long enough."

She spent a second frustrating day trying to pin down what Wilhelm expected of her. The best she could figure out was that he wanted whatever she had *not* done.

Josh stopped by Wilhelm's office late that afternoon. "How is it going?"

"Fine," Wilhelm said. "Of course, it'll be a steep learning curve, but we'll bring her along."

"Do you need anything?" Josh asked her.

"An office would be nice," she said, looking around the cramped space.

"It's almost ready. My dad's taken it on as his personal project, and I'm happy to have him occupied."

"Could you show it to me?"

"I don't think that would be kosher. He's pretty invested in the surprise. Hang in for a couple more days, okay?"

"Sure." Did she have a choice?
"Great. See you tomorrow."

*

On Friday afternoon, Wilhelm said, "I think it's been a good week, considering what we're starting with. Of course, you have a long way to go, but eventually, I think you'll catch on."

The first thing she was going to hang in her new office was her diploma, maybe even on the door, so he'd have to see it every time he walked in.

"I'll certainly do my best."

"I'm disappointed you haven't had more to offer. You've been here a week without giving me a single suggestion or idea."

Maybe this was the way to get through to him. "I do have an idea for an event I believe would be a wonderful opportunity for the Princess."

"Oh? And what might that be?"

"I call it the Bridal Ball. It's a dance, of course, that would give a woman a second chance to wear her wedding gown, and dance with her husband in beautiful surroundings, without the stress and expectations that accompany every wedding."

"A bridal ball?"

"The thing is, a woman spends more on her bridal gown than on any other dress she ever buys. She only wears it once. She..."

"And you think that would somehow help us out here?" He could not have sounded more condescending if she had suggested mud wrestling on the mezzanine.

"Yes." She cringed at the hesitancy in her own voice. "The Crown Ballroom is the perfect place for..."

"For a disaster," he interrupted. "For a glittering event planned by someone who has no idea how a hotel works."

THE BRIDAL BALL

He sat back, his face not masking his distain. "Thank you for your idea. I'll give you six months to realize why it's so bad. When you do, I'll know you've made some progress."

A slap in her face could not have hurt more.

"That's all for today," he said.

Dismissed.

"What time do you want me here tomorrow?"

"I'll run the events this weekend; you're far from ready."

"How do you expect me to learn if I'm not here?"

"I've been asking myself that exact question. How will you learn? Certainly not by dreaming up events that would ruin our reputation." He picked up a stack of work orders. "I'll see you on Monday," he said, and walked out of his office.

She sat, staring out the window at the busy street corner. Cars, trucks, buses, and pedestrians crowded Van Ness every day of the week, but it was particularly busy on a Friday afternoon. She wished she had plans for the evening; somewhere to go or someone to talk to. She pulled out her cell phone and called Heather.

"Hi, Kristi. What's up?"

"Not much. I'm off this weekend. I was wondering if you could use some help tomorrow."

"Are you serious? I'd love it. You could do the event at MOMA with Matthew and Lexi."

"Would they be offended?"

"Actually, I think they'd be thrilled."

"Okay then, what time?"

"Three-thirty at the office?"

"I'll be there. Could we have a drink afterward?"

"Sure. Is anything wrong?"

"Wilhelm is..." she began, then thought better of it. "I'm still at work. We can talk tomorrow."

"Fine. I'll see you at the office when we're finished, probably around eleven."

"Great. Thanks, Heather."

*

Kristi was marvelously tired by eleven the next night; the kind of tired where her body said *stop,* but her brain still said *go;* a happy exhaustion that she loved; one that always followed a successful event. She, Matthew, and Lexi worked easily together, after much experience with Heather.

"Nice having your help tonight," Lexi told her as she was leaving the Current Events office. "We've missed you."

"I've missed you, too. And we still haven't gotten together. I probably have some free weekends coming up. I'll call you."

"The new job not what you expected?" Lexi asked.

"Not exactly."

"I'm sure things will improve once you settle in."

"I hope so. If not, I'll be back here, applying for a job as a server."

"I'd hire you," Lexi said. "Do you want me to wait with you until Heather gets back?"

"No. She's on the way. She just texted me."

"Okay. I'll take off then. See you soon."

"Thanks, Lexi."

"You bet," she said, and left, checking to make sure the door was secure behind her.

Heather arrived ten minutes later, and Kristi helped her unload the van.

"I sure do miss you," Heather said when they were finished. "Do you want a glass of wine?"

"Not really. I'm tired. I probably shouldn't drink."

"You didn't sound happy on the phone yesterday."

"No. Things aren't exactly going brilliantly." She told Heather about her week, and Wilhelm's not-so-veiled sabotage.

"I knew there was a chance he might be difficult, but I

didn't imagine he'd be a bastard."

"I told him about my Bridal Ball idea. He was so negative and condescending, I felt like a complete fool."

"That's too bad, because it's a good idea."

"He didn't think so."

"I think he's wrong. But, you need to do your homework to prove it. Work it out from start to finish—every detail, every cost, every possible aspect. Then, present it to him again, with your ducks lined up like plucky soldiers. I think he might change his mind."

"You do?"

"Yes. As long as you give him concrete reasons."

"Thanks, Heather."

"No problem. I hope it works. You sure you don't want some wine?"

"I'd better not." She was quiet for a bit, and then asked, "Do you seriously think the ball could work at the hotel?"

"I do. With plenty of planning on your part. Are you prepared for that?"

"I'll get prepared."

"If you want, you can run your new ideas by me. I'll give you more feedback."

"Heather, you're the best."

"That's what I hear."

CHAPTER 6

"I have a surprise for you," JT said to Kristi on Monday morning when he met her coming out of the stairwell. He led her down the hall to a door halfway between the lobby and the administration offices. A sign in a holder on the wall read *Event Coordinator*. He swung open the door to reveal a space not much larger than a general supply closet.

"What do you think?" He looked to her like a kid ready to launch a boat.

"I love it."

And she did.

Two tall, narrow windows looked out onto the tree-lined street, and gave the room both light and focus. A maple desk and chair sat to one side; across from the desk were two upholstered side chairs that might have been appropriated from the dining room. A bookcase and credenza, which she suspected were not new, completed the suite.

"I know it's small, but I thought you'd be better off here, where you'll have some autonomy. Clients can find you easily, without having to wander around the entire first floor."

Kristi sat at the desk, where a laptop, a notebook, and a

phone occupied the otherwise bare surface. The only decorative touch was a large fern sitting on the credenza.

"Did you put all this together?"

"Debby helped. She's the one with the flair. She wanted something for there," he said, pointing to the wall behind the desk, "but she wasn't sure about your taste. You can talk to her about it."

"This was so thoughtful of you, Mr. Townsend. I appreciate it very much."

"I know you had a rough time last week. I spoke to Wilhelm after the function yesterday, and I think things will improve now."

"I'm afraid he's not impressed by my credentials."

JT paused as if weighing a thought. "He has a long history. I'll tell you about it one day." His face brightened. "But, not today. Let me know if you need anything else. And, try to be patient with Wilhelm. He can teach you a lot."

"Thank you, sir. I'll do my best."

"I know you will, Kristi."

After he left, she put her purse in the bottom desk drawer, locked it, and dropped the key in her jacket pocket. She took the notebook from the desk, a pen from the drawer, and walked to Wilhelm's office. "Good morning."

"Have you seen your office?"

How did he deal with clients with such a dearth of cordiality?

"Yes. It's lovely."

"It certainly is. I would have preferred to have you closer, but no matter. We'll manage." He handed her several sheets of paper. "Those are the work orders for the events this week. I'll run them, but you can observe, providing you don't interfere. We do things in a particular fashion at the Princess. Regardless of what you've done in the past, you'll need to learn our procedures."

"That's why I took this job: to learn."

His look said her response was utterly unsatisfactory.

She tried a different approach. "What can I do to help?"

"Learn quickly."

She stifled a laugh. When it came to dearth, a sense of humor was at the top of Wilhelm's list.

The second week was an improvement over the previous one, though only slightly. She observed every event, and on Friday morning, Wilhelm informed her she would be seeing her first client the following week.

"Mr. and Mrs. Bailey's older daughter was married three years ago. The reception was the most talked-about social event of the entire year. Invitations were coveted like winning lottery tickets. Now, their younger daughter is having her reception here. They are friends of the Townsend family, so we'll want an especially memorable event."

"Of course."

"From what I can recall, Rebecca is an extremely sophisticated young woman, well-schooled and widely-traveled. She will expect a flawless event with careful attention given to every detail."

He said it as though it were a new concept for her.

Spitting at him was not an option, so she smiled.

*

When Rebecca Bailey walked into Kristi's office, she was sure someone was playing a joke. "Rebecca?"

"The one and only," the young woman said.

"I'm Kristi Peyton-Scott. It's nice to meet you."

Kristi wondered how long it had taken Rebecca to have the jeans air-brushed onto her lithe frame. The girl walked easily in her strappy, black, four-inch heels; heels that would have sent Kristi teetering even on a tether. Her hair was spiked with tinges of pink and purple, and the large piercing above her left eyebrow made Kristi wince.

"Please sit down." Kristi nodded at the chair. "Are your parents here?"

"No. It's just me today."

Kristi got up and closed the door. She wanted no distractions. "So, you're getting married. First let me give you my best wishes." She sat at her desk and pulled out a blank form. "Tell me about yourself, Rebecca. What do you do? Where did you meet your fiancé?"

"I'm a nurse. I graduated last year, and I work at a clinic in South San Francisco. Yancy and I met three years ago at a club downtown."

"And what does he do?"

"He has a band. He's a musician, and he writes music. In fact, he writes most of the songs the band performs."

Kristi made one note on the form, and another in her head. "I understand your sister's reception was here at the Princess."

"It certainly was."

"Did you have something similar in mind for yourself?"

"Anything but."

Kristi had looked at her sister's file, which was long and elaborate. "Something more simple, then?"

"Way more simple."

Kristi sat back, put down her pen, and smiled at the girl. "Tell me your vision of your wedding day, from beginning to end. I'd like to see what you see."

Rebecca glanced out the windows, squinting at the late afternoon sun. After a long silence she said, "Yancy and I would like a small, private wedding on the beach. Ideally, right about this time, when the light is long and low on the horizon, and the ocean looks like the sun just fell in. I'd have a simple dress; I don't need any attendants. After the ceremony, we'd eat dinner at a nearby restaurant. Then we'd have some champagne and cheesecake, and go home."

"That sounds beautiful. And very romantic."

Rebecca's smile was soft and sweet, and it struck Kristi that the harsh exterior was the antithesis of a gentle spirit.

"If that's what you want, then why are you here?"

"My father wants to replicate my sister's wedding. Mira Lang dress, morning coats, seven-course meal, full orchestra, more bridesmaids than Kim Kardashian. He thinks five hundred guests is a reasonable number."

"What about a simple wedding here? Perhaps we could do something casual that didn't feel like such a reality show production."

Rebecca looked out the window again. "Could you bring the sun inside?"

"There's a beautiful patio on the roof."

"It's not quite the same."

"No, it isn't." Kristi studied the unhappy girl. "You know, your wedding day is supposed to be one of the happiest days of your life. Is there a way to compromise so you can have your dream wedding, and at the same time, not disappoint your father?"

"My father's idea of compromise is when you do things his way, just not as fast as he'd like."

"So, Rebecca, I'm going to ask you again: Why are you here?"

"My mother made the appointment, but realized she had a conflict this afternoon. She asked me to cancel this one and reschedule. I thought I'd come and meet you, and tell you what I'd like. When I come back with them, my father will make sure you know that his opinion is the only one that matters."

"I see."

Rebecca stood. "It was nice to meet you."

"You too, Rebecca. I hope we can figure out a way to create your vision of a perfect wedding. It does sound beautiful."

"Thank you." She started to leave, and then stopped in the doorway. "You know, you're the first person who's ever actually listened to what I'd like on my own wedding day. I meant it when I said thank you."

"You're welcome, Rebecca. Don't give up hope. I'm

sure we'll figure out something."

Heather had catered several weddings on the coast, some small; some not so small. She would be the ideal person to put Rebecca's vision together. However, Kristi couldn't very well refer Rebecca to her, since the Baileys were friends of the Townsends, and had specifically chosen the Princess.

Not to mention, these were her first clients since being hired at the hotel.

How did she handle a situation where the bride wanted one thing and her parents wanted something so completely different?

Kristi was sure she knew Wilhelm's answer: whoever was paying made the decisions.

Josh stopped by her office, as he had almost every day since she'd started work. Much as she wanted to think otherwise, she felt sure he was merely doing his job.

He looked around the room and grimaced. "I suppose we could have found a smaller space for you, though not without some effort."

"I love it. It's perfect for me."

"I think my dad had fun with it. It's been a while since he's had a project to tackle." Josh sat down. "You'll need something for up there," he said, nodding at the empty wall behind her.

"My mom's an artist. She'll have a piece that'll work."

He smiled, and she had to struggle to keep her mind on her side of The Line.

"You met with the Baileys?"

"Just Rebecca."

"She's quite a character. She and her sister are like yin and yang gone bad."

"So I gather."

"Does Rebecca have an idea of what she wants?"

"She does. It isn't what I would call the standard wedding package."

"Nothing Rebecca ever did was what you'd call standard. Don't let her looks fool you. She's as tender as a new leaf. It doesn't take much to crush her."

"I'll be careful."

He glanced out to the hallway, and then spoke more softly. "Dad mentioned Wilhelm was less than cordial when you came on board."

She didn't know how to respond.

"I wish you'd come to me. I would have spoken to him."

"I doubt that would have improved our relationship much. He wants to protect the hotel's image, which is understandable. Eventually, he'll realize I'm capable of doing the job, and that I know when to ask for help." She sounded more confident than she felt at that moment, considering the dilemma with the Baileys. Who would she ask about that?

He stood.

Don't go, she thought, but of course, she didn't say it.

"I'll be curious to see what you choose for the wall."

"I'm sure I'll need help hanging it."

"We'll call someone from maintenance. Let me know."

"I will, thanks."

With one final smashing smile, he left.

Kristi sat still, waiting for the air to return to the room. If he were the concierge she'd ask him out faster than he could say beurre blanc. She turned back to her computer.

How many cups of coffee had she had that morning? Her heart was pumping like she'd just finished a Costa Cappuccino.

*

She was no closer to solving the Bailey reception puzzle when Rebecca and her parents arrived for their appointment on Thursday. Kristi had brought a third chair into her office to accommodate the family, but she needn't have bothered; Rebecca may as well have stayed home.

"Please say something, Rebecca," Mrs. Bailey said after nearly an hour. Her voice was low and controlled, but her irritation grated like unexpected eggshells.

"Why bother? You've already made up your mind how it's going to be."

Dr. Bailey gave his daughter a baleful look. "Please don't start."

The prominent surgeon was clearly accustomed to having things his way. Although Mrs. Bailey did most of the talking, she glanced at him periodically, and received a nearly imperceptible nod when he agreed. When he did not, the woman tried again. Kristi was shocked to see that sort of archaic paternalism still existed.

The event was shaping into a grand spectacle, the opposite of the wedding Rebecca had described. Kristi watched the girl shrink into herself as layer after layer of excess was added.

That must be why she dressed the way she did—so they'd notice her. Otherwise, she might be completely invisible.

"You're sure you have the right date on the calendar?" Mrs. Bailey asked. "I know you're new here. I wouldn't want any slip-ups."

"It's in the system, Mrs. Bailey. I'll send you a printout of all the details."

"Please send one for each of us," Dr. Bailey said.

Rebecca shifted in her chair. "I don't need one."

"Of course you do," her mother said. "It's your wedding."

Tell them, Kristi encouraged her silently.

Rebecca struggled to respond and finally settled on, "Whatever."

Dr. Bailey stood and extended his hand. "It was nice meeting you, Ms. Peyton-Scott. We'll discuss the menu selections, and look into an orchestra."

"There's still plenty of time," Kristi said. "We'll probably have entirely new menu items by this time next year. The important thing is reserving the room."

"The Crown Ballroom is the only place we'd consider for a reception. It's the most beautiful venue in the city," Mrs. Bailey said.

"I couldn't agree more," Kristi said. "It's the best."

But, not the best for everyone.

*

On Friday night, once the event dinner was finished, Kristi left her supervisor in charge of the cleanup, and went to meet her friends for GNO. They had chosen a seafood café on the wharf, so that Kristi wouldn't have far to travel.

"Hey," Nicole said, "you're early."

Kristi slid into the comfortable, red, faux leather booth. "It was going smoothly, so I left Queenie in charge. She's perfectly capable of wrapping it up."

"I love it that someone named Queenie works at the Princess. She should be in charge, don't you think?"

"She's been there so long, she probably could be. Say, where's Laura?"

"Chloe is sick. Laura didn't want to leave her with Ethan. What's that about? He's a doctor, for heaven's sake."

"He's a dentist."

"Same thing."

Kristi ordered a bowl of clam chowder and a glass of white wine. "So, what's new?" she asked, relaxing for the first time all day.

"Not a whole lot. What about you?"

"I saw my first clients this week. Their event is shaping into a nightmare." Kristi took a grateful sip of wine and sat back. "The bride wants a simple beach wedding; her parents want an epic production in the Crown Ballroom."

"I can't imagine planning wedding after wedding; one was hard enough."

"I don't plan them so much as I facilitate them. Most brides have a pretty clear idea of what they want."

"Although they don't always get it," Nicole said.

"You mean Laura?"

"Exactly. The dance that never happened. She'll never get over it, I'm afraid. It's been almost four years, and she tears up every time she talks about it."

"You know," Kristi said, "I have an idea I've been toying with, and this is the perfect time to tell you about it."

"You mean without Laura?"

"Yes. It's something I've been thinking about for months, but I've never mentioned it because I couldn't figure a way to pull it off."

"Don't tell me you're planning a surprise wedding reception," Nicole said with a laugh, "you know, like a surprise birthday party?"

"It's not a reception, and it wouldn't be a surprise. It's a dance, a ball, created for brides, so they can wear their wedding dress again, and dance all night, without the pressure of their wedding day."

While Nicole ate her chowder, Kristi shared every aspect of her idea, detailing as much as she could. She told her about Wilhelm's response when she spoke to him, and about Heather's advice. "I'm not sure where to go from here, but there must be some way to get the word out, and find out how many women would be interested."

"Did I hear someone calling my name?" Nicole asked. "What do you think I do all day? I create web pages to give companies, businesses, and *events*, visibility."

"But it isn't any of those; it's only an idea."

"An idea you want to turn into a reality. So, we frame it that way. We make it interactive. Women can give us their ideas. We get local sponsors, like hairdressers, caterers, and spas who serve the wedding industry. We convince them to give a flyer to every patron, in exchange for an ad on our site. This is Webpage One-O-One. It sounds like fun."

"Can I hire you?" Kristi asked.

"Are you nuts?"

"But I thought..."

"Laura is my friend as much as yours. We were both in her wedding. You're not going to hire me. We're going to do it together." She pointed at Kristi's soup bowl. "You haven't had a single bite. It's probably cold. You should ask them to warm it up."

"I don't care." She took a bite of the soup, which was indeed cold. She pushed it away. "I'm too excited to eat."

"What a waste."

Kristi picked up a piece of sourdough bread and took a bite. "This is enough."

"You sure? It wouldn't be for me." Nicole said.

"I'm fine."

"Okay then, back to the ball."

"I know a lot of business owners in the Sunset. I'm sure at least some of them would be interested."

"We'll make a list of our favorite shops: beauty salons, spas, florists, bakers, travel agents, and so on. Then, we'll create a brochure to explain our idea, and what we're offering. I'll start working on the layout. You need to come up with the description of the ball, how and where it would be, and all the details of the evening."

"Do you really think this can work?" Kristi asked.

"We'll make it work. It's that, or see that look on Laura's face every time the subject of weddings comes up for the rest of our lives."

Kristi spread a liberal layer of butter on another piece of bread. "When do we tell her?"

"After it's all put together. Maybe we'll have her run the site," Nicole said. "She could do it from home, whenever she has some free time; during Chloe's nap, or in the middle of the night, for that matter."

"Okay, we wait to tell her. But, it won't be easy, now that you know. She's going to be so excited. I'm curious, would you want to wear your wedding dress again?"

"I would, if I could get into it. My dress hasn't been out of the bag since it was cleaned. I've heard those bags make dresses shrink. Maybe we should have an alterations shop for a sponsor."

"A cleaner," Kristi cried. "Add a cleaner to the list. They'd get repeat business if a woman wore her dress again."

"Of course, even if I could get in my dress, Blake has no more idea of how to dance now than he did at *our* wedding."

"Dance lessons!" they said at the same time.

"Not only as a sponsor," Kristi said. "We could offer them at the hotel the afternoon before the dance. A refresher course: the basics for the ball."

"You should be writing all this down, Kristi. We both should make notes of our ideas and combine them."

"Yes. We need a master plan. I'll put something together, exactly the way I would if I were coordinating an event at the hotel."

"By the time we're done, Wilhelm won't be able to turn it down," Nicole said.

"Thanks, Nicky. This is great. I appreciate all the effort this will take."

"A Bridal Ball," Nicole said. "This means I'm going to have to lose ten pounds." She looked at the calendar on her phone. "Can we meet next Sunday?"

"Next Sunday works for me. And, I'm serious about not telling Laura yet. I'd hate to get her hopes up before we have a better sense of whether we can do it. "

"If we want her to manage the site, we have to tell her."

"True. But, not until it's ready."

"I'll email you the client questionnaire I use for a new website," Nicole said. "Fill it out, and add anything you think might help to bring in users. Eventually, we'll need a newsletter. We should probably have freebies occasionally, like tickets to a fashion show or a convention. I imagine we'll have brides-to-be, as well as already marrieds, following us. We want to keep them all coming back to the site."

"Do we need a domain name?"

"Yes. But I doubt that will be a problem. If it hasn't already been used, The Bridal Ball dot com will say it all. Simple, straightforward, and strategic."

"I hope it catches on. Unless Wilhelm is impressed, it won't mean a thing."

"You should tell JT about it. He was the one who hired you, after all. From what you've said, he already thinks you're the golden girl."

"Technically, Josh hired me. And, Heather warned me not to jump rank, so that's the way it's going to be. I'll have to pitch it to Wilhelm."

"Then, Wilhelm it is."

"I'm finally making some progress at work. Wilhelm has me booking nearly all the catering events. This week I'm meeting with a client who is having a twenty-year reunion dinner for a private school in Marin. Very wealthy, very highbrow."

And very difficult, Kristi soon discovered.

"I asked for Wilhelm," the client said to her when he was escorted into her office on Tuesday afternoon.

"I apologize if there's been a misunderstanding," Kristi said, "but I was told you wanted to book an event."

"Precisely."

"Then you'll want to see me. I'm the Event Coordinator."

"What I want," he said as if she were stupid, "is to see Wilhelm. I've worked exclusively with him in the past. What I want is his experience."

"I'm sorry, sir," Kristi said, doing her best to sound

calm, "Wilhelm no longer handles event planning. He is now the Assistant to the General Manager; I was hired to take on his former duties."

The man made no pretense of being polite. "I have no intention of dealing with a fledgling employee. If I can't work with Wilhelm, I'll go elsewhere."

Kristi had no idea what to say. Wilhelm and Josh were gone that afternoon. She wasn't sure if JT was at the hotel, or whether it was wise to refer this angry man to him.

"I'm sure Wilhelm would be happy to call you..."

"If it isn't too much trouble for you, Ms. Peyton-Scott," he said from her doorway, "have him do that." His tone was so patronizing that her teeth hurt.

She slumped in her chair. How did that turn into such a disaster? What in the world had she done wrong? She stared out the window. The sunshine outside didn't reach the gloom in her office. She would have to explain the debacle to Wilhelm, who would surely add this to her list of inadequacies.

JT stopped by her office an hour later. "I heard you had a rough meeting a while ago."

"From whom?"

"Debby was walking by and heard the exchange. Don't worry about him. Wilhelm will call him and sort it out. You probably didn't kowtow to him sufficiently."

"I've met with more than a dozen clients here, and not one has ever been rude to me."

"It happens," JT said. "Not very often, but it happens. Most of our clients are considerate and cooperative; a handful are hell on a Harley." He grinned at her. "Don't be discouraged. You're doing a fine job."

"Thank you, sir."

She left a voicemail for Wilhelm, explaining what had happened and asking him to contact the client. After that, she braced for the fallout.

CHAPTER 7

Kristi worked until eleven on Tuesday night, and came in late the next morning. Josh told her to offset her hours when she could; if she had big evening events with nothing scheduled the next morning, she should adjust her time accordingly.

She had barely put down her purse when she noticed the boldly written note on her desk.

See me immediately.
Wilhelm

She hung up her coat, freshened her lipstick, and walked down the hall to his office.

"Good morning. You wanted to see me?"

"Yes. Sit down." He checked his watch. "You're late."

"Josh told me to offset my hours..."

"You don't work for Josh, you work for me. In the future, please advise me of any schedule changes."

She nodded, not trusting herself to speak.

"I had a message from a very unhappy client this morning. Do you think you could possibly have made more of a mess of yesterday's meeting?"

It was the classic *have you stopped beating your wife* dilemma—yes was as damaging as no.

"He wanted you to run the event," she told him, "and I explained that you no longer work as the Event Coordinator."

"Do you dictate what I do?"

"I was hired to manage events here."

"And some day you might be qualified to do that. But clearly, that day has not arrived. At the Royal Princess, we do our utmost to please our clients. It goes without saying we give them what they want whenever possible. What possessed you to tell him he couldn't see me?"

"That's not exactly what I said. I…"

"Whatever you said, it was the wrong thing. We've lost a valuable client thanks to you."

"I'm sorry that…"

"You're obviously not skilled enough for your position here; I regret you were hired without my involvement. My only option now is to monitor your meetings more closely."

Or, he could support her, and tell his former clients she was fully capable.

"Have you nothing to say for yourself?"

Why, when he would twist anything she said and make things even worse?

"No matter. The damage is done. As I said, I'll have to check in with you regularly from now on. Please keep me apprised of all your client meetings."

"Yes, I'll do that." You controlling…

"That's all," he said, looking at her as if he expected a salute.

She left his office with a huge hole shot through her confidence. She'd quit, except that that was what he wanted, and she'd be damned if she'd give him the satisfaction.

"Good morning," Josh called out as she passed by his office.

His warm smile drew her heart in; her feet had no choice but to follow.

"How did the dinner go last night?"

"Very well, I think."

"Good. It looks like you're getting used to our particular way of doing things."

She was glad someone thought so. "Yes," she said, not trusting herself to say more. In truth, she was content to stand there, soaking up the pleasure of his company.

"Did you need something?"

She felt the crimson flush of embarrassment crawl up her cheeks like mercury in a candy thermometer. "No." Telling him about Wilhelm's latest rant would not be wise. "I'll see you later."

"Right," he said, almost as if he were disappointed. But that couldn't be. She knew how busy he was. His gaze fell to the work on his desk, and the light in the room seemed to dim.

Walking down the hall, she wished again that he was the concierge instead of the heir apparent. But, she pushed aside the "if onlys", knowing that a relationship with the boss's son was not going to happen.

Back in her office, Kristi reviewed the schedule for the remainder of the week, and sent Wilhelm a memo detailing her hours. Once that was done, she put her frustration aside. She would not allow him to ruin her days with his supercilious pettiness. She didn't know how she could win him over, but she was determined to keep trying. Until then, she would just have to tread water.

*

Once again, on Saturday afternoon, Kristi was a silent observer at a wedding reception managed by Wilhelm. She had to admit he ran the function smoothly, quietly directing staff and responding to the client's needs. The employees clearly respected him, and did his bidding eagerly.

Why did he dislike her so much? He didn't treat anyone else with such disdain.

She watched the bride and groom's first dance from a discrete corner of the ballroom. "Can't Help Falling In Love" was one of Kristi's favorite selections for a first dance.

The bride's gown swept gracefully across the dance floor as her husband, vigilant of the long skirt, carefully twirled her.

She wanted to see Laura and Ethan dancing there, just like these two. She had to make the Bridal Ball happen. Her resolve made it necessary to stay at the Princess and endure Wilhelm's ridicule.

As the couple finished their dance, Kristi looked up at the domed, stained-glass ceiling that soared overhead. Ten four-foot-high crystal chandeliers hung at the perimeter, as if the room was enclosed in a giant crystal snow globe.

"You can stay for the breakdown," Wilhelm said from behind.

She turned. "I'd be happy to."

The look he gave her said that if he'd thought his directive would make her happy, he wouldn't have given it. He walked away without another word, and she turned back to the room. The wedding party joined the bride and groom on the floor, and were performing a well-rehearsed dance, which brought their appreciative guests to their feet.

Kristi found herself swaying to the music. The DJ was good, no doubt about it. Still, for the ball, *their* ball, recorded music would never work. The Bridal Ball *had* to have live music. A group that played pop music as well as old standards…music that appealed to all ages.

"It's a good party," JT said.

"Mr. Townsend. Good evening." She blushed that he'd caught her all but dancing. "I'm so glad to see you. I want to thank you again for all the work you did in my office. It's a lovely space, and I'm so comfortable there."

"I'm glad. I'm convinced that employees work best when they're in comfortable and attractive surroundings."

"I couldn't agree more."

"Please let me know if you need anything else. I'd like to see a piece of art hanging behind your desk, but you should be the person to choose it, not me."

"My mother is a watercolorist. She said she'd paint something for me to hang."

"That would be perfect. I'd better get out of your way now. I'm sure you're busy."

"Have a nice evening, sir."

"You too, Kristi."

Kristi turned back to the ballroom as the bride and groom walked across the dance floor, holding hands and laughing. The groom looked down at his new wife as if she were the only other person on the planet.

When she drove home late that night, Kristi pictured the groom looking his bride with complete joy. During one of their meetings, the bride had told Kristi details of sweet things he did for her regularly.

A man who knew how to treat a woman like a princess. Were there guys like that still around?

Josh's face came to her, his smile wide as the world. Not him, though. She banished the vision. There'd be no relationship with Josh Townsend. Kristi understood who the real boss was, even if Wilhelm did not.

*

Kristi knocked on Nicole's front door far later than she'd intended on Sunday night. "I'm sorry I'm so late," she said when her friend answered. "I should never make plans for after an event."

"If you adopted that policy," Nicole said, "you'd never plan a thing. You work every day, for heaven's sake."

Kristi followed Nicole up to her spacious office on the second floor. Five computer monitors lined a wall-to-wall desk on one side of the room. Each one had a different picture of a wedding dress with the words The Bridal Ball highlighting the frame, each with a separate and distinct character.

"What do you think?" Nicole asked.

"They're beautiful, Nicole."

"Which one do you like best?"

Kristi looked from the screens to her friend's face. "I have to choose?"

"Uh, yeah. The site needs a personality that wows the user. We want it to be memorable, so they'll come back. We want it to be interactive, so they're part of the process."

"You want all that from a picture?"

"The picture, the font, and the design. They've done studies that show we're drawn to certain elements. The best pages use color, contrast, and contour to get viewers to engage."

Kristi took several moments to look at each screen. "They're all wonderful. I don't know how to choose one."

"Go over to the door and close your eyes. When I count to three, open your eyes. Look quickly at all the screens and then walk to one of them. Don't think about it, just do it." She paused and asked, "Ready?"

Kristi stood with her eyes closed. "Yes."

"One ... two ... three."

Kristi opened her eyes, panned across the five monitors and walked straight to the image of a groom with his hands clasped behind his bride's back. The ornate, Art Nouveau design that framed the page reminded her of the Crown Ballroom.

She tapped the screen. "This one."

"That one it is."

"That wasn't very scientific."

"No, it was intuitive, which is better, particularly when

you consider the majority of our users will be women."

In mere seconds, the design she had chosen was on Nicole's largest monitor, where her friend sat at the keyboard. The navigation ribbon at the top said: Home, The Dream, Sponsors, Your Story, Comments, and Contact Us. Nicole clicked on the second one, The Dream.

Over the softened photograph of a beautiful wedding dress, Kristi read the text.

Your bridal gown: the most beautiful dress you've ever worn—the most romantic dress you've ever owned—the most expensive dress you've ever bought.

Have you ever dreamed of wearing your wedding dress again—of waltzing around a spectacular ballroom with the love of your life?

We have.

Help us make the dream come true. Help us create an evening you'll remember the rest of your life. Help us design The Bridal Ball.

We're looking for a ballroom, we're looking for an orchestra, and we're looking for your help. Tell us what you would include to make this romantic evening the second most memorable night of your life.

Share your ideas with us on our Comments page.

Check back regularly for updates on our progress. We will post information as plans are solidified, but the event won't be complete without you. Tell your family, tell your friends.

Our goal is a ballroom filled with brides. And one of them is you.

"It's perfect, Nicole." Regret rose in her throat, a solid sadness that made it hard to swallow. She'd never been a bride; never known the wonder of wearing a wedding gown.

"Now, tell me what you liked on the other designs, and I'll see if I can pull them into this one. Remember, our target

THE BRIDAL BALL

audience can afford a weekend at the Royal Princess, and that demands a level of sophistication. We want the site to be friendly, but not folksy; sweet, but not saccharine."

"It shouldn't be stuffy," Kristi said. "The whole point is for everyone to enjoy themselves without all the pressure."

"Yes, of course. But, it's a ball, not a prom. These are grown women, not teenagers. We're aiming for a cosmopolitan market."

"I see what you mean."

They worked for three hours, adding and refining elements. With each change, the site improved. With each change, the idea expanded. With each change, the Bridal Ball morphed from concept to content, from dream to design, from fantasy to fact.

"How do you get users to engage?"

"By asking them to give an opinion or tell us about themselves. Every bride has a story. We want to fold every one into the collective story of The Bridal Ball. Wouldn't it benefit the Royal Princess if this were a yearly event like the Black and White Ball?"

"Absolutely."

"Then we need to create a forum where users think of each other as family—as sisters—who talk to each other on our site, look forward to meeting each other at the ball, and promise not only to keep in touch, but to meet at the ball the next year."

Nicole clicked on the third button in the navbar and brought up a list of sponsors. "I talked to these business owners. They all want to be involved. I still need to add images, and website links. I expect we'll have twenty or thirty businesses before we're finished."

"I'll canvas my local shops this week."

"I need to finish the brochure; an explanation of what we're trying to create, and how the shop owners will benefit by being involved from the beginning. If it works, we'll all gain referrals."

She clicked on Tell us Your Story.

"Here's where we get our users involved. We'll start with Laura's story. Most brides will appreciate the disappointment of not dancing in her wedding dress. We'll ask a few other brides to add their stories, to gain momentum."

"I wish I could go through the files at the hotel and call every woman who had her reception in the ballroom. I'll bet there are dozens of good stories there."

"I hadn't thought of that."

"I can't…"

"No. But later, when we get it going, once the hotel is on board, we can email former clients and tell them about the ball. I bet they'd be thrilled to dance in the ballroom again."

"I'm not sure how that would work privacy-wise."

"If the Royal Princess hosts the event, I imagine former clients are fair game."

"Maybe. But, that's a way down the road."

Nicole turned back to the computer. "The Comments page is for users to tell us their ideas about what they would like to be included at the ball."

"I've been thinking about that. We should offer two packages: one for the dinner and dance only; and one for the dinner, the dance, a night at the hotel, and the Sunday buffet. The complete package would be considerably more expensive and may be harder to sell."

"The first year, maybe. After that, I bet they'll go like cupcakes."

"I sure hope so," Kristi said.

"Users can email us questions through Contact Us," Nicole said, "like a business owner who sees the site and wants to be involved. Can you think of anything else we should include?"

"I think you've covered it all."

"Okay then." Nicole took a drink from the designer

water bottle that was a permanent fixture on her desk.

"So, that's it?"

"For the moment. I need the rest of the sponsors from your neighborhood. I'll have a few from Chestnut Street. Once the images and links are added, we can go live."

"I can't believe it's happening so fast."

"It will take a while for it to catch on. You'll have to be patient, Kristi. These things rarely take off overnight."

"I just thought of something. Heather has a huge client list. I'm sure she'd send everyone an announcement."

"Of course we'd add her link on the site in exchange. For now, anyway. If it's taken over by the Princess, they probably won't want another event coordinator involved."

"True."

"We need to make it clear that The Bridal Ball will be in San Francisco. We don't want women in New York, Dallas, or Los Angeles getting excited about it, only to discover they'd need to add airfare to the cost of the weekend."

"If the idea catches on, who knows where the next one might be."

"There's only one Crown Ballroom."

"True. Nothing compares with The Princess."

"Except maybe Versailles." Nicole's smile was impossibly impish.

Kristi covered a yawn. "Are we done?"

"For tonight. You need to get me info on your local businesses. I'll order the flyers this week." She took another drink of water. "When shall we tell Laura?"

"On the day we launch."

"That'll take some coordination."

"We can have GNO here. I'll bring take-out."

"Sushi?"

"Sure. Could Laura do the launch?"

"I'd have to do it a couple of days ahead if you want it live for GNO."

"That would be better. I want her to be able to see it up and running. Are you going to write her story?"

Nicole looked like she was debating pros and cons. "No. You write it. She can redo it if she wants."

Kristi pictured Laura's face, surprised, excited, joyful at the possibility of finally dancing in her wedding dress. "If we can pull this off, she's going to be ecstatic."

"I talked to two clients about it this week, and they thought it was brilliant. They said they'd love to wear their wedding dresses again. I imagine a lot of women would."

"Let's hope we can find every one of them."

Before she left, Kristi gave Nicole a huge hug. "Thanks for all you've done, Nicky. The site is beautiful. I just hope it's successful."

"Are you kidding? Brides are gonna beg to go to the ball."

"You're sure about that?"

"Of course. I'm the expert."

Kristi drove home, her joy tinged with jealousy. Laura and Nicky were in an exclusive club. Would she ever be a member?

What would it feel like to be a bride?

And, who'd be at the end of the aisle for her?

*

Kristi carried a cup of coffee to Wilhelm's office on Monday morning, ready to discuss scheduling for the upcoming events.

"Are you sure there is plenty of coverage for this weekend?" he asked. "I don't want things falling apart while we're in Yosemite."

"Everything is covered."

"You're sure?"

"Yes." She swallowed her next words. Nasty was unnecessary.

No major events were on the calendar that weekend, a fortunate coincidence. Kristi wasn't sure how, but it had worked to her advantage.

"I'll drive," Wilhelm said as Kristi stood to leave. "We can leave here at six on Friday morning."

She hadn't considered them traveling together.

He looked up at her. "Do you have a problem with that?" His face was more smirk than smile.

Why were all his questions challenges? "No."

"Fine. Then we're done."

She turned and left his office. Hours alone in a car with him? She should have said she would drive herself—or fly—or walk. Anything but be stuck with his sorry soul for six hours.

She cheered up when she remembered that Georgia Markham was her first appointment. In four weeks, Georgia would be marrying Josh's best friend, Wyatt Warren. Kristi had already met with her once, and had been drawn to the exuberant young woman. Most of the clients Kristi had inherited from Wilhelm were the parents of brides-to-be. Working with a bride was way more fun.

She was surprised to find Georgia waiting in her office.

"Hi," the young woman said, rising to greet her. "I know I'm early. I hope that doesn't mess you up. I have a house to show in the Marina District, and I wanted to get there early."

"It's nice to see you," Kristi said, extending her hand. "It's no problem at all."

Georgia took her hand and pulled Kristi close for a quick hug. "We're practically family," she said. When Kristi frowned, Georgia said, "Since you work at the Princess, I mean. It's like you're part of Josh's family."

"Do the Townsends adopt their employees?"

"Only the special ones." Georgia's smile was warm and intimate. "I think you've made quite an impression on Josh."

Kristi waited for Georgia to tell her more.

Was Josh interested? Had he said something?

But, Georgia merely sat down, crossed her long legs, and pulled out her phone.

Kristi was left to wonder.

She pulled up Georgia's file on her computer. "What have you got for me?"

"Final menu counts. All the RSVPs are in."

"Wow. A month in advance? How did you manage that?"

"I called the malingerers. They all know better than to mess with me when I'm on a mission." She gave Kristi the numbers. "I think that's the last thing."

"Unless someone cancels. You can change numbers up until the Sunday before."

"I'll call you with any last-minute problems."

Georgia glanced at her watch. "Drat. I'm way too early. Do you have time for a cup of coffee?"

"Sure. My next appointment isn't until ten."

"Let's go into the dining room. I love it there."

They seated themselves near the doors to the ballroom, which were closed. After the waitress poured their coffee, Georgia leaned forward. "So, how do you like your new job?"

"I love it. There's a lot to learn, of course, but I'm enjoying it." She gestured around the room. "How could I not?"

"I was grateful I didn't have to work with Wilhelm anymore," Georgia said in a low voice. "He's such a pompous patoot."

Kristi was sure Georgia would have said something worse if the waitress had not walked by.

"I told Josh time and again they needed to hire someone else for that job. The man never smiles. What a vision for a bride on her wedding day. Grim."

"Have you been to many receptions here?"

"Probably eight or ten."

Eight or ten brides. A goldmine. Of course, asking her about them would be utterly unprofessional.

"Something wrong?" Georgia asked.

"No. Nothing. Tell me about your wedding gown."

Georgia sat back, smiling as if the dress were hanging before her. "It's beautiful. It's long, with a drop waist, a sheer bodice, and tiny straps that cross in back. The skirt has miles and miles of chiffon and it makes me feel so feminine I could almost cry. I adore it. It's like the designer had me in mind. I can't wait for Wyatt to see it. I can't wait to dance in it."

Her words melted the professional reserve Kristi had struggled to maintain. Unable to restrain herself, she leaned forward. "Would you like the chance to wear it again?"

"You mean after the wedding?"

"Yes."

"Absolutely."

"Maybe you could," Kristi said, and she shared the secret she'd just promised Nicole she would not divulge.

CHAPTER 8

That evening, Kristi called Nicole to check on the website progress. She began telling her about her meeting with Georgia when Nicole's voice exploded in her ear. "You told who?"

"Her name is Georgia Markham. Her wedding reception is at the Princess next month."

"And what possessed you to tell a client?"

"I didn't intend to. She was talking about her wedding dress, and she was so happy and excited about it, I got carried away."

"For Pete's sake, Kristi, couldn't you have waited until the site was launched?"

"I'm sorry. I know I should have kept my mouth shut. But, you talked to your clients about it."

"I know my clients. This woman is practically a stranger. Please, don't tell Laura until we're all together. I want to see the look on her face."

"Of course. We agreed on that."

"Thank you." Nicole's voice was stiff and formal, one Kristi had seldom heard.

"I really am sorry, Nicky. I didn't spoil anything. I

won't mention it to anyone else, I promise."

"Thank you."

"Here's the good part. Georgia grew up in the city. She told me she's been to eight or ten wedding receptions at the Princess. She probably knows a dozen brides. She'd be a great addition to our team. And, she's a real estate agent, so she works with dozens of couples."

"Do you think she'd want to be a sponsor?"

"She might. The problem is, now I'm worried about it getting back to Josh. I told Georgia it was a secret, but…"

"Let's hope she's better at keeping them than you are."

"Okay, okay."

"It's done now. With luck, we didn't lose anything, and we may have gained something."

"Let me think about the sponsor part. I'm not sure about involving someone so close to Josh."

"If you ask her, and if she says yes, get her business card and website as soon as you can."

Late that night, Kristi climbed into a bed big enough for two with pillows for one. Her thoughts followed a familiar path from the ball, to Georgia, to Josh. More and more often, she found herself day dreaming about him.

She knew it was foolish. She knew it was pointless. She knew it was dangerous. She knew countless stories of employees who had crashed and burned on the road to romance with their boss. She did not want to jeopardize her future at the Princess with a dalliance with Josh.

But he pulsed like a laser beam in a dark night, blinding her every sense, especially her good sense.

She forced herself to focus on the following weekend.

Maybe she'd meet someone special in Yosemite.

*

She spent the next three work days double-checking every event, every supervisor's list of responsibilities, the food and beverage orders, the florist's orders, and the linen supply. By Thursday, she felt as though she'd done a month's work in less than a week.

"I'll meet you here at six in the morning," Wilhelm told her as he was preparing to leave that evening. "Try to be on time."

He walked away without another word, and Kristi couldn't resist sticking out her tongue at him.

JT dropped by her office not long after Wilhelm left. "I want to wish you a safe trip. According to the news, the weather in Yosemite this weekend will be perfect."

"I'm afraid we'll be inside most of the time. But fair weather is certainly better for driving."

"I think you'll be comfortable. Wilhelm drives a new Mercedes. He insists no car manufacturer can rival a German maker."

Naturally. "I hope he likes to listen to music. I can't imagine what we'll find to talk about for three and a half hours."

"Maybe you should take a book on CD, or tell him you need some extra sleep."

"Or both. It's only three days. What could go wrong?"

*

Kristi arrived at the hotel at five forty-five the next morning, surprised that Wilhelm's Mercedes was not already in the garage. She left her suitcase in her car and went upstairs to check her voicemail. Nothing. She was about to call him when Josh walked into her office.

He flashed an adrenaline-shooter grin straight to her heart. "Plans have changed a bit." He was dressed in jeans, boots, and a black polo shirt, and looked so sexy, she could barely concentrate on his words.

"What do you mean?"

"Wilhelm called me this morning. He's picked up a flu

bug, so he won't be able to go with you this weekend."

A smile sailed from her heart to her lips. "That's too bad."

"I thought if you didn't mind, I'd tag along instead."

At that, the smile broke free. "That'd be great, Josh."

"I'll drive, if that's okay with you. My car is downstairs. You about ready?"

"I'm ready. I came up looking for Wilhelm." Imagine her luck finding Josh instead.

Josh put her suitcase into the trunk of his car. "It's no Mercedes. I hope you're not disappointed."

"Cars are all the same to me."

"Don't let Wilhelm hear you say that. He'd consider it blasphemy."

Josh's BMW had a moon roof, which he opened the minute he turned on the engine.

Kristi didn't recognize the music on the radio, but saw on the screen it was from the forties.

"I love Sirius," he said, pulling out of the garage. "I can listen to forties music all day if I want to." He glanced over at her when she didn't reply. "You can change it if you don't like it."

"It's fine." Her mind had still not caught up with the unexpected twist of the morning. She had anticipated being with Wilhelm for three or four hours, and then stuck with his disagreeable company for three days. Instead, she was leaving the city with the most attractive man she'd ever had the opportunity to ogle.

Maybe she should buy a lottery ticket. She'd hit the jackpot; maybe her luck was running strong. How could this possibly have turned out any better?

"You're very quiet," Josh said. "Do you need some coffee?"

"I'd love a cup of coffee. We have plenty of time. They don't expect me—us—to be there until one o'clock."

They stopped at a nearby coffee shop, bought lattes and

sweet rolls, and were soon on the Bay Bridge heading east.

Josh turned the volume down on the radio. "I love the view of the Campanile." He pointed toward the tallest building on the Cal Berkeley campus. "More than anything, that was why I wanted to go to school there." He laughed at himself. "A mature reason to choose a university."

"Had you been there?"

"No. But, it was in the center of my bedroom window at the hotel when I was growing up. At night, the light in the tower called to me like Circe's sirens."

"You lived at the Princess?"

"Yes. My grandfather died when I was seven. The apartment was way too big for my grandmother, so she moved downstairs, and we moved in."

"It must have been wonderful."

"At first, I hated it. I associated living there with my grandfather dying. It was a terrible year."

"How sad for you."

He exited the bridge and maneuvered through the traffic to Highway 580. "Eventually, I understood that moving there didn't cause my grandfather's death. He'd been a heavy smoker, and it caught up with him. You'd think my father would have learned from the experience, but he won't give up his cigars."

"Apparently smoking is a tough habit to break."

"I'm glad it never appealed to me."

"Me, either."

"What about you? Did you have a happy childhood?"

"For a while. My father died when I was eleven; after that, my mother wanted to be closer to her parents. That meant we had to leave everything I'd ever known in Seattle, and move here, where my grandparents were the only thing I knew."

"Tough."

"It was. But, then I met Laura, who became my best friend, and things improved."

"No brothers or sisters?"

"Two older brothers. They're both back in Seattle."

"But not you."

"No. As it happened, I fell in love with San Francisco. Now, I wouldn't want to live anywhere else." She glanced over at him, trying not to let her eyes linger too long on the shirt that rounded in all the right places. "And you? Any siblings?"

"Nary a one. I kept hoping when I was a kid. I'm not sure why there were no more. My parents seemed happy, so maybe one was enough." He was quiet for a while, as if trying to figure it out.

"Seemed?"

He hesitated, and finally said, "My mom left when I was in high school." There was no humor in his laugh. "I guess she wasn't all that happy after all." His voice fell off and then changed. "Your mom couldn't have had it easy, and yet you went to Cornell."

"I was lucky enough to win several scholarships."

"From what I remember about scholarships, you don't get them because you're lucky. You must have worked hard. What made you choose hotel management?"

"Heather Ames is my mom's best friend. I worked part time and summers for her during high school and loved it. There was a certain excitement—somehow always being at the edge of disaster—that was intoxicating. By the time I graduated, I knew that was what I wanted to do."

"And you chose Cornell."

"Heather said they have the best program in the country."

"Good advice."

The sun peeked over the east bay hills with blinding brightness. They both reached up and pulled down their visors.

"What did you study at Cal?" Kristi asked.

"Political Science."

"Which segued right into hotel management?"

He laughed, and Kristi shivered at the delicious sound: a low, rumbling explosion of joy that wrapped around her like experienced arms.

"Hardly. At the beginning of my senior year, I was considering my options and realized I didn't like any of them. Government work, law, teaching, politics; none of it appealed to me. At Christmas, when I was home on break, it all fell into place. I belonged at the hotel."

"I bet that made your father happy."

"It did. He insisted I get my Master's, so I went to University of Nevada in Las Vegas, and got an MBA and a Master's in Hotel Administration."

"But did not run off with a showgirl."

"I considered it."

"Was her name Bambi?"

"You know her?"

"She was only working there to save money for college. She was my roommate at Cornell."

"I thought you were kidding. What are the odds? You must have seen as much of her as I did."

She started to say something even more suggestive, but checked herself.

Watch That Line.

"You win," she said. Better safe than sexy.

The silence that followed was completely comfortable. Kristi sat back, relaxed, and watched the landscape melt from inner-city, to urban, to rural.

Josh turned up the radio. "What do you like? I only listen to the big-band stuff."

"Does it remind you of your grandfather?"

"No. I played in the Cal Band, more by accident than anything else. I took clarinet lessons when I was a kid and was okay. I quit playing in high school. One of the guys in my dorm played in the band at Cal, and he was always having so much fun. I dragged out the clarinet, practiced the rest of the year, and auditioned that fall."

"And got in."

"Barely, I imagine. But I improved. I had to. The prof worked us hard. He expected a lot, particularly when you consider it was an elective. Zeb was a big influence on me. We're still in touch, in fact. He considers me one of his greatest accomplishments."

"I bet teaching is most satisfying when a student goes on to be so successful."

"Probably most of the time, a teacher doesn't have a clue what happens to students after they graduate."

"Are you always so optimistic?"

"Only when I'm making a point."

A giant grey cloud slipped in front of the sun, stealing the heat from the morning. Kristi hoped it didn't mean a storm was coming. She didn't want any dampers on the weekend.

"I like your music. It reminds me of my grandparents. My Nana used to say this was when music sounded like music and not like two raccoons fighting over garbage."

"What kind of music do you like?"

"Show tunes. Something I can sing. My Nana took me to a lot of musicals when I was a kid. I like them the best."

"Which shows?"

"Mostly her favorites. The old ones. She took me to see *Grease*, *Annie*, and *The Music Man*. I still love those three the best. Later, in New York, I saw *Phantom of the Opera*, *Cats*, *Mamma Mia*, and *Wicked*. I'm a wimp, though. I like bright shows like *Mamma Mia* more than the dark ones like *Phantom* or *Les Mis*."

"Then you probably don't care for opera."

"I've never been to an opera."

"How about the symphony?"

"A few times."

"It's a shame to live in San Francisco and not go to the opera."

"Ah, but I've been to the Dragon Boat races."

"Did that get Olympic status yet?"

"Not yet. We're in line behind fire batons and balloon-animal making."

"It's only a matter of time."

He did a search for show tunes on the radio, and Kristi was soon humming along with the music from *Chicago*.

"Do you consider this dark? It's about a murderer."

"He wasn't a nice man—the guy she shot. He probably deserved to die."

"Remind me never to let you off for jury duty."

CHAPTER 9

The winding highway narrowed to two lanes when they passed the park entrance. Pine trees and spring green foliage scattered along the road, splashed shadows on the car like a flashing flipbook. Kristi wished they were headed to Tahoe, or Tennessee, or Tallahassee. The trip was ending too soon.

"We're early," Josh said. "Is there anything special you'd like to see before we check in?"

"Do we have time to hike up to Half Dome?"

"I'm afraid not."

"What a relief."

His eyes never left the road, but Kristi saw the half-dome-grin that climbed up his face.

"Something a little less strenuous? We could rent hammocks at Curry Village."

Her turn to smile. "What about the museum in Yosemite Village?"

"I don't think it opens until ten."

"We could ride around in the car and take pictures."

"We'll be sitting for two days. We ought to get out and walk around. Let's look for a meadow that isn't already crowded with tourists, and take a hike."

"Hike?"

"Walk."

"That I can do."

Half an hour into the park, Josh pulled into a broad turn-off at the side of the road and parked the car. "This looks good." He unbuckled his seat belt, and then slid his hand over just far enough to unbuckle hers.

The gesture was so unexpected, so subtle, so intimate, that it bordered on provocative. Her entire body tingled as if she'd been caressed.

Get a grip, she warned herself. He was being a gentleman.

He pointed across the highway. "No people; lots of meadow. It's still early enough that we might see some wildlife."

Kristi scanned the meadow, the wide expanse peaceful and inviting. "How wild?"

"If you count the tourists, it's all wild. But, it looks pretty safe to me. I'll leave my gun in the car."

"You have a gun?"

"I'm kidding. We're fine. Come on."

He led her across the meadow toward a dense stand of trees, thick with underbrush. The damp grass glistened, and smelled wild and sweet. Tiny yellow flowers dotted the meadow like confetti sprinkled from one of the towering mountains surrounding the valley.

When they had nearly reached the trees, Kristi turned to look at the view back toward the car. "Is that Half Dome?" she asked, pointing to the west.

He walked back to her. "No. I think Half Dome is farther east." He peered at something in the grass and walked even farther toward the car.

He was twenty feet away from her when he turned. His head jerked, and he drew in a short, sharp breath. "Kristi…"

His voice sent cold coursing through her body, turning her fingers to ice.

In a barely audible tone, he said, "Listen to me. Do exactly what I say. Walk toward me. Slowly. Don't turn around. Don't talk."

She moved forward as if Satan himself followed, ready to grab her. When she was only a few steps away, he pulled her close, and pushed her behind him.

He drew in a massive breath and let out a spine shivering scream.

Kristi whirled.

Josh stood stretched up, arms reaching overhead, his voice a mind-bending, primal screech.

Thirty yards away, at the edge of the trees, stood a black bear, its nose high in the air.

Kristi's heart thumped and thumped and thumped again, then thammered with a desperate, erratic beat.

The bear shook its head, and took a threatening step toward them.

Josh waved wildly and yelled even louder. "Go! Go! Go!"

With a mere heart-breath of hesitation, Kristi arched up beside him and shrieked, "Go! Go home! Go!"

The animal stared at them, giving no ground.

Kristi screamed until her voice quit. Sweat dripped down her back, and puddled, cold, at her waist.

After what seemed like forever, the animal turned toward the woods. It took a few steps, then glanced back at them, as if to make sure they were not following. Turning once more, it lumbered into the forest.

Josh put his arm around her. "Time to go."

Her body refused to move. Her heart banged madly in her chest and echoed in her ears.

"Kristi?"

She searched for her voice.

"Kristi?"

"Yeah, I hear you." But, she was paralyzed. She leaned against him.

He held her briefly, and then said, "We need to get back to the car."

She glanced back toward the trees, looking for movement.

"Now, Kristi," he said, urging her with a strong arm around her waist.

He was right beside her until she slid into the car seat. Moments later, he got in on the driver's side and handed her an open bottle of water. "That's enough wildlife for one day." He started the engine and pulled onto the road.

After a long, slow drink of water, Kristi leaned back. Her heart pounded, the image of the bear seared on her eyelids. She wished Josh had held her a little longer. She'd felt safe with his arms wrapped around her.

"You okay?"

"I'm fine," she said, sure she was not. "What do you think he wanted?"

"He was just curious. The wind was blowing in that direction. He probably smelled your hair."

"Would he have come after us?"

"Only if he felt threatened. Or, it could have been a female. Maybe she had cubs and we were getting too close."

"Which means she felt threatened."

"Yes, possibly."

"Which means she might have attacked."

"Yes."

"Which means you saved my life." She let her eyes linger on his face. "If you hadn't been here, I might be dead."

The half-dome smile reappeared. "If I hadn't been here, you would have been with Wilhelm; I doubt he would have stopped in the first place. I'm the one who put you in danger."

"There's always that."

She wanted to reach over, to touch him, to thank him.

Not good.

Not good at all.

Instead, she pulled out her phone and found a site on bears in Yosemite. "'When preparing for hibernation, bears consume twenty thousand calories a day—the equivalent of a human eating forty hamburgers.'"

"Forty hamburgers. Do you think they mean with fries?" He glanced toward her briefly, smiling again. "Speaking of food, I'm hungry. How about some breakfast?"

"Back from the hunt..."

"Empty-handed."

When they reached the hotel, they left the car with the valet and walked into the massive entrance to the rustic Ahwahnee.

Josh gave their names to the clerk at the front desk, who told them their rooms would not be ready until eleven o'clock.

"I'll text you if something comes available sooner," she assured Josh, her practiced smile perfect.

"Thanks. We'd appreciate that."

Kristi noticed the clerk's smile fade at the word *we*.

He rested his hand on the small of Kristi's back. "Breakfast?"

"Sounds wonderful."

They were soon seated in the dining room, where a vaulted, beamed ceiling and floor-to-ceiling windows framed a stunning view of a verdant meadow.

"It's nothing like the Princess," Josh said, looking around the cavernous room, "but it's regal in its own way. It was quite an accomplishment to build this huge room in a mountain valley during the twenties. I wonder how many engineers worked on the plans."

"And who approved them?" Kristi leaned over and spoke softly. "Do they have earthquakes up here?"

"There are earthquakes all over these days. I think the gods of the underworld are unhappy about something."

"Fracking," Kristi said.

The waitress stopped at their table. "Coffee?"

They both said yes.

Josh opened his menu. "What looks good?"

Kristi read down the page. "Everything."

After they ordered, Kristi stared out the window at a world more brilliant and full of wonder than it had been an hour before. They'd faced down a bear and survived.

She was sure that Josh's quick thinking had saved her life. He was as capable in the woods as he was in the hotel.

*

The conference attendees ate dinner in the Solarium, a room offering a majestic view of Glacier Point. They broke into small, informal groups after dinner and Kristi watched Josh drift from one group to another, meeting and greeting friends and strangers alike.

Had he been at other conferences where she would have met him?

Doubtful.

She never could have forgotten those eyes.

She watched him work the room, giving out business cards, making people smile or laugh with his comfortable banter. He'd changed into slacks and a sports jacket. He looked great, every bit the professional. But, Kristi preferred him in jeans.

Stop!

Thinking that way was not a good idea. She shouldn't even imagine crossing The Line. It wasn't safe, it wasn't smart, and it certainly wasn't going to help her career.

"How about a drink, Kristi?"

She turned to the chairman of the conference. "Hey, Don. Sure. I'd like that."

"Let's duck into the bar. It's quieter there."

They spent nearly an hour at a table next to a window, discussing details for the next day. It wasn't long before others from their group drifted into the bar.

"Is there room for one more?" Josh asked, looking down at Kristi.

"Of course," she said. "Do you two know each other?"

"We sure do," Josh said. "Is this a business meeting?"

"It was, but I think we're done. Unless you have something else, Kristi."

"No, I'm set."

Don stood. "If you don't mind, I'm going to turn in. I want to be up early in the morning to do my run."

"Stay out of the woods," Kristi said.

The man nodded toward the window. "How?"

"I think she means be careful," Josh said. "We ran into a bear earlier."

Don looked out the window and then back at them. "Maybe I'll use the gym."

"I read they're more active in the early morning. The gym might be safer."

"If I don't show up tomorrow," Don said, "you'll know why." He laughed and left.

A waiter came over and asked Josh, "Can I get you something to drink?

"A sparkling water. Whatever you have is fine."

"And you, miss?"

Kristi nodded at her half-full glass. "I'm good, thanks."

Josh sat back, looking like he wanted nothing more than to put his feet up on the other chair. "It's been a long day."

"Fraught with danger."

"Nearly facing a grisly death."

She shivered, imagining the bear's tilted head. "Yes. Life-threatening danger takes a toll every time." Remembering, her body pulsed with exhilaration. It seemed like the encounter with the bear had heightened all her senses.

"All I could see was that bear dragging you into the woods."

"Like a bad version of Little Red Riding Hood."

"How would I have explained it to my dad?"

"Or my mother?"

He lifted his drink and raised it toward Kristi. "Here's to survival."

"Of the fittest."

"Not unless we go running tomorrow morning."

"Not happening. I've done enough running for one weekend."

"We didn't run, remember?"

"No. We stood tall."

"And yelled 'go, go, go'."

"Thanks again for saving my life."

"Any time."

"And if I ever go to the Kentucky Derby, I want you with me. That tactic might be just the ticket."

He laughed, her stomach tumbled, and The Line blurred.

They sat at the same table late the next night, Kristi drinking champagne, and Josh, another sparkling water.

"You did a nice job today," Josh said. "I was impressed. The panel was enthusiastic and informative."

"At least nobody fell asleep."

"Everyone was especially keen on how to incorporate current design trends into corporate events."

"I'm glad. I put a lot of hours into that."

A waiter stopped at their table. "Just to let you know, if you want to go out to the patio, there's a meteor shower tonight. It's the Lyrids. It happens every year at the end of April."

"Thanks," Josh said. He looked at Kristi. "Interested?"

"Absolutely."

They found two lounge chairs on the patio and lay back to watch Mother Nature's fireworks display. Sparkling diamonds fell from the sky, like luminous gifts from heaven.

"It's beautiful," Kristi whispered.

"Amazing."

But he was not looking at the stars.

*

She woke later, stiff and disoriented. Something warm covered her; it took several moments to realize it was Josh's jacket. She sat up and looked around. They were the only ones left on the patio.

"How long have I been asleep?"

"Not long."

What an idiot. How could she have fallen asleep in front of her boss? Her mouth was dry and her eyes, scratchy. She reached for her glass, grateful for the last sip of champagne.

"I'm so sorry. Were you asleep, too?"

"No. One of us needed to keep watch for the bear."

"Shouldn't she be home reading those little ones a bedtime story?"

"Saturday is her night out."

"What time is it?"

He checked his phone, the glow blaring into the intimate darkness. "Two-thirty."

She pulled herself to her feet, and he adjusted the jacket around her shoulders. She couldn't help wishing it were his arm instead.

"Thanks. I guess I was more tired than I realized."

"It was a long day. I'm tired, too."

"Why didn't you wake me up?"

"You were comfortable; I was enjoying the night. I figured you'd wake up eventually. Especially if it got any colder. I was just about to take back my jacket."

"You should have it," she said, letting it slip from her shoulders.

He wrapped it back around her. "I was kidding." But this time, he left his arm draped loosely around her shoulders.

They walked up to the first floor, their shoes clicking and echoing in the stairwell. Kristi turned too quickly on the landing and slipped on the highly polished floor. She grabbed for the railing but missed, and crashed into Josh.

She cried out, and he caught her just before she hit the floor.

"Are you okay?"

She recognized the anxious voice from the meadow. "I'm fine." But, her face had exploded into a fiery blush. "That was just an example of my well-honed clumsiness."

"Let's get you to your room before you break a leg." He wrapped his arm around her waist, and she leaned into the embrace that she'd longed for all day.

Once there, he took the key card from her hand and opened the door.

She entered the dark room, and turned to give him his jacket. "Thank you…"

His lips met hers and silenced her words and her thoughts. The splendor of the Lyrids paled in contrast to the explosion of his kiss, which flamed through her body.

The door squeezed shut with a loud crunch.

He kissed her again, and she felt his chest pounding against her own.

"I need to go." He unwound his jacket from her shoulders. "I'll see you in the morning." When he opened the door, the hallway light chased his shadow across the room. "Turn on the lamp." His voice was the antithesis of the one that had chased the bear.

She switched on the lamp by the bed.

She barely heard him say, "Good night," before the door swallowed his shadow.

Kristi toppled, speechless and shocked, onto the bed.

CHAPTER 10

Kristi's heart hammered, her hands shook, and her breath came in short gasps. She collapsed against the bed pillows.

What the hell was that about?

What was he thinking?

And why did he stop thinking it?

Her mind jumped back two minutes, back into his arms, the arms she wished were still around her. He could have let the door close with him right there.

"No, he couldn't." She sat, stiff and resolute. "This cannot happen. He's my boss."

With fireworks like falling stars sparking in her blood, she stood on unsteady legs and found her nightshirt. She brushed her teeth and her hair, avoiding her own eyes in the mirror. She slipped under the lofty duvet, turned off the light, and curled up in the luxurious linens.

But sleep was far from her mind.

Josh Townsend owned every thought.

Had she given him some message? Maybe after the bear, when she'd been scared half to death and wanted him to hold her. Had he sensed that?

She couldn't imagine how. She had pulled out her phone the moment she realized she was imagining his arms wrapped around her.

Then what was it?

It wasn't the booze. He'd only had water after dinner.

She flashed on his tall, lean body, stretched up high as he yelled at the bear. She remembered his explanation in the car. "The bear probably smelled your hair."

The bear?

I think not, Mr. Townsend. I think you smelled my hair.

So, it wasn't just her.

Now what?

She lay, wide-eyed and wondering, until the east offered up a dazzling sun.

*

The morning provided no time for explanation or exploration. They ate breakfast with three other board members, and then immediately went into the conference wrap-up session. As soon as that was over, they had to pack and check out.

Josh met her at the front desk, pulled out his wallet, and said, "This is on the company."

"I'm happy to pay my way."

"My dad would have a fit. This is business."

The night before certainly wasn't.

But what was it? A dream? A mistake?

The thought of his kiss thundered through her, stealing her breath and her balance. She leaned against the counter and waited for the weakness to pass.

The car was brought to the portico, where Josh loaded the suitcases into the trunk.

Traffic was heavy on the valley floor, and Kristi didn't want to distract Josh with a conversation—or questions—or assumptions. But once they were out of the village, she found she needed to say something.

He beat her to it. "About last night..."

"Yeah..."

"I was entirely out of line."

Okay, mistake. "You mean that's not the way you usually tell your employees good night?"

His smile stalled somewhere between half-hearted and Half Dome. "Can we forget it ever happened?"

Forget that kiss? Not in her lifetime; not in his lifetime; not in a hundred lifetimes. "Of course," she said. What choice was there?

"I think I was unduly influenced by the meteor shower."

"It was spectacular."

"The last thing I want is for things to be awkward at work."

Too late for that. "I agree. We'll forget it happened." The words of self-betrayal tasted bitter.

He turned on the radio and they listened to show tunes all the way back to San Francisco.

Periodically, Kristi glanced at him. Each time, he looked back with a smile that said he had done nothing but remember.

Would he kiss her again at the hotel?

Sure. In front of half a dozen employees. That's going to happen.

Not.

The Bay Bridge was jammed, so they inched along, watching impatient drivers move from lane to lane, making more problems than progress. They crept off the bridge at last, and turned up the Embarcadero. By the time they reached the hotel, Kristi was ready to explode.

Or grab him and tell him that kiss had not been a mistake.

She stretched her cramped legs and arched her back as best she could. The seatbelt felt suddenly confining. "I feel like we've been gone forever. It's only been three days."

"A lot can happen in three days."

Was that a message?

Would she be second guessing everything he said now?

This was going to be impossible.

Josh greeted the garage attendant when he drove into the Princess parking lot. He pulled in next to Kristi's car, turned off the engine, and unbuckled her seat belt before undoing his own. She shivered from his hand so close to her.

She opened the door quickly and jumped out. He had her suitcase out of his car by the time she popped the trunk on hers. Wasting no time.

"Thanks for the ride," she said, just as her phone rang. She glanced at the screen. "Sam," she cried, answering it before the third ring. "Where are you?"

Josh looked at her, frowned slightly, then pointed up in the general direction of his office.

"I have to take this."

"No problem. I'll see you." He headed for the elevator.

Samantha's voice was crackly, and faded in and out.

"Where are you, Sam? I can barely hear you."

"I'm in Florida, on my way home."

Kristi watched Josh disappear into the elevator and cursed her phone for working, today of all days, in the underground garage. "How long will you be here?"

"Three days."

"Do we get to see you?"

"Why else would I be calling? Will Tuesday night work?"

"Yes," Kristi said, without actually knowing. "We'll make it work."

She knew she had at least one function to run that night, but Queenie would help out.

"Great. I'll call you in the morning."

Sam considered anything before two PM, morning.

"Super. Talk to you then. Safe travels."

One last crackle and she was gone.

What miserable timing. She stood next to her car, uncertain what to do. Follow Josh upstairs? Wait for him to come down again? Hang out near the elevator and attack him when he stepped out?

All good ideas.

Instead, she got into her car and drove home. He was her boss. He'd stepped over The Line; encouraging him would only cause her grief.

*

Josh didn't come by her office the next morning, as he had nearly every day since she had come on board. He didn't drop in on her meeting with Wilhelm, or seek her out in the kitchen, or leave a phone message. By late afternoon, she found herself inventing excuses to go by his office, asking Debby inane questions, which she imagined were completely transparent.

By the time she left, she still hadn't seen him.

A guy not calling 'the day after' was never good. Was he going to avoid her all week?

She'd hoped he would come to a different decision. A decision that would have included her. He'd checked out, and all she had were memories that lingered on her lips like bittersweet chocolate.

*

On Tuesday, she took a stack of outdated folders into Debby's office, intending to ask her about Josh's whereabouts. Once there, she stood tentative and tongue-tied.

"Do you need something?" Debby asked when Kristi lingered by the file cabinet.

Kristi felt an incriminating blush creep up her cheeks. "No, thanks." She made the most graceful exit she could muster. Josh's absence was none of her concern.

Queenie agreed to fill in for Kristi at the dinner that evening. A small group from a local businessmen's organization met at the Princess regularly to discuss upcoming election issues. JT told her they always reserved the same room, ordered the same entrée, and left at the same time. The function would practically run itself.

"I really appreciate you doing this for me, Queenie. I owe you big time."

"Go meet your friends. If this Sam person only comes to town once in six months, you can't afford to miss her. Besides, the dinner is almost over. Go."

When she arrived at the restaurant, Kristi found her friends had ordered for her. She slipped into the booth next to Sam, and hugged her slim, tanned friend, who was so attractive, she could easily have been a model.

"It's about time," Sam said, checking her ever-present waterproof watch.

"She's always late these days," Nicole told her. "Kristi is the new Laura."

"Wait until you have a baby," Laura said.

Nicole leaned over. "Eat your salad, Kristi, or I will. It looks too good to resist."

"I want to hear about the Great Blue Hole," Kristi said.

Sam nodded at the salad. "Eat."

Kristi took several bites. "Come on, Sam. What was it like?"

"Exciting beyond belief. I saw marine life that I've never seen anywhere. The dive is like gliding down a rocky mountainside. There were caves I wanted to explore, but my guide wasn't having it."

"What's down there?"

"Fossils, boulders, stalactites, speleothems—those are mineral deposits. It's an historical and geological treasure trove." Her eyes sparkled as she spoke, like crystals in sunlight.

"Weren't you scared?" Laura asked. "Or nervous?"

"What's there to be scared of? We had a safety diver with us."

"Why would you want to take chances like that?" Laura asked. "I don't get it."

"Me either," Nicole said, picking a shrimp off Kristi's plate.

"What's next?" Kristi swatted Nicole's hand.

The sparkle faded. "The magazine wants me to do this train ride thing. Boring, but it promises to pay well."

"Where?" Kristi asked.

"China to Russia: the Trans-Mongolian Express."

Nicole reached for another shrimp, and Kristi slapped her hand. "Stop."

"That does sound boring compared to The Blue Hole," Nicole said.

"No doubt. We'll see the usual tourist dreck: the Gobi Desert, the steppes of Mongolia, the Great Wall, Saint Basil's Cathedral."

"Dreck," Kristi repeated. "Right."

"Sounds wonderful to me." Nicole tried to take the last shrimp from Kristi's plate and was met with a threatening fork. "I'd love to visit Moscow."

"How long is the trip?" Laura asked.

"Twenty-one days."

"Maybe you'll meet some nice guy who likes dreck." Laura gave her an innocent smile.

"I'm going to meet overweight, retired couples discovering that they don't like Mongolian food."

"Do you?" Nicole asked.

"I will," Sam told her confidently. "I've never met a meal I didn't like."

"Neither has Nicole." Kristi pushed the remainder of her salad toward her friend.

Nicole looked hard at Kristi. "You're awfully quiet tonight. Is anything wrong?"

"Not at all." Kristi sounded too bright and she knew it.
"There's a lot happening at work."
"How's your hunky boss?" Sam asked.
She'd been at the bottom of the ocean. How did she know about Josh? "Hunky?"
"Don't be coy. Laura told me all about him."
"Actually, our paths don't cross all that often."
Laura shot her a look. Liar.
They talked until, one after another, they began to yawn.
"Could you give me a lift home?" Laura asked Kristi. "No point in Nicole driving me."
"Sure." Kristi knew what was coming.
They walked out to the parking lot, extracted a promise from Sam that she would email more regularly, and were all soon pulling away from the restaurant.
"What gives?" Laura asked before Kristi had a chance to say a word.
"Nothing."
"Shall I remind you how long we've known each other? Out with it."
Kristi thought a moment. "The weekend wasn't exactly what I expected."
"How's that?"
"Wilhelm didn't go with me...Josh did."
"You spent the weekend with Josh?"
"I wouldn't put it like that."
"How would you put it?"
"It was a business trip."
"A business trip with benefits?"
"Good Lord, Laura. I just got this job. Do you think I'd risk it by sleeping with my boss?"
"I bet you thought about it." Laura's laugh said how well she knew her.
I bet you're right.
When Kristi didn't say that out loud, Laura said, "Tell

me everything, from beginning to end. And slow down; I don't want to miss a single detail."

Kristi told her about the weekend, from bear sighting to meteor shower. "He apologized the next morning, of course. Although what I would have preferred him to say was, 'the kiss last night was only the beginning. Let me fire you, and we can take a cruise around the world'."

"Does he live at the hotel?"

"No."

"So you won't be sneaking up to his room for some afternoon delight."

"Uh, no."

"It'll be interesting to see what he has to say the next time you see him."

"It's strange. He's come by my office every day since I started. This week, I haven't laid eyes on him."

"Uh, oh; morning-after regret raising its ugly head? Not good."

"I know." Kristi pulled up in front of Laura's house.

"Don't let it discourage you. He probably just needs time to sort it out. He'll be back."

"I hope so."

But Kristi didn't see him the rest of the week. The longer it took for him to face her, the harder it would be. For about two seconds, she considered making an appointment to see him. In the end, she didn't have the nerve.

He'd kissed her, not the other way around.

Besides, they'd agreed to forget it.

As if.

CHAPTER 11

Kristi took the stairs down to the garage on Friday evening. The minute she stepped out the door, she saw Josh's BMW pull in next to her car. He got out, dressed in his impossibly sexy jeans and boots. Her heart began rapid firing in a conspicuous rat-a-tat.

"Hi," he said. "No events tonight?"

"No," she managed to slip in between beats.

The back door of his car swung open, and Georgia Markham peered out. "Hey, Kristi."

"Hi, Georgia."

"We're going to North Beach for drinks. Come with us?"

Kristi looked at Josh, sure he could hear the tympani hammering in her chest. "I don't know…"

"Come on," Georgia said. "Josh and Wyatt are going to rehash their fishing trip, and I'll be bored beyond belief. Come keep me company."

Fishing trip? Fishing? Not avoiding her?

A delicious-looking man got out of the passenger seat. "Hi, Kristi. I'm Wyatt. Please, come with us. Give Josh and me a foil."

She looked at Josh, the guy to whom "morning after" etiquette meant going fishing.

"By all means, if you don't have plans, come with us."

What his invitation lacked in luster, Georgia's balanced in brio. "Oh yes, Kristi, please, please come with us."

She let Georgia's encouragement persuade her. "If you're sure I'm not intruding." She had told her mother they could go to a movie that night. Her mother would understand.

Especially if she saw him in those jeans.

"I need to check on a couple of things in my office." Josh opened the door to the stairwell. "Go ahead and hop in. I'll be right back."

Kristi walked to her car. "I think I'll drive myself," she told Georgia.

"If you don't mind, I'll go with you," Georgia said. "I've heard enough fish tales."

Kristi followed Josh's car, noticing how careful he was not to lose her in traffic. Georgia answered a business call and was on her phone during the entire trip. They found parking two blocks from the main street in the Italian district, and wound their way through the crowded sidewalks to the pub.

"Hey, Josh," the bartender said when they entered. "Long time no see. Did you and Wyatt get out for salmon season opener?"

"Sure did. Caught our limit every day."

"So, fishing trip, huh?" Kristi said as they slipped into a booth at the rear of the bar.

"Yep. Wyatt has a terrific little boat he keeps at Half Moon Bay. We have a long-standing tradition of going out for the season opener every year."

"A tradition that's never been broken, right buddy?" Wyatt said.

"And you caught your limit? What will you do with all that fish?"

"We had most if it flash frozen. But, I have a couple of friends who expect a visit tomorrow. I still have three good sized pieces, if you're interested."

"I love salmon."

"Yes, I remember."

Kristi blushed, the orgasmic comment dangling between them like an impaled worm.

The arrival of the waiter couldn't have been more timely.

"What would you like to drink?" Josh asked her.

"Champagne."

"Me, too," Georgia said.

"A beer for me," Wyatt told him.

Josh ordered Pinot Noir.

"Have you two been friends for long?" Kristi asked Josh.

"Since high school. Then, we roomed together at Cal, where we met Georgia. Wyatt studied law and has a practice in Berkeley."

Kristi felt herself sliding into the comfort of his voice, floating on his inflections like a small boat on a calm sea.

Georgia leaned toward Kristi. "When Wyatt and I were first dating, I was jealous of Josh. Back then, I resented how much time they spent together."

"And now?" Kristi asked.

"Now it's a relief when he takes Wyatt off my hands." She put a loving hand over Wyatt's and Kristi watched unsaid words pass privately between them. "What about you, Kristi? Do you have a bestie?"

"I do. I met Laura when our family moved here from Seattle. We both live in the Sunset. She's married now, and has a baby girl named Chloe. Still, we do our best to see each other every week."

When their drinks arrived, Josh raised his glass. "Here's to best friends."

"Best friends," the others echoed.

While Josh and Wyatt reviewed the highlights of their fishing expedition, Georgia took one business call after another.

"I'm so sorry," she said to Kristi after the fifth call. "I've got a bidding war on my hands, and if we lose this house, my client will have a nervous breakdown."

"No problem."

"I thought you asked her to join us to keep you company," Josh said.

Wyatt put his arm around Georgia and said, "All she needs for company is her phone."

"Darling, if this deal falls through, we'll be spending our honeymoon in Sonoma instead of Samoa."

"Don't knock Sonoma," he said. "We've made some nice memories there."

"We have. And, we'll make even more in Samoa."

Josh's phone buzzed and he read a text. "They're ready for us at the restaurant."

"We're meeting some other friends," Georgia said to Kristi. "Can you join us?"

"I'm afraid not. I told my mom we'd go to a movie if it wasn't too late."

"I'll walk Kristi to her car, and meet you at the restaurant," Josh said.

"You don't need to do that, Josh."

"Let him practice being a gentleman," Georgia said. "It's good for him."

"It was nice meeting you," Wyatt said.

"You, too. I'm looking forward to your wedding reception."

"I hope you'll have time to enjoy it," Georgia said.

"I'm sure I will."

Josh escorted her out of the pub and down the crowded street. When they neared the end of the block, he said, "I want to apologize again for my very inappropriate actions last weekend. I assure you it won't happen again. I don't want you to be uncomfortable at work."

Her disappointment tasted bitter after the sweet champagne. "I'd all but forgotten it." Who knew the skills from Children's Theater would be so useful?

"Good. Then I'll do the same."

He stood watching as she drove up the street.

Kristi glanced in the rear view mirror, and saw Josh's head drop forward, as if he had just lost a fortune—or a friend.

Was he lying, too?

If so, what could she do about it?

*

Wedding receptions kept Kristi moving at full speed all weekend, but whenever there was a quiet moment, she saw Josh's slumped silhouette. Why so downcast? She could ask him. That is, if he wasn't her boss.

Better to let sleeping bears lie.

Her phone rang late Sunday night. "Hi, Nicole."

"Hi. Do you have a function Friday night?"

"I'm fine, thanks for asking."

"You never have time for pleasantries. Well, do you?"

"I don't think so."

"Good. We'll have GNO here. I'm ready to unveil the Bridal Ball website."

"Really? Oh Nicky, that's fantastic."

"Let's hope Chloe won't be cutting teeth, or taking her first steps, or preparing for her SATs."

Nicole had never done any babysitting and had no clue about small kids. "That's not fair. Laura wants to be with us. Babies are unpredictable; that's not her fault."

"I'm only kidding. Sort of. Anyway, I'll call Laura."

"Let me bring food," Kristi said.

"Sushi?"

"Not this time. I'll have Tony fix us something special."

"They won't mind?"

"No. If anyone asks, I'll tell them I'm trying a new recipe."

"Okay then, I'll see you on Friday."

"I can't wait."

*

Josh dropped by her office on Monday, as he had before their trip to Yosemite. But, Kristi felt a palpable difference in his demeanor—a formal greeting that lacked the casual camaraderie they'd once shared. He came by every day, but on Friday, merely waved a quick hello as he passed.

She knew that if she expected to be successful at the Princess, it had to be that way. But, the loss of the fragile beginnings of friendship was so disappointing that she almost wished he wouldn't come by at all.

Tony prepared cold salmon with fresh dill sauce, and a tabbouleh and mango salad for GNO on Friday night.

"You're a genius," she told him when he brought it to her office.

"I expect a full critique in the morning."

"You'll have one."

Wilhelm stopped her at the elevator. "Leaving so early?"

"Yes. There aren't any functions this evening."

"I thought you might want to be better prepared for the weekend."

He made it sound as though she hadn't been previously.

Kristi held the elevator door open and said, "Everything is in order."

"Very well. I suppose you'll manage," he said, his inflection implying impending disaster.

When the door closed, she sighed, relieved that he had not asked what she had in her tote bag. Tony had given her food to sample many times, but Kristi did not relish the thought of explaining the meal to Wilhelm.

If Josh had known, he probably would have said, "Good for you. Enjoy." If JT had known, he probably would have thrown in a bottle of wine.

How in the world did someone as gloomy as Wilhelm end up at the Princess?

Kristi couldn't make sense of it.

Traffic was horrendous. A serious accident on Lombard Street prompted a nightmare of impatient drivers to weave precariously in and out, trying to escape the backup. The trip from the hotel to Nicky's house would normally take five minutes; that night it took nearly forty.

"Thank heaven you're here," Laura said, meeting her at Nicole's front door. "Nicky is acting like she hasn't eaten in weeks. If we don't feed her soon, she may chew off her arm."

"I've got the antidote right here." Kristi handed her the tote.

"I offered her some Goldfish," Laura said, grinning. She pointed to a zip-top bag on the kitchen counter that contained the crumbled remnants of Chloe's favorite treat.

Laura opened the tote bag and pulled out the three carefully wrapped meals. "Oooh, yum. You're the best."

"Tony is the best," Kristi said.

Nicole came in from the small balcony. "It's about time."

"Sorry. There was an accident on Lombard."

"I've told you, never use Lombard."

"I know. Next time I'll remember."

They carried their meals out to the table on the balcony, where Nicole refreshed everyone's wine before sitting down.

"This is so fancy," Laura said. "What's the occasion?"

The other two looked at each other. "We're celebrating," Nicole said.

"What? Tell me what we're celebrating."

"We're celebrating a new venture," Nicole said, and

raised her glass. "Here's to the Bridal Ball."

Kristi raised her glass and repeated, "To the Bridal Ball."

Laura's look reminded Kristi of Chloe when she'd first discovered her toes.

"What the heck is the Bridal Ball?"

CHAPTER 12

Laura sat in front of Nicole's computer screen, wiping away tears as quickly as they slipped down her cheeks. "This is beautiful. Really beautiful. Do you think you can make it happen?"

"*We* can make it happen," Nicole corrected her. "We're all part of it now. You're going to manage the website."

Laura sat back, eyes big as basketballs. "Me? I don't know a thing about websites."

"By the time we're done, you'll be an expert," Nicole said.

"You should leave a comment, Laura," Kristi said. "It's only right that you're the first."

Laura clicked over to the comment screen.

"Not there," Nicole told her. "Go to 'Tell Us Your Story'. That's where the first post should be. I was going to write it, but I decided you should be the one."

Laura clicked the button and then sat immobile, her hands hovering above the keys like a drone. "I can't. I have to think about it. I want it to be perfect."

"Don't wait too long," Kristi said, "or someone will beat you to it."

Nicole nudged her. "Put your name there. You can edit it later, after you've had time to consider what to say."

Laura typed, "Thanks to two wonderful friends, my dearest dream may be coming true."

"There's still a lot of work to do," Nicole said. "I had the flyers printed for the businesses who've already agreed to sponsor us. We've got to hit up our neighborhood shopkeepers and try to get them involved. This is a soft launch. We're depending on word of mouth to get the site initial recognition, so talk it up."

"Will people say advertising something that doesn't exist, is fraud?" Laura asked.

"I've made it clear that we're trying to create the ball," Nicole said. "Let's hope nobody who visits the site is so mean-spirited that they'd sue us."

Laura swiveled in Nicole's chair. "How can I ever thank you for this?" Fresh tears streaked her face and fell onto her shirt.

Kristi leaned down and hugged her. "We'll get our thanks when we watch you dance in your beautiful gown."

Laura looked at Nicole. "Will you go too? In your wedding dress?"

"Sure. As long as I can fit into it."

"Maybe we can get Kristi married by then," Laura said. "Speaking of which, how are things going with the concierge?"

"That relationship is strictly business," Kristi said, knowing Laura was not fooled. "Did you get us dessert, Nicole?"

"I did."

"Well, what's the holdup?" Kristi was thankful that Nicole could be so easily sidetracked.

Laura held Kristi's arm as they followed Nicole into the kitchen. "Strictly business?"

Kristi jabbed her in the ribs. "Hush."

Kristi stepped up to the hostess at the Royal Princess dining room and smiled. "Good morning, Abby. I have a reservation for two."

"We're not really ready yet, Kristi."

"Couldn't we sneak in before the rush? It's always so busy on Mother's Day."

"Why not? Come with me."

Kristi and her mother followed the woman into the beautiful room that Kristi loved so much. Too late, she realized that Josh, his father, and an elderly woman were seated at the rear.

"Kristi," JT called to them. "How nice to see you. Come join us."

"Thanks, but we wouldn't want to intrude."

"Nonsense." JT said, standing. "I insist."

As they neared his table, Kristi put her arm around her mother's waist. "This is my mom, Victoria."

"And, this is my mother, Rose," JT said, resting his hand on the older woman's shoulder.

"Please, sit here, Victoria." JT pulled out the chair next to him.

Kristi had no choice but to sit next to Josh. "I had no idea you'd be here this morning."

"Family tradition," Josh said. "I was branded a traitor years ago when I suggested we go to the buffet at the Hyatt." His laughter reached into her heart and coaxed out a grin.

JT ordered champagne, but the bubbly golden beverage that she loved didn't help Kristi relax. Why was this so different from Yosemite, where she'd been perfectly comfortable?

Until Saturday night, anyway...

The food stations that surrounded the room were soon filled with fragrant offerings.

JT stood. "Shall we?"

His mother leaned toward Victoria and spoke in a conspiratorial whisper. "Come with me. I assure you I know all the best dishes."

Josh smiled indulgently as his grandmother led Victoria to the salad station. "I'm heading for the oyster bar," he told Kristi. "I intend to get my money's worth."

"I'm going for an omelet," Kristi said.

JT went directly to the prime rib station.

Kristi was surprised, two hours later, that time had evaporated as quickly as the champagne.

"Thank you, again," she said to JT. "We certainly didn't expect to be treated."

"You wouldn't have been charged in any event." His smile was generous and genuine. "Management has its privileges."

"Good to know. We'll be inviting two hundred to our next family reunion," Kristi said.

Victoria extended her hand to JT. "It was lovely meeting you. And you, Mrs. Townsend."

"Please, call me Rose. I hope we can do this again. You're much more interesting company than these two. Perhaps one day I can see some of your paintings."

"I'll have one in my office soon," Kristi said.

"We'll look forward to seeing it," JT told her.

They said goodbye at the stairs, and Kristi and her mother walked down to the garage.

"He's a nice looking man," Victoria said when they were headed back home.

"JT?"

"No. The concierge."

"He is."

"Too bad he's your boss."

"Yes."

"If I were you, I'd consider quitting."

*

Georgia Markham knocked on Kristi's door late Monday afternoon. "Got a minute?"

"Of course. Come in. How are you doing? It's only five days now. Are you nervous?"

"Not especially. But, I have a problem I'd like to talk to you about." She closed the door and sat down across from Kristi. She looked more like a troubled teenager than a successful real estate agent. "Wyatt's Uncle Max has a serious drinking problem. He originally declined our wedding invitation, but he called yesterday to say he's coming after all."

Georgia's unhappiness spilled over and puddled around her on the floor. "We've been planning on an open bar, but if there's an unlimited supply of liquor, he'll be drunk before dinner. I don't know what to do."

"I take it Wyatt's parents aren't willing to talk to him."

"They talk to him before every family event. It doesn't help. He agrees to behave, but never does."

"Why don't they tell him not to come?"

"I guess blood is thicker than booze."

Kristi pulled up Georgia's reception on her computer. "What's his preferred drink?"

"Bourbon."

"Don't serve it. In fact, don't serve any hard liquor. Offer red and white wine. It might not stop him, but it'd slow him down. Your guests won't care, especially if he has a reputation."

Georgia nodded, a small smile erasing the tension on her lips. "I think that might work. It's a start, anyway."

"And, what about a friend or bridesmaid to distract him? They could talk to him about his work or a hobby, if he has any."

"I have a cousin who would absolutely do that. She's a psychologist. If I phrase it right, she might consider it a challenge."

"Great. You solved your problem."

"Hardly. You came up with the solution."

As Georgia opened the office door, Kristi said, "One more thing."

"Yes?"

"On Saturday, remember that you're the honored guest, not the hostess. Let other people do for you. Enjoy your special day. It's the only chance you'll get."

"Yes. That is until the Bridal Ball."

*

Every day, whenever she had a free moment, Kristi checked the Bridal Ball website. Every night before she went to bed, she pulled it up on her laptop. Every time, she checked the traffic count. By Friday afternoon, she was so distressed she texted Nicole a 911/411.

When Nicole called minutes later, Kristi asked, "Is the site still live? It only shows eleven page views and I think I was ten of them."

"Of course it's live. I warned you it would be a slow start. As soon as the business owners give out more flyers, it'll start to pick up. You have to be patient."

"I'm trying. Don't blame me for being anxious."

"Anxious won't help. Be productive. Distribute flyers."

"In my spare time, right?"

"None of us has any spare time, Kristi. You have to make time. What about tomorrow?"

"We have a huge reception tomorrow. In fact, the groom is Josh's best friend."

"Isn't that the bride you told about your idea?"

"Yes."

"Maybe you should talk to her again now that the site is up; see if she wants to be a sponsor."

"I'll find an excuse to call her after their honeymoon."

"So, what about the flyers?"

Kristi looked at her calendar. "Tuesday is a light day. I'll take the afternoon off, walk around my neighborhood, and see how many businesses I can recruit."

"Good girl. Do you have enough flyers?"

"Hundreds."

"Let me know how you do."

"Of course."

*

The Crown Ballroom was never more beautiful than during a wedding reception. Kristi observed her staff, serving and clearing tables, their training evident in every move. She kept to the side, watching for problems, ready to step in and solve any issue. Happily, there were none.

Except Wyatt's uncle.

The biggest person, the loudest person, the most annoying person at Georgia and Wyatt's reception, was the infamous Uncle Max. He looked just like Wyatt, save for his screaming red hair.

The wait staff was trying to clear the dinner dishes and serve coffee; Max was trying to engage anyone who passed nearby.

"Come on, honey," Max said to one of the servers, "I need a decent drink."

Kristi looked at the head table, but neither Wyatt nor Georgia was paying attention.

"I'm sorry, sir," the young woman said, "but wine is the only beverage available tonight."

"Bull. I wanna see your supervisor."

The girl looked around for Kristi, who was already on her way to his table. "Can I help?"

"Yes. You can get me a drink. A real drink."

"We have red and white wine this evening," Kristi told him. "Or coffee, if you prefer."

"I'd prefer bourbon. I know you have a full bar here, so

I don't understand the problem."

"The bride and groom have limited the bar to wine this evening."

"I asked to see the supervisor."

"I am the supervisor."

"The manager, then. Somebody with some clout."

"What about the owner?"

Kristi recognized JT's voice, and turned. He looked almost as handsome as Josh in his dark suit. "I'm sorry, sir."

"It's not your fault," JT said. He looked down at Wyatt's uncle. "Sir, the bride and groom have chosen to offer red or white wine, or coffee this evening. Can we get one of those for you?"

"If you're the owner, you can get me a bourbon, neat."

"I'm afraid that isn't possible."

"Why the hell not?"

JT leaned toward him as if the man were hard of hearing. "Because bourbon is not being offered tonight. The bride and groom have chosen to serve red and white wine. Which would you prefer?"

"Forget it."

"Let me know if you change your mind," JT told him, and walked away.

Kristi glanced up at the head table, and let out a slow breath. They hadn't noticed. Heather always put troublemakers at the side of the room. Better yet, she'd say, don't invite them.

"Ladies and gentlemen," the emcee said, "please direct your attention to the dance floor, where Mr. and Mrs. Warren will share their first dance as husband and wife."

Wyatt put his arm around Georgia's waist and escorted her out to the dance floor. Kristi was fascinated, as she often was, watching a couple's first dance. Their steps were simple and uninspired, but they moved with exquisite intimacy. They had obviously danced together often. Some couples struggled through the first dance with painful uncertainty.

Georgia's elegant designer gown was every bit as stunning as Kristi expected, and looked as if it had been created especially for the beautiful woman. The delicate neckline showed-off Georgia's creamy skin; the low-waisted V-bodice, her tiny waist. A fingertip veil hung from a wreath of petite white rosebuds.

When the song ended, the emcee said, "And now, we'd like the rest of the wedding party to join our bridal couple."

Josh walked the maid of honor out to the floor and exchanged a few words with Wyatt. His tux suited him well, but could not compare with the way he looked in jeans and boots.

Georgia's maid of honor was a striking beauty. Her sleek, ebony hair stopped abruptly at her long, delicate neck, and emphasized her height. She wore a full-length black gown, much like the dress Kate Middleton's sister, Pippa, had worn at the Royal Wedding.

Although every attendant was dressed in black, each gown was different. Georgia looked like a luminous, white star spinning in a night sky.

"And now, the parents," the emcee said.

Kristi moved around the ballroom, directing servers and watching every table for any needs their guests might have. But, her gaze kept drifting back to the dance floor where she wished she could be, wrapped in Josh's arms.

Josh and his partner talked and laughed as they danced. They looked so comfortable that Kristi was sure they'd known each other before, perhaps even dated.

Was he interested in her, or just being an obliging best man?

She tried to shake off her jealousy. Be professional, she told herself.

"Kristi..."

She turned.

"You wanted me to let you know if Wyatt's uncle left," the server said.

Kristi glanced toward the man's table. His chair was empty.

"Thanks. If he comes back, please tell me."

The girl nodded, and returned to her station.

The dance floor was crowded for the next hour. Kristi tried not to focus on Josh. But, every time he danced, she noticed. Every time he laughed, she noticed. Every time he sat alone, she noticed.

She seriously couldn't stop noticing.

Many guests left after the cake was served, and Kristi sent half the staff home. She instructed the head server to dim the chandeliers and turn on the lights above the stained glass ceiling. The room morphed from ballroom to fairyland.

The orchestra began playing "Make You Feel My Love," and the emcee said, "Once again, Mr. and Mrs. Wyatt Warren."

Kristi's attention was fixed on the couple, leaving her unprepared for the rough hand that grabbed her arm.

"Wine or coffee?" Wyatt's uncle said, his voice mocking.

She whipped around, trying to shake off his hold.

"Your bartender didn't have any problem finding the bourbon." His upper lip curled like a snarling dog. He pushed her behind one of the huge columns. "Nothing to say for yourself?"

Kristi pulled as close to him as she dared. "Nothing you want to hear."

"Then let's dance," he said, his arm crushing her waist. He loomed over her like a mountain. "You made me look like a fool, begging for a drink."

His breath was foul and she gagged. She pushed on his chest. "Let. Me. Go."

He snorted, turning her roughly.

Kristi looked around for help, but nobody was nearby. She pushed at the man again, his massive frame not the least impacted by her effort.

"You're not going anywhere."

Suddenly, Georgia was at Kristi's side, pulling roughly on the man's arm. "For God's sake, Uncle Max, let go of her."

"We're just having a little dance."

Wyatt grabbed his uncle's jacket and nearly toppled both him and Kristi. "You're out of here, Max!"

"I'm only…"

"Shut up! It's time for you to go." Wyatt pushed the huge man toward the lobby.

Wyatt's father joined them, and helped muscle Max out of the ballroom.

"Are you okay?" Georgia put a protective arm around Kristi. "Did he hurt you? Thank heaven I saw him. I was just going to the ladies' room."

"I'm fine, Georgia. Please, don't make a fuss. He isn't the first drunk I've had to deal with. Go back to your party."

Josh came up to Kristi. "What the heck is going on?"

"Nothing." Kristi kept her voice level, trying to cover the tremble.

"My uncle was manhandling Kristi," Wyatt said, joining them.

"Please, I'm fine. Go back to the party."

Josh turned to Wyatt. "You two go dance. Let's not have everyone else wondering what's wrong."

Josh flagged down a waiter. "Would you get me a glass of champagne, Brendon. Thanks."

"Of course."

Josh pulled out a chair. "Kristi, you need to sit down."

"I'm fine," Kristi insisted, but her heart was quaking and her hands were quivering. The minute Josh handed her the champagne, she spilled it.

"Please, Kristi, sit down." Josh eased her into the chair.

"I'm sure he wouldn't have hurt me."

"Not if he'd been sober. I've seen him drunk before. He turns into a complete bully." He nodded at the glass. "Drink

THE BRIDAL BALL

some champagne. It'll help."

"I'm working, Josh."

"Not any more, you're not." He motioned to Brendon. "Kristi is off the clock. Consider her one of the guests. Tell your supervisor. If anyone has a problem, they can come to me."

"Yes, sir." He looked down at Kristi. "I can take you to your car when you're ready."

"Thanks, Brendon, but I'll walk her down," Josh said.

The champagne did help. After a time, she began to relax.

"Feeling better?" Josh asked.

"Yes. I should get back to work."

"Not tonight."

"But..."

"Not tonight."

Georgia and Wyatt stopped at the table, their arms wrapped around each other's waists.

"How are you doing?" Wyatt put a gentle hand on Kristi's shoulder.

"Much better."

"Come and dance," Georgia said.

"No." The word jumped out of her mouth like a hyperactive jack-in-the-box.

Georgia took Kristi's hand. "Come on. I want you to dance at my wedding."

Wyatt patted Josh on the back. "That's your cue, buddy."

"Please?" Georgia urged.

"One dance," Josh said to Kristi. "Let's keep our clients happy."

"I'm wearing a suit. It isn't at all appropriate," Kristi said.

"You look adorable," Georgia said.

Kristi stood on wobbly legs, realizing how un-fine she was. "You may have to hold me up."

Josh put his arm around her. "I think I can manage that."

As they walked out to the floor, Georgia went to talk to the band leader

Kristi didn't recognize the music at first, but when the vocalist began singing, she felt relieved and disappointed. "You've Got a Friend in Me" was a swing number; Josh wouldn't be holding her in his arms the way she'd imagined.

He smiled down at her. "We can do this."

And they did. Beautifully. Amazingly. Wonderfully.

And then, it was over.

But, Josh didn't walk her back to the table. "Wait here."

He went up and spoke to the band leader, who grinned at Kristi.

The strains of "The Beer Barrel Polka" brought nearly every guest to the floor. Josh whirled Kristi around the ballroom with ease, avoiding couples careening in every direction. By the time the music stopped, he was laughing, and Kristi was gulping for a breath.

"No more." She grabbed for air. "I can't breathe."

Josh got them two glasses of water. "Here," he said, handing her one. "Not too fast."

Georgia rushed up to them and kissed Josh on the cheek. "That polka was the best. Kristi, where did you learn to dance like that?"

"We did *The King and I* when I was in Children's Theater. All the kids learned the polka along with the leads."

The orchestra began playing a slow song.

"How about something a little less challenging?" Josh asked.

"Are you sure this is a good idea—me dancing at a client's wedding?"

"Why? Do you think the staff will mutiny?"

"I think it sets a bad example."

"At the risk of sounding elitist, it's my hotel; I get to do what I want."

"You're right. That sounds elitist." And, it didn't sound like Josh. He was usually so modest. Discomfort nibbled at the corner of her consciousness, and then dissolved when she saw him grin.

"How about, the Event Coordinator is the best partner here, and I'm not going to miss a chance to dance with her?"

His compliment was all she needed. This wasn't real life anyway—it was fairyland. She knew; she'd had them turn on those lights.

Josh led her to the dance floor, and then, no matter how hard she looked, she couldn't see The Line. He slipped his arm around her waist and pulled her close. There was no place for her head except on his shoulder. Her heart exploded, beating like she'd run up and down the stairs to the parking garage half a dozen times.

They danced as if they had danced a hundred times before; as if they had known each other for a lifetime; as if they belonged together.

She wanted to dance with Josh all night; to waltz around the room in his arms like a real-life princess. She wanted...

Kristi kept her eyes wide open, trying not to imagine herself in a bridal gown. Trying to see Laura and Ethan there, center stage, instead of her and Josh.

This was nuts. Moreover, it was bound to lead to a miserable end.

"You're an amazing dancer." Josh leaned even closer. "We should do this again."

She had no plans that week. But of course, she didn't say so. Besides, she wasn't sure if he was asking her out or just complimenting her.

Half an hour later, she was no closer to knowing.

She and Josh sat together, watching the six couples who were still dancing.

Brendon came up to her. "Sorry to interrupt. We're pretty much cleaned up except for a few wine glasses and coffee cups." He glanced toward the dance floor. "Some of these folks are never going to leave."

"Thanks, Brendon. I'll be right there." She stood, wishing she could send a text. Or a carrier pigeon. "I need to go check on the staff."

"Okay, Cinderella," Josh said. "I'll be right here."

She followed Brendon into the kitchen, gave the crew instructions, and then went to her office. Normally, at this point, she would leave. The staff was perfectly capable of wrapping up.

One more dance. How could that hurt?

"And then what?"

She shook her head.

She turned off her computer, grabbed her purse, and walked to the elevator.

In the bright light of the hotel hallway, The Line was unmistakable.

CHAPTER 13

Kristi drove to work on Monday, her heart heavy with dread; dread of the awkwardness that was inevitable after dancing with Josh at Georgia and Wyatt's reception.
 She should never have agreed. She'd known it then; she knew it now. Bad idea.
 Very bad idea.
 The driver in the car behind her honked. "Sorry," she muttered, giving an embarrassed wave.
 She wanted to be driving anywhere other than work. But, she hadn't been able to conjure up an excuse to stay home, so she was on her way.
 Another honk; different driver.
 On her way, clearly distracted.
 She had been at her computer for less than ten minutes when she realized someone was standing in her doorway. She looked up.
 "Good morning." His voice said it was not the least good.
 "Good morning." She tried to smile but her lips felt broken.
 "I thought we'd agreed that I was going to walk you

down to your car on Saturday night."

"Did we?"

"Yes, we did. I kept waiting for you. I finally came here, and found the door was locked. I called downstairs to the garage, and they said you'd left."

"Was there a problem? Queenie didn't call me."

"The problem was Wyatt's idiot uncle. I wasn't happy about you going down to your car alone. When someone is that drunk, and that—stupid, there's no telling what he might do."

"I appreciate your concern, but I was fine."

"Next time, let's err on the safe side." He shook his head, obviously not happy. "What would you have done if he'd been downstairs waiting for you?"

Kristi stood, stretched her arms high above her head and yelled, "Go! Go! Go!"

His laugh rumbled up from deep within and ricocheted off the wall behind her. "I'm glad bear training one-oh-one wasn't lost on you."

Kristi heard his laughter all the way down the hall.

Nothing from that trip was lost on her.

*

Kristi left work early on Tuesday and drove to the Sunset District to canvas her neighborhood business owners about the Bridal Ball. She saw her own hairdresser, Peg, first.

The woman was both supportive and enthusiastic. "I love it. Sign me up. I want to be a founding member."

Her manicurist was every bit as keen to be a part of the website. "We do entire wedding parties," she told Kristi. "I'll have no trouble getting the word out."

Later, Kristi was glad that she had started with them first; if she hadn't, she might have given up by the fourth store. Many shopkeepers were not in the least interested.

"How will this help me?" she heard several times. "I have plenty of customers already."

"Don't get discouraged," Nicole told her on the phone that night. "The Sunset isn't the only neighborhood in town. Try the Haight; try Pacific Heights; try Russian Hill. And try not to worry! The idea is going to take off."

"Has Laura written her post yet?"

"No. She's having trouble with it, which is strange, given how much she enjoys writing. Maybe you could help her."

"I'll call her."

"I noticed there's going to be a Bridal Faire here in the city next month. I think we should go. We might get some ideas, or make some useful contacts."

"Okay. I'm game. Anything we can do to get some momentum going." Kristi was still smarting from the shopkeepers' lack of enthusiasm.

"We're going to get there, Kristi. Maybe not next week or the week after, but it's going to catch on. And, I'm convinced it's going to be big. I've seen my share of website ideas, and I have a really good feeling about this one."

"I hope you're not just saying that."

"Would I lie to you? Stop worrying. Call Laura. Recruit more businesses."

"Take two aspirin and call me in the morning."

"Exactly."

"Okay, Doc."

Nicole's laugh lifted her spirits. "I have to go. I have a deadline, and I'm way behind."

"Talk to you soon," Kristi said, and hung up. She glanced at the clock. Chloe was normally in bed by eight, and it was after nine.

Laura answered the phone in a whisper. "What's up?"

"Did I wake you?"

"No. But, Chloe was fussy from her inoculations, so we have her in our room."

Kristi heard her moving, presumably to the living room. "Nicky said you were having trouble writing your story for the website."

"I am. When I put it in words, I sound like a whiny brat; like it was a trifling inconvenience even though for me, it was a total disaster."

"Maybe it would be better if you made it funny."

"Funny? What was funny about it?" Laura's voice was tinged with hurt.

"Absolutely nothing. But they say humor is tragedy with time added."

Laura was quiet for a moment and then said, "Maybe not enough time has passed."

"Laura, I wasn't saying it was funny."

"I know. I'm tired. Unless there's something else, I need to get to sleep."

"No, there's nothing else."

"I'll talk to you soon."

"G'night." Kristi hung up, and thought, note to self: never talk to an exhausted woman about an emotional subject when she's half asleep.

She grabbed her laptop and curled up on her bed. First, she opened the file of Laura's wedding photos. She considered the events on the day that had begun with such promise and ended with such pain.

Then, she opened a new word document.

The day was beautiful: heaven's puffiest cotton-white clouds decorated an arctic blue sky, and held no hint of what was to come.

I put on my wedding gown, filled with hope and anticipation. I hoped my father wouldn't step on it as he had my sister's, three years before. She may have been the only bride in our church ever to arrive at the altar all tattered and torn.

No, that would not be my fate. My fate was much more

THE BRIDAL BALL

noxious—literally. My fate was gas, and not the kind caused by beans.

We had just finished our dinner, and the emcee announced that my new husband and I would now share our first dance. My husband helped me from my chair, careful not to step on the voluminous train I had so ably kept away from my father's feet.

When I stood, I noticed a distinctly unpleasant odor. I glanced at my groom. "Was that you?"

"No. I thought it was you."

"Thanks," I said, and flashed my best smile, to cover my dismay.

As we walked toward the dance floor, the hotel manager rushed up to my father and spoke quickly to him, waving his arm in a sweep across the entire room.

My husband and I took our place in the center of the floor, well-rehearsed and prepared to enjoy our first dance as husband and wife. But before the orchestra could play the first note, my father grabbed the microphone from the emcee. "We've got a gas problem," he said gravely.

And I'd thought a torn dress was bad.

"That's pretty indelicate," my husband said.

"I've been told we need to evacuate immediately," my father said. "Please, take all your belongings and move as quickly as possible."

"What?" I cried.

Our guests were already standing and looking around for the nearest exit.

"But we haven't had our dance," I protested.

My husband and protector pushed me roughly toward the large doors that led to the patio. "Laura, the place could blow up. We have to leave."

The room was cleared in less than three minutes. The fire department arrived in four. In five, ninety percent of our guests had vanished.

The building did not explode, but my father did later,

when they handed him the bill.
But that's another story.
The saddest thing is that I never got to dance in my wedding dress. All the planning, practicing, and preparation, all in vain. I cried for days. For years I have dreamed I could somehow relive that day.
At last, The Bridal Ball promises to make my long-held dream come true.

She read it over, and then emailed it to Laura.

She looked at the wedding photos once more before turning off the light. But when she closed her eyes, she didn't see Laura. She saw herself dancing with Josh. She knew it had been foolish; knew it could ruin her position at the hotel. But, once he took her in his arms, she'd felt at home, right where she belonged.

She fell asleep and dreamed of white dresses, black tuxes, and waltzes.

Laura called first thing in the morning. "I don't know whether to laugh or cry. It's perfect, Kristi. And, you're absolutely right: it's funny. Thank you."

"I'm glad you like it. I never meant to hurt you."

"I know."

"Okay. Fix the wording however you like, and send it to Nicky."

"I need to run. Chloe is in her crib yelling. Or maybe she's singing. I'm not sure."

"Hugs from Auntie," Kristi said. "I'll talk to you soon."

That night her mother made dinner for the two of them.

"How is the website doing?" Victoria asked, setting plates of spaghetti on the table.

"Not very well. Unfortunately, none of us has had time to recruit the support we need from local businesses. I guess I'll have to beg Wilhelm for some time off in the middle of the day for a couple of weeks."

"Don't do that. I can easily take three or four mornings

to canvas our local businesses. Not to mention there are a few shopkeepers who owe me a favor."

"Oh, Mom, would you? That would be fantastic." She adored the way her mother was always willing to make an effort in her behalf.

"It would be fun. And it would get me out of the studio."

"You hate getting out of the studio."

"Everybody needs an adventure now and again. Even a recluse."

*

Two weeks later, the Bridal Ball website had twenty-seven enthusiastic sponsors scattered throughout San Francisco.

Nicole called Kristi long after she'd gone to bed, delighted with their progress. "Your mom is amazing. Our viewer rate is increasing daily. There have been four stories posted, as well as twelve comments."

"That doesn't sound like much." Kristi was barely awake.

"Slow start, big finish. Give it a couple more weeks. Like I told you, I have a good feeling about this. Can't you start talking it up at work?"

"I have to be careful. I'm not ready to tell Wilhelm about it yet, and I certainly don't want it to get back to Josh."

"Don't wait too long, Kristi. The word is going to get out. It would be better if you told them."

"I agree, but I want to wait until the site is getting a little more attention."

The next day, after meeting with three brides, Kristi began to reconsider. The Princess hosted wedding receptions throughout the year, but June was by far the most popular month. If she wanted the ideal time to talk to women about the ball, June was it.

She didn't like asking a client to keep a secret. It felt risky and somehow disloyal. Telling Georgia had probably been unwise, but, she was so supportive, and had promised not to mention it to anyone else. Besides, Georgia would make a terrific sponsor.

By Thursday, Kristi was still wavering. A young, web-savvy bride took the decision out of her hands.

"Have you seen this?" the woman asked Kristi when she arrived for their final appointment before her Saturday reception. "My maid of honor heard about it." She waved her phone in front of Kristi, and when she finally held it still, Kristi saw the home page of The Bridal Ball.

"If this happens, I could wear my dress again! I would love that! I've never had a dress that I loved so much. Do you have any idea how much that thing cost?" She laughed at herself. "Of course you do. You work with brides every day."

"So you think this ball is a good idea?"

"Good? It's absolute genius," the woman, who was not shy of superlatives, said. "I don't know who put this together, but whoever it is, he's brilliant."

"What makes you think it's a he?"

"It was a figure of speech." She sat in the chair across from Kristi and looked at her closely. "You never answered my question. Do you know about it?"

"As a matter of fact, I do."

"Do you know who's doing it?"

"I do."

"Well, tell me."

Kristi got up and closed her office door, trying to decide how much to share. When she sat at her desk, she said, "I'll tell you, but for the time being, I need you to keep it between us."

The woman leaned forward and whispered, "I love secrets. Tell me. Who is it?"

"It's me. The Bridal Ball was my idea."

"You? The Bridal Ball is your idea? Oh my gosh, Kristi, that's fantastic!"

If she yelled any louder, someone would call 911.

"Yes, well, thank you. But seriously, no one at the Princess knows about it, and I'm not quite ready to tell them."

"I understand. But, we've already told all our friends. I have two friends who want to go as much as I do."

"I'm glad." Kristi's heart galloped, hearing the woman's enthusiasm. She had been right after all. "We have to make sure we have enough interest to make it successful, and then find somewhere to hold it."

"Somewhere? Have it here. In the Crown Ballroom. It's the only place."

"That would be ideal, of course. But it might not be possible."

"Why not? This is the perfect spot. Who should I talk to?"

"Nobody. Absolutely nobody. We're in the earliest stages of the project. We can't afford to disclose too much so soon. You promised."

"Okay. You're right. I don't want to mess anything up. But, you'll tell me as soon as you firm up a date, right?"

"Yes. Meanwhile, if you want to help, you and your friends can leave comments or stories; and you can support the businesses that are sponsoring the site."

"Absolutely. Anything we can do to make this happen. It's so exciting, Kristi. Congratulations."

"Thank you. Now, let's talk about your reception."

CHAPTER 14

Kristi met Nicole at a small Chestnut Street trattoria the next night for GNO, and told her about the excited bride.

"Really?" Nicky asked. "She'd already seen it?"

"Yes. Her MOH told her about it."

"That's terrific. It's exactly what I hoped would happen. It means the keywords are working."

"Or the flyers," Kristi said.

Laura rushed into the restaurant, looking anxiously for them. Kristi waved her over.

"Sorry, Chloe was..."

Nicole raised her hand to stop her. "We know—Chloe was going out on her first date, and you were taking pictures."

"Funny," Laura said. "That's coming, you know."

Kristi pushed a glass of wine in front of her friend. "Since we're having pasta, I ordered white."

Laura took a sip, and sighed. "Perfect."

"Tell her," Nicole said.

"What?" Laura asked, turning to Kristi.

"Well," Kristi began, and then gave Laura the details of the meeting the previous day. "This woman was so excited about the prospect of wearing her dress again, I could hardly get her to focus on her own reception."

Laura looked at Nicole with a smile that held a dream. "It's starting to happen, isn't it?"

Nicole nodded. "If brides are coming to us to tell us about *our* website, I think the word is on the wires."

"More like the rumor is on the router," Kristi said.

"So, now what?" Laura asked. She and Nicole looked at Kristi.

"June is the busiest time of the year at work. Let me get through the end of the month, and then I'll talk to Wilhelm. If the site continues to grow, the next three weeks will only serve to show that the Bridal Ball idea is viable."

"You're both reading the stories and comments, right?" Laura looked from Kristi to Nicole. "Right?"

Nicole looked like the cat who'd scored the final fish bone. "Do you have any doubt?"

"So, you read the one where the best man spilled red wine all over the bride's dress?"

"He went from best man to biggest idiot in six seconds," Kristi said.

"It got me thinking—we're going to have an entire ballroom full of white dresses. Let's limit the drinks to colorless cocktails."

Nicole looked unsure. "But what about…"

Laura cut her off. "People can live without red wine and hard liquor for one night."

"There's always gin and vodka," Kristi said. "I like the idea. I guarantee the women will love it."

"The men won't," Nicole said.

"Some may not. But they'll be a minority," Kristi said. "Men won't book this event anyway. This whole evening will be about the women—the brides."

"If you're going to get the men on board, you'll have to give them something. Otherwise, couples will come once and that will be the end of it," Nicole said.

Laura looked at Kristi, disappointment dampening her bright eyes. "She has a point."

"Men attend the Black and White Ball year after year," Kristi said. "What's the difference?"

"Colorful cocktails," Nicole said.

The waitress put salads down on the table. "Enjoy."

"I think we're getting ahead of ourselves," Kristi said. "Let's worry about having the first one before we get carried away worrying about the next one."

Nicole took a bite of salad and said, "We could offer the men in-room massages."

"You and your massages," Laura said.

"If you'd try one once, you'd see why I like them so much."

"It's an option," Kristi agreed, "but I'm not sure it's much of a selling point."

"We can ask women what their men would like once we get the newsletter going," Nicole said. "They'll know best."

When the waitress set steaming bowls of pasta on the table, Nicole said, "Time to eat."

Kristi lifted her fork and then said, "I forgot. Sam texted me. She's in Iceland doing a photo workshop. She'll be home the weekend after the Fourth of July, and wants to see us all before she leaves for China."

"Let's do something special," Laura said. "There's no telling when we'll see her again. Let's celebrate her birthday."

Kristi looked sideways at her. "Sam's birthday isn't until November." She pushed her salad aside and took a bite of carbonara.

"She hates parties," Nicole said. "How about a nice, simple dinner at our house? Maybe Tony could fix us something new."

"Ooh, yum," Laura said. "I like that idea."

"I'm sure he'd be happy to try a new recipe for us to critique," Kristi said.

THE BRIDAL BALL

"You can tell Tony that anytime he needs a critique," Nicole said, "I'm there for him."

"If you knew anything about food besides how to eat it, that might be tempting," Kristi said.

When Kristi got home, she found a text from Lexi. "Call me. Let's get together for a picnic. I'll meet you in the city."

Much as she wanted to see Lexi and Tori, June was not the time. "Can't this month. I'll call when I figure out July. Hugs to Tori."

Her career offered her many advantages; one of them was not a social life.

*

Kristi's week was packed from sunrise to sunset to moonrise. On Wednesday, she was so busy she had to look for time to breathe. Her phone rang late in the afternoon, and she was going to let it go to voice mail, when she recognized the familiar number. She grabbed it just in time. "Heather?"

"Hi there. How are you doing?"

"Good. Busy, of course, as I'm sure you are. What's up?"

"Norma Russell came in to see me yesterday."

Norma was one of Kristi's favorite clients. Current Events had done both of her daughters' wedding receptions, as well as a huge anniversary bash for her and her husband.

"She was waving her computer tablet around like a matador's cape, insisting that I must know something about a new website the girls had shown her, called The Bridal Ball."

A smile crept across Kristi's face. "What did you tell her?"

"I told her I'd ask around."

"Did you check it out?"

"The minute she left my office. It's beautiful, Kristi. I

guess you didn't need any more help from me after all. I assume Nicole put it together."

"Yes."

"I figured. It has her fingerprints all over it. You've gotten a lot of responses already. Some of the stories are really touching. When did you launch?"

Kristi closed her office door. "Five weeks ago. It was slow at first, but it has started picking up in the last week. Nicky is convinced it's going to be a big hit."

"I can see why. It's very appealing. Have you talked to Wilhelm about it again?"

"Not yet."

"Don't wait too long. You don't want a client to show it to him. He might take it as a threat—as though you've gone behind his back. Which, of course, you have."

"I have not. Going to Josh or JT would have been going behind his back. I went to him first. He blew me off. So, I pursued it on my own."

"As you should have. Call me after you tell him about the site. I'm curious what he'll say."

"What can he say? There's obviously a market for it. Women want to wear their wedding dresses more than once."

"Yes. Well, let's hope he sees it that way. Regardless, call me after you talk to him."

"I will. Tell the crew hi for me, okay?"

"Will do. Talk to you soon."

*

Kristi had been in her office less than five minutes Friday morning when Georgia peeked around the door. "Got a minute?"

"Of course. How are you? How was the honeymoon?"

"Wonderful. Quiet. Relaxing. Probably the first and last relaxing days of our marriage. We're both back to the grind, trying to make up for lost time."

"I'm glad you enjoyed the honeymoon, at least."

"Have you got time for a cup of coffee?"

She didn't. Her calendar was a study in overscheduling. "Sure," she said, and walked with Georgia to the dining room.

"I came by to pay the remainder of the bill," Georgia said, pouring cream into her coffee, "and to thank you for the wonderful job."

"You're so welcome."

"I also wanted to apologize for the way Uncle Max behaved. He called us and said he was sorry, but that's nothing new. We never should have invited him, but he's family. What can you do?"

"There's not much choice when it comes to family. Don't worry about me. I've had worse run-ins with drunks."

"I knew you'd say that. Still, I am sorry." She smiled. "On a brighter note, Wyatt and I are having a Fourth of July housewarming, and we'd like you to come."

"That's so kind of you." Kristi had heard Heather use the exact phrase with clients dozens of times.

"No excuses. I already checked with Josh, and he told me there are no events here that day."

"I'm not sure..." Kristi began, but she wasn't sure what she wasn't sure of.

"Come on. We have some great friends. They're fun. You saw that at the reception, right? And, I promise Uncle Max won't be there."

"It isn't a question of fun, Georgia. But, mixing business with pleasure isn't wise."

"Our business here is done; so we can be friends now. I like you, Kristi. Come meet some of my other friends. You'll have fun, I promise. If you don't, you can always leave." Georgia gave her an impish grin. "Of course, that would hurt my feelings."

"When you put it that way, how can I refuse?"

"Perfect." Georgia leaned toward her. "I was on the net looking for a place to get my wedding gown cleaned, and found a site called The Bridal Ball. Is that you?"

"Yes."

"Oh my gosh, Kristi, it's beautiful. I love it! I see you have several businesses sponsoring you. I'd love to be one of them, if you aren't already maxed out."

"I would love to have you sponsor us. I wanted to ask you, but I wasn't sure about the ethics."

"None of that applies anymore. We're friends now. How can I help? What would you like me to do?"

"I'll need your business card for the website. I have flyers that explain about the Bridal Ball and direct people to the site. If you'd give one to any of your clients who might be interested, that would be great."

"That's easy enough. What else?"

"That's all for now. Remember, Josh doesn't know anything about it yet. I'm going to meet with Wilhelm next week and pitch it to him. He wasn't too enthusiastic the first time, but that was before we had the website."

"If he doesn't love the idea, he's a fool."

Kristi glanced around the room nervously.

"Oh, sorry. I should be more careful." She took a business card out of a rich leather case and handed it to Kristi. "Do you have some flyers for me?"

"Not here. I'll drop them by your office."

"Great. So, can I count on you for the Fourth?"

"Yes."

"Thanks for the coffee." Georgia stood. "I'll see you soon. Watch for an invitation in your email," she said, and breezed out of the room.

As Kristi walked back to her office, she thought about that pesky Line she was trying so hard to avoid. Wouldn't this make it worse? Was it a bad idea?

Her life seemed as intricate as bridal veil lace.

CHAPTER 15

A week later, Kristi called Nicole on her way to work. "I just had my nails done…"

"Nice life," Nicole said.

"I'll be working until midnight tonight and tomorrow night. Want to trade jobs?"

"No. So, if you didn't call me to gloat, why did you call?"

"My, but you're grumpy this morning."

"Sorry. No coffee yet. What's up?"

"Peg, the owner of the shop, told me she's already booked three wedding parties for women who saw her ad on our site. It's working, Nicky."

"Did you ever doubt it?"

"Uh, yes, as a matter of fact, I did."

"Well, have a little faith. We're getting more first-time visitors every day, and the click-through rate is increasing as well. We're starting to get more return visits, probably looking for updates. Maybe we should add a blog to the page."

"A blog about what?"

"Anything and everything wedding." Nicole paused and

then said, "We could feature one shop every week."

"Sounds like a lot of work. Does Laura have time for that?"

"I told you, none of us have any extra time. But Laura loves to write, so this is a perfect allocation of talent."

"Once a week would be a lot of added pressure in her life, don't you think?" Kristi pulled into the hotel driveway and drove down the ramp to the garage.

"I suppose, although for the life of me I can't understand what's so difficult about taking care of a baby. They sleep most of the time, don't they?"

"Have you ever taken care of Chloe for an entire day?"

"No."

"I think you'd find those moccasins more confining than you imagine."

"What?"

"Never mind. I'm at work, and you need to go have your coffee. I'll talk to you later."

Kristi rechecked the event calendar on her computer and breathed a giant sigh of relief. Just two more June wedding weekends and then life would be less hectic.

*

By Sunday night, Kristi felt like she had gone through a wringer and been left in a wet heap in a hotel laundry basket. She could barely keep her eyes open as she drove home. Before she crawled into bed, she left Wilhelm a message that she wouldn't be in until ten the next morning. He wouldn't like it, but that was too bad.

She needed sleep.

Wilhelm arrived even later than Kristi on Monday morning, and stopped at her office door to say good morning. He was so rarely pleasant that she was caught off guard.

"How did the receptions go over the weekend?"

"Really well."

"That's good. Maybe you're getting the hang of it."

His compliment, halfhearted as it was, gave her a measure of courage.

Fearing she might not get a better opportunity, she said, "There's something I've wanted to speak to you about."

"Oh?"

"Two of my friends and I have put together a website to explore the possibility of having a Bridal Ball. Do you remember I told you about the idea a while back?"

"Yes." His voice changed from bright to bored.

"We've had many enthusiastic responses, and already have businesses throughout the city sponsoring the site."

"Really? And where do you intend to have this ball?"

"I'd always hoped to have it here."

"I already told you that that is not practical." He turned to go and then looked back at her again. "And of course, if you try to have it somewhere else, we would naturally consider that a conflict of interest." He gave her a look of supreme condescension, crushing her heart and her dreams.

*

She called Nicole and Laura that evening, patching them in together for a three-way emergency summit.

"He can't tell you what you can do outside of work," Laura said. "What a jerk. He's full of hot air."

"He's full of something nastier than that," Nicole said. "He's jealous because it's a great idea, and he knows it. You can't get discouraged. We're going to keep right on going."

"What if he fires me?"

"Would JT allow that?" Nicole asked.

Kristi tried to imagine JT firing her. "No."

"Then don't worry. Besides, I've got some great news that may put the Bridal Ball on Josh's radar and completely bypass Wilhelm."

Kristi was afraid to ask. "What's that?"

"I got a call from a local radio station. I guess the station manager's wife gets her nails done at one of the shops Kristi's mom recruited. She's all jazzed about the Bridal Ball idea, and they want to interview one of us."

"Not me," Kristi said quickly,

"Me either," Laura said.

"Fine. I'll do it," Nicole said. "You guys are such wimps."

"Don't mention my name, Nicole. If it got back to Wilhelm, I'd be in big trouble."

"I don't believe that, but I won't mention your name, if that's what you want."

"What will you say?"

"That I have silent partners." Nicole's chuckle made Kristi laugh.

"I'm serious."

"I'll tell them all about our idea; how we've found most women would love to wear their wedding dress again, and how we need an appropriate place to hold the ball."

"No names," Kristi said.

"No names," Nicole repeated.

"Why don't you just tell JT?" Laura asked. "He likes you, after all. Who better to champion our idea?"

"Heather said going over Wilhelm's head is a mistake, and I agree."

"Nicole," Laura said, "did they set a date for the interview?"

"They did. It's this Saturday at eleven."

"Oh good; then I'll be able to hear it," Laura said.

Kristi knew her calendar was packed. "I won't. Would you record it for me, Nicky?"

"Of course."

Kristi was so busy all week that by Saturday, she had forgotten entirely about the interview.

On Monday, Nicole called, ecstatic. "The site is going

through the roof. I don't know who was listening on Saturday or who they told, but we are in business."

"Have people written more stories?"

"Yes. And they've left dozens of comments. These women are excited. They're offering all sorts of ideas about where to have the ball. But Kristi, seventy-five percent of them are saying it should be at The Royal Princess."

Pleasure wrapped its warm arms around Kristi. "Really? In the Crown Ballroom?"

"Yes. And you know what that means, right?"

Kristi knew, and the warmth waned. "Josh."

"Yes. He's going to hear about it sooner rather than later. You need to tell him."

"If I do, Wilhelm is going to be furious."

"If you don't, Josh may be furious. Who would you rather have mad at you?"

"I have to think about it. I wasn't expecting this."

"What were you expecting?"

"I don't know. Just not this." Not total, open-armed acceptance.

It was time. She had to make a move.

"Call me when you decide what you're going to do. Meanwhile, I'll talk to Laura about a new blog post."

She worried about it all day long. She checked the site several times to confirm what Nicole told her. Each time, two or three new comments or a new story had been posted.

By late Tuesday afternoon, her anxiety was greater than her fear. She had to talk to Wilhelm. With feet heavier than her heart, she walked to his office.

"Do you have a minute to talk?" Her heart pumped at twice its normal rate, and made her words sound choppy.

"What do you need?"

Civility, for starters.

"I wanted to speak to you again about the Bridal Ball. On Saturday, my friend Nicole…"

Condescension coupled with contempt curled his lips.

"I've heard all I want on that subject."

"But..."

He raised his hand and waved her off. "Enough."

She turned and left. Anger burned in her like butter in an overheated skillet. When she reached her office, her hands were balled in tight fists. It took every ounce of willpower not to slam the door.

I won't let him ruin it. I will not let the Bridal Ball fail.

But, her heart was heavy all the next day. She didn't call Nicole, or Laura, or Heather. She couldn't stand the thought of telling them about Wilhelm's rude dismissal.

First, she had to figure her next step.

*

On Wednesday morning, Kristi woke to the explosion of firecrackers. The one day she could sleep in, shot. Once she was awake, she couldn't stop thinking. Her body yearned to rest, but her mind wouldn't cooperate. Frustrated, she dragged herself from bed and took a shower.

Laura called her just before noon. "Happy Fourth. You're off today, right?"

"I am."

"Would you like to come over for a barbecue?"

"I'm afraid I can't."

"Did Nicole beat me to it?"

"No. One of our brides, Georgia."

"Josh's friend's wife?"

"Yes."

"Oooh. Is the hunk going to be there?"

"She says he will."

"Wear something splashy. Make him notice you."

"I'll do my best. Listen, I wanted to tell you something. I tried to talk to Wilhelm again about the ball. He didn't even let me finish my second sentence. He waved me away like an annoying gnat."

"Don't let it bother you, Kristi. Talk to JT. That's really all you had to do all along."

"Just click my heels together, right?"

"Yep."

"I'll think about it. It still doesn't seem smart."

"Oh, there's the baby. Gotta run. Have fun today."

Her conversations with Nicole and Heather went much the same way. No one was going to let Wilhelm discourage them.

All well and good. But, what now?

The site was getting more attention every day. When they reached critical mass, they'd have to make a decision: where would they have the ball if they couldn't have it at the Princess?

After two excruciating hours of no answers, she put it out of her mind.

Today was her day off and she intended to enjoy it.

She looked in her closet, trying to decide what to wear to the party. Shorts, sundress, suit? Certainly not a bathing suit. She didn't intend to have Josh see her in a bikini.

She needn't have worried. The pool in the backyard of Georgia and Wyatt's beautiful hillside home would have been ideal for Chloe and three of her friends. One foot deep, and five feet across, it sat in the center of the lawn in bright pink, polyvinyl splendor.

"Georgia insisted she wanted a house with a pool," Wyatt told Kristi when he escorted her out to the back patio, "and I always try to make my wife happy."

"Kristi!" Georgia cried. "You came." Georgia hugged her. "I'm so glad."

Kristi handed her the small housewarming gift she had brought. "It's not much."

"We don't need much. That whole gift registry thing was my mother-in-law's doing." She took Kristi by the hand. "Let's put your stuff in our room," she said, and lead Kristi back inside.

The house and yard were crowded and noisy; Kristi recognized some of the people from the reception. Georgia introduced her to several couples, mentioning that Kristi was the event coordinator at the Princess.

"I love the pool," Kristi said. "Do you have a maintenance service?"

"No. Wyatt just turns it over." She grinned with amusement. "When I was growing up, one of my friends had a pool; that's where we always hung out. I wanted to be that house. Turns out there are fewer than a dozen private swimming pools in all of Berkeley. So, after we fell in love with this place, Wyatt promised we'd have a pool. I came home from work one night, and there it was."

"You have to respect a man who keeps his word."

Georgia poured Kristi a glass of champagne, and they went out to the patio, where Georgia's beautiful, dark-haired maid of honor was standing.

"Did you meet Inez?" Georgia slipped her arm around the woman's waist. "I can recommend her highly if you need a maid of honor."

"Hi, Kristi. You did a great job at the reception, particularly with Wyatt's a-hole uncle."

"Thanks. I think the reception was one of the best we've done since I've been at the Princess. Of course, Georgia was responsible for most of the decisions."

Georgia took the empty glass Inez was holding. "White?"

Inez nodded. "Thanks."

"So, no weddings on Independence Day?" Inez's laughter was light as air. "I guess that would be a contradiction of terms."

"I hadn't thought of it that way, but you're right."

"Hello, ladies."

The familiar voice grabbed Kristi's gut and she shivered. She turned and smiled.

Jeans, check. Polo shirt, check. Boots, check.

Check. Check. Check.

"Hey, Josh," Inez said, and leaned toward him for a kiss.

He obliged her, and then turned to Kristi.

She felt like someone had dropped a hot potato in her lap. Kiss? No kiss? Hug?

Josh smiled. "I'm going to jump in the pool and swim a few laps. Want to join me?"

"I'll join you later," Inez said in the sexiest version of sultry Kristi had ever heard.

"I would, but I forgot my suit," Kristi said.

"Yo, Josh!" Wyatt called from the kitchen. "How 'bout a beer."

"Coors calls," he said, and headed toward the house.

Kristi dragged her eyes away from Josh and back to Inez.

"Gorgeous, isn't he?" Inez said. "Ah, but he's your boss. Maybe you don't see him the way the rest of us do."

Georgia returned with a glass of wine. "Here you go," she said, handing it to Inez.

Inez took a gulp and said, "I think I'll go make another play for the best man." She walked toward the kitchen, her heels probably not the best choice for the day.

"Some things never change," Georgia said.

"What do you mean?"

"Inez has been after Josh since the first time they met. Josh, not so much. He told me once she reminded him of his mother, whatever that means. I've never met his mom. I guess he's never gotten over the way she left without any warning."

Kristi could see Inez talking to Josh in the kitchen, hands flying, and head bobbing.

"The Jimmy Choo heels probably sealed her fate," Georgia said.

Kristi turned to her. "Jimmy Choo?"

"Inez was wearing a pair when they met. Apparently

that was all his mom ever wore; he's quite astute at recognizing them. If I were a psychologist, I'd say he associates Jimmy Choo with abandonment."

So, that was it.

"Do you have a special guy, Kristi? I didn't think to ask when I invited you."

"Not at the moment."

"Well, let's introduce you around, and see if we can't make a few sparks. Wyatt has some nice friends."

I know, she thought, glancing back to the kitchen.

By the end of the evening, Inez was hanging all over Josh, while he was doing his best to fend her off. Kristi felt sorry for the woman, who had clearly had way too much to drink, and was missing all of Josh's polite rebuffs.

"I really should get going," Kristi said to Georgia.

"Oh, don't go. Stay and watch the fireworks."

"You're going to set off fireworks?"

"No, but we can see the show in the city from here."

"You're dreaming," Wyatt told her. "There's no way with those trees across the street."

"It's late," Kristi said, "and I'm tired. I think I'm going to take off."

"I'll walk you out," Josh said, extracting himself from Inez. "I should get on the road, too."

"No," Inez whined, pulling on his arm.

"I'm so glad you came, Kristi," Georgia told her.

"I am, too. You have some lovely friends."

"We're so fortunate. We've known most of them since our days at Cal. It's a fun group."

"Thank you for including me," Kristi told the couple as they said goodnight.

Josh put a tentative arm around Kristi's waist, guiding her down the steep, dark road to their cars. "These country style neighborhoods without streetlights are great," Josh said, "until you're walking around at night."

"Give me city lights any day. That is, unless it's the

Fourth of July. Fireworks lose something in translation when the night is bright."

"We have the perfect view of fireworks at the hotel."

"Really?" She turned to look up at him and her shoes skidded on the loose gravel.

"Careful." He tightened his hold around her waist. "For years, we'd take popcorn up to the roof on the Fourth, and pray for a clear sky."

"How fun."

Kristi dug to the bottom of her purse, pulled out her keys, and unlocked the door.

"Listen, if you'd like, we could go check it out—the fireworks, I mean."

She hesitated.

"I understand if you're too tired."

Should she?

Of course she shouldn't.

"That sounds like fun."

The night was far too dark for her to see The Line.

*

The sky was clear and black and made walking across the rooftop patio at the Princess precarious.

"There's no point in turning on the lights," Josh said. He reached into his pocket and pulled out his phone. "This should help." He turned on the flashlight.

"Thank you, Steve Jobs," Kristi muttered.

They found lounge chairs near the glass partition facing the bay. Josh adjusted the backs on two of them, and they sat. The fireworks had barely started when he said, "It's not the same without popcorn."

"I'm sure Tony could whip something up."

"That's a good idea." He sat up.

She stopped him with her hand. "I was kidding; don't bother him. He's probably gone anyway."

"The bartender isn't. How about a glass of champagne?"

He paid attention. "Sure. If you're going to have something, too."

"We just got in a new bottle of scotch I wanted to try. I think it's about thirty-five years old. Anything else while I'm at it?"

"Not for me."

After the elevator door closed, Kristi got up and walked around the perimeter of the patio roof, looking at San Francisco from every angle. She had been to the Top of the Mark many times, and loved the city skyline. The vantage point from the Princess was lower, more intimate. Here, she hovered over the rooftops like one of the parrots on Telegraph Hill.

Josh brought back two glasses of champagne. "He hasn't opened the scotch yet, and I didn't want to answer a bunch of questions."

She lifted her glass toward him. "Here's to a clear night."

"And a minimum of visits to the E.R."

A small explosion lit the sky with a red, white, and blue starburst that glittered, twinkled, and expanded into a fine grey mist. The next one sent a red jet trail high into the sky, and then exploded, showering the sea with golden sparkles.

"Have you ever watched fireworks from a boat?" she asked.

"No. But it sounds intriguing. It would probably be good from Alcatraz, too."

"I bet it would be spectacular from the Campanile."

She couldn't see his smile, but she heard it in his voice. "Yes, the Campanile." He turned to her. "You win."

"Good! What's the prize?"

"A trip to the Campanile. Have you ever been?"

"I've been on the Cal campus, but I didn't go up in the tower."

"Have you ever been to the Big Game?" he asked.

"The football match between Cal and Stanford? Nope."

"That's a travesty. Never been to an opera; never been to the Big Game."

"Have you ever been to the Dragon Boat races?"

"Tragically, no." He took a drink of champagne and said, "You know, Georgia says people come into your life for a reason. Maybe I'm in yours to rectify some serious deficiencies. You should go with us to the Big Game. There's a group of about twenty alum. Wyatt, Georgia, and that whole bunch. We always have a tailgate party beforehand. It's at Cal this year."

Was he asking her out on a date? Where was The Line?

A huge starburst lit the sky, sending red, white, and blue streamers in every direction. Then, each streamer exploded in yet another dazzling star.

"Well, what do you think?" he asked, finishing his champagne.

"Will Tony cook?"

"We have something much better than that. We have our own rendition of the Oski-burger. I think you'll find it rivals any of Tony's masterpieces."

"That's hard to believe."

"It is a culinary treat. If you can identify all the ingredients when you're eating it, you'll win another prize."

"I'm beginning to feel like I'm on a game show." She was quiet a moment and then asked, "If Georgia's theory is true, why am I in your life?"

"Simple. To take me to the Dragon Boat races. When are they this year?"

"End of September."

"Good thing."

"Why?"

"I wouldn't want to have to choose between that and the Big Game."

"When is this momentous game?"

"The weekend before Thanksgiving."

"Oh, look." She pointed to a brilliant, three-part explosion of red, white, and blue concentric circles. "How in the world do they do that?"

"They use computers."

"Thanks. You just ruined the magic."

"There's one more thing before we finalize our deal."

"What's that?"

"Is there a Dragon Boat Burger?"

"Afraid not."

"Reason number two for me to be in your life. Together, we have to drag the festival food into the twenty-first century. You and I have to save the Dragon Boat ethos from sinking into the cultural abyss."

His playfulness filled her with pleasure. "And why were we, of all people, chosen for this momentous task?"

"I think it has something to do with the bear."

"Oski?"

"No. Yosemite."

CHAPTER 16

Kristi drove home with achingly unkissed lips.

Had he forgotten Yosemite after all? She never would. Never could.

It had turned cold, and she was glad for her comforter when she crawled into bed.

She closed her eyes and saw Josh. Was he interested in her? If not, why had he invited her back to the hotel? If so, why hadn't he kissed her good night? Would he take her to the Big Game? Would they go to the Dragon Boat races together?

All she knew about the dragon boats, she had heard from Sam, who had seen them in China. Sam believed the only place to attend any folk celebration was the country where it had originated: all else were faux festivals.

Faux or not, if he wanted to go, she'd go.

"Tell me everything about the Dragon Boat races," Kristi said to Sam the following Saturday night. GNO was at Kristi's apartment, and the four friends had just finished the delicious stroganoff Tony had prepared.

"Why? Have you decided to go to China with me?"

"That'll be the day," Nicole said. "We can barely blast

her out of this apartment, much less out of California."

"Excuse me," Kristi said, "but I went to college in New York."

"Where else have you been?" Nicole challenged.

"Chicago."

Laura glanced at her, a confused frown on her face. "When did you go to Chicago?"

"I didn't exactly go there, I...uh..."

"You changed planes there, right?" Nicole said.

"I was there, wasn't I? Anyway, I love San Francisco. I can do anything I want to right here, so I'm happy. Don't lecture me, please."

"The Dragon Boat Festival," Sam said loudly, "started in southern China more than two thousand years ago. The legend says the townspeople paddled out in boats on the Miluo River, looking for Qu Yuan, an exiled official and patriotic poet. He was in despair because his beloved state had fallen to neighboring conquerors. Although the villagers tried to save him from drowning, they could not."

"What else do they do to celebrate?" Kristi stacked the plates in the dishwasher.

"I'll bet there's food involved." Nicole scraped the last morsel of rice from her plate before handing it to Kristi.

"The traditional food for the festival is a sticky rice dumpling called *zongzi*. They're rice balls filled with meat, beans, or vegetables, and wrapped in triangular or rectangular shapes with bamboo leaves. Some are sweet and some are savory. My favorite is the ham *zongzi*, but lots of people prefer the sweet ones."

"Tell us about the boats," Laura said.

Sam lit up like a kid telling a tale in front of the classroom. "The old ones are beautiful, works of art, really. They're carved from wood, with a dragon on the prow, painted brilliant colors. They can be seventy-five feet, and need forty people to paddle. A drummer, who sits in front, is the heartbeat of the team; he sets the pace, and the rowers synchronize their efforts to his tempo."

Nicole listened carefully and then said, "Drummer sounds like my kind of job."

Sam ignored her. "A sacred ceremony is performed each year before the competition, when the eyes of every dragon are painted to 'bring it to life'."

"Hand carved and painted?" Laura repeated. "I bet they're extraordinary."

"They used to be. Those are the real gems. These days, many are made of fiberglass and aren't nearly as charming as the antiques. Of course, the boats in China are far more elaborate than the ones they have in the States."

"Have you ever been in one?" Laura asked.

"I have. I did an article on Chinese dragon myths years ago. I interviewed a fellow who was a drummer. He invited me to a practice session, and they let me paddle for about half an hour. I was exhausted. And let me tell you, there's nothing comfortable about those boats."

"Will you go to the races while you're in China this month?" Kristi asked.

"In China, races are held on the fifth day of the fifth month of the Chinese lunar calendar."

The others looked at her blankly.

"That would be in either May or June. The date changes from year to year, the way Chinese New Year does." She looked at Nicole. "And no, I can't explain the Chinese calendar to you." Nicole kicked her and she laughed. "Nor can I use an abacus."

"I'm glad you cleared that up," Nicole said.

"So, why all the interest in Dragon Boats, Kristi?"

"I bet it has something to do with the concierge," Nicole said.

"He's not a concierge," Kristi said, perhaps a tad too quickly.

"What's up, Ms. Peyton-Scott?"

"I just thought it might be fun to go to the races."

"And you thought Dragon Boats rather than horses?" Nicole asked.

"It was just an idea," Kristi said as offhandedly as she could manage. She looked at Laura. "Didn't you say you wanted to read us one of the stories from the website?"

"Nice segue," Nicole said.

Laura took a sheet of paper from her purse. "I printed it out," she said, looking embarrassed. "I don't have one of those tablets everybody carries around these days." She unfolded the paper and began reading.

"*The Bridal Ball would be a dream come true for me. Five years ago, I married my wonderful husband in the most perfect wedding you could imagine. Well, almost perfect. It would have been, if I hadn't been a perfect idiot two months before. Against my parents' advice, I entered a downhill ski race at Northstar. I should have known better.*

"*You see where this ended up, right? In the hospital, in traction for a month. My fiancé only laughed. It didn't matter to him if we got married in a shack, in jeans. My mother was another matter—her daughter's dream wedding was turning into a nightmare.*

"*In the end, my gown covered the brace I had to wear after I got out of the hospital, and my limp was minimal. But, dancing was out of the question. My husband and I swayed back and forth on the dance floor during our first song as husband and wife. After that, I sat.*

"*Since I made the decision to enter the race, I had only myself to blame. I've shed buckets of tears over that stupid choice, which robbed me of a night of dancing with my husband in a dress I love more than any I've ever owned.*

"*Sometimes my husband teases me about it. He has no idea how jealous I was that night when he danced with my bridesmaids. I hope that I'll finally be able to replace that memory with a romantic evening in my bridal gown, dancing in my husband's arms.*"

"Aww," Sam said.

"Be nice," Nicole told her in a voice cradled in caution.

"I think it's touching," Laura said.

"Which? The stupid decision or the jealousy?"

"Sam!" Kristi hit her. "Don't be nasty."

"Why do women get so whiny? Put on the damn dress and go dancing."

"Where?" Laura arched a delicate eyebrow at Sam. "Where, exactly, do you wear a bridal gown to dance? Believe me, if there were a suitable venue, I would have found it."

Sam shrugged.

"And I'm not whiny. I'm sad about a big disappointment in my life, the same as this woman is." Laura shook the paper before putting it back into her purse. She stood. "I need to go."

"Come on, Laura." Sam reached out to her. "I didn't mean…"

"You don't understand. Maybe you never will. And I don't understand about China, or Iceland, or Belize. But, I hope I never make you feel foolish, because those are your dreams." She kissed Kristi's cheek. "Thanks for dinner. I'll talk to you soon." Then, she walked out.

"Nice job," Nicole said to Sam.

"She couldn't be any more explosive if she were a redhead," Sam complained.

"Laura, wait." Kristi followed her friend to the front door.

"No. I should go. She's going to make me feel worse with a halfhearted apology."

"You're absolutely right. She doesn't understand. None of us do who haven't been married. A wedding gown is so much more than a beautiful dress. It's all tied up with love, and hope, and a little girl's dream of Prince Charming. I see it all the time with the brides at the hotel."

"Do you think I'm whiny?"

"Maybe a bit. But, I would be too. All that energy,

planning, expectation, and money is poured into one night; to have it end in disappointment is a lot to accept."

Sam came into the entry and put her arm around Laura. "I'm sorry. You're right. I don't understand. I've never had a man or a dress I really loved. The Bridal Ball will make it all right for you. Kristi and Nicky are going to make it happen."

"I hope so," Laura mumbled.

Sam hugged her. "Forgive me?"

"Don't I always?"

"Maybe if you didn't, I'd be a nicer person."

"Not likely," Nicole said, joining them.

Laura took her keys from her purse. "When do you leave for China?"

"A week from Sunday."

"Don't forget you're coming for dinner Wednesday night."

"Six o'clock. I'll be there," Sam said. "I'd never miss seeing Chloe."

"No more toys, please," Laura said, opening the front door.

"Not if you don't want me to."

Laura looked at her closely. "You already got something for her, didn't you?"

"It's just little. I saw it in Iceland. I couldn't resist."

"We'll have to buy a bigger house to accommodate all your gifts."

"I don't keep a journal. It's my way of remembering my travels," Sam said, with no apology in her voice. They hugged again. "See you Wednesday."

Laura started down the stairs. "'Bye," drifted back up as the lock on the downstairs door slid open.

"You're bad," Nicole hissed after it closed. She pushed Sam into the living room. "You're so mean to her."

"She used to take teasing better."

"She's been a bundle of hormones ever since she first got pregnant. I keep thinking it's going to wear off," Nicole said, "but it hasn't."

"Her reception, or rather the lack thereof, is a super emotional issue for her," Kristi said. "Tease her about it after the ball; it'll probably go over better then."

"What did you get Chloe in Iceland?" Nicole asked.

"Oh, it's the most adorable little folk costume, with a white blouse, red jumper, an apron, high socks, and a little cap. She'll look precious."

"You should have gotten her a flag, or a book," Nicole told her.

"Why?"

"She wouldn't outgrow them in three months."

*

Josh stopped by Kristi's office a couple of times the following week, but both times she was on the phone, and they didn't have a chance to talk. Wilhelm was with Josh when he walked by once, but Josh merely waved. By Thursday, she considered going to see him in his office, but decided against the idea. There was A Line.

Kristi was turning on her computer on Friday morning, when she smelled a delicious, familiar scent.

"Good morning." Josh stood in front of her desk.

"Hi." Everything that she had intended to talk to him about all week long flew out of her head, like steam from a pot of boiling water. She searched for a thought, but could only come up with, "What's new?"

"Not much. You?"

Her brain found traction, and grabbed hold. "I saw my friend Sam over the weekend. That's the travel writer I may have told you about."

He seemed almost to recoil. "Oh?"

"She assured me that China is the only place to see the Dragon Boat races. The festival started there more than two thousand years ago, and they've pretty much perfected it."

"She?"

"Yes. Samantha."

"Ah," he said, and then he laughed. "It took two thousand years to perfect?"

"They might still be working on it. Anyway, it looks like there is no Dragon Boat burger."

"A serious oversight. But, that does leave the field wide open for us. I suppose it should involve rice. And some sort of meat?"

"Are dragons an endangered species?"

"The fire-breathing dragon is protected. I think it's only available on the black market."

"I'll ask Tony to check with our vendors," Kristi said.

He frowned. "You're not supposed to eat dragon during months that start with a J."

"I'm glad the FDA is on top of that. I guess we'll have to wait until August."

"Maybe we could practice with ground turkey. I hear dragon tastes a whole lot like chicken, which, of course, tastes almost the same as turkey."

"Chicken would keep our food cost down. Besides, is an Oski-burger made from bear?"

"No. I think they're made from chicken, too."

She loved the banter; loved how their teasing spiraled up and up and spilled out in sheer joy.

"Chicken and rice don't sound like the makings of a Dragon Burger," he said.

"We'll cook them with a flame thrower."

The laughter started in his eyes, moved to his mouth and settled in his chest.

Score!

"Yeah," he turned to leave, "a flame thrower."

He walked out, laughing and trailing dragon dust.

CHAPTER 17

Nicole called her late the following afternoon. "Busy?"

"No. In fact, Wilhelm gave me the weekend off."

"I want to read you a story that was posted on the site late last night. It'll break your heart. It almost made me cry."

"Wait, let me sit. I need to prepare." She folded herself into her favorite living room chair.

"Okay, wise apple. Are you ready?"

"Go."

"*Dear Bridal Ball organizers: You have reached into my heart and pulled out my fondest dream. I would love to dance with my husband again, in my wedding gown. In a way, it would be honoring a dress that helped me through some of the darkest days of my life.*"

"That sounds grim."

"Hush. *My fiancé and I bought a house six months before our wedding. It wasn't big or fancy, but we worked hard to improve our new home with our limited resources.*"

"Is there a dress somewhere in this story?"

"Kristi."

"Okay. I'll be quiet."

"We moved into the house two weeks before our wedding. There were boxes everywhere when we left on our honeymoon, but we were young, and happy, and undaunted by the prospect of the job that faced us when we returned. A month after our wedding, we had nearly finished the Herculean task, and were finally able to relax."

"She must be an English teacher."

"If you say one more word, I'm going to hang up."

"I'll go online and read it myself."

"I'll hide it from you."

"Can you do that?"

"Shut. Up."

"Okay."

"My mother insisted that I take my wedding dress to a specialist to have it cleaned and stored in acid-free paper. The day I went to pick it up, our house burned down due to frayed wire we hadn't noticed. I drove up to a chaotic scene of fire engines, gargantuan hoses, and my life reduced to wet ruins.

"Everything was gone! Everything, except the clothes I was wearing, and my wedding gown."

"Geez!"

"My husband and I stayed with my parents until we found an apartment, and began to save for another house. My husband took a second job, and for months, we rarely saw each other. But we were lucky: neither of us was hurt, and we could start over.

"I confess there were times when I was discouraged. Usually it was late at night, when my husband still wasn't home, and I was lonely. One night, I got my wedding dress out, put it on, and danced around our living room. I thought about our beautiful wedding, and all our friends and family who had been there to celebrate with us.

"Somehow, they were all there in the living room, keeping me company and lifting my spirits.

"*For months, that magical dress raised me up from despair when the burden felt too heavy. We finally moved into another house about a year ago, and I took my dress to have it cleaned again.*

"*I've never told anyone this story before; not my husband, my best friend, or my family. My little ritual seemed childish and embarrassing. But somehow, I knew you would understand. Thank you for giving me both the courage and a platform to share it.*

"*I'll be watching for a date and place for the Bridal Ball.*"

There was a long silence.

"Are you crying?" Nicole asked.

Kristi swallowed the lump in her throat. "No."

"Pretty touching, don't you think?"

"I do. Has Laura seen it?"

"I doubt it. She'll call me when she does—probably bawling."

"Maybe we should give a prize for the best story."

"Like what?"

"I don't know…a couple's massage?"

"I'd go for that."

"We can give it some thought. Maybe a few of our sponsors would be interested in donating services for raffle prizes at the ball, provided it even happens."

"Why so pessimistic? Of course it's going to happen."

"I hope so."

"I don't have time to give you a pep talk. We're leaving for a concert in fifteen minutes, and I have to get changed. Go on the site and read some of the other stories. I'm sure you'll be surprised."

"Maybe it'll inspire me how to proceed at work." Kristi went into the kitchen and got a soda out of the fridge. "I'm nervous Josh will find out from someone else. But, I can't figure out how to tell him without ticking off Wilhelm. I don't want to create an enemy who'll make my life miserable."

"Talk to JT, Kristi. You can do no wrong in his eyes. He's going to support you because he likes you. And, of course, because the ball is a fabulous idea."

"I'm counting on that."

"I have to run. I'll talk to you later. Don't forget: Italian food with Sam next Friday night."

"Right. I'll see you then. Who's playing tonight?"

"Maroon Five."

"Oh, I love them. Have fun."

"I'm sure we will. Call me next week, after you talk to JT."

"Okay."

But as soon as she hung up, she dismissed the idea. The risk of Wilhelm making her life miserable for going over his head, was all too real. Until she figured it out, Nicole would have to wait.

*

The summer season at the Princess revolved around conferences and vacationers. Europeans and Asians loved to visit San Francisco, and the hotel was typically full to capacity during July, August, and September.

Conferences generally hosted one major dinner at the hotel; other nights, attendees were on their own. Kristi was grateful for the evenings when she could leave work early. After the June wedding madness, she needed a break.

On Friday, she had intended to take off by four-thirty. Sam was leaving for China on Sunday. GNO was in North Beach for a bon voyage dinner. An unhappy sous chef meant Kristi had to postpone her departure until feathers were smoothed and the kitchen staff had been appeased.

She made a last minute dash to Wilhelm's office to drop off an equipment catalog, and overheard him talking to JT.

Rather than interrupt, she stood outside his door, waiting for them to finish.

"How is your mother?" JT asked.

"All right, I guess."

"Any luck getting her to move here?"

"No. She's too set in her ways to leave Germany. Besides, she has so many health problems, I doubt I could afford her medical care here. There, everything is covered."

"I'm sure that's a relief."

"Yes," Wilhelm said.

It seemed like a good time for Kristi to speak up, but then Wilhelm said, "Who could have imagined money would ever be a concern?"

She knew she should leave, but she didn't.

"It wasn't entirely her fault, Wilhelm. The times were bad."

"It had nothing to do with the times. She didn't understand the first thing about business. She should have let me run the hotel. If she had, we would have been fine. She had no idea what she was doing, and she ruined a gasthaus that had been in our family for generations."

"Do you know if it's still there?"

"I'm told it is one of the most popular in all of East Berlin. Not that that helps us, of course. My mother practically gave it away." Bitterness flavored his words. "She was desperate by then, and she wouldn't listen to anyone, particularly me."

After a long silence JT said, "Please tell her hello for me the next time you speak to her. I will always be grateful for her kindness when I was there years ago. And Wilhelm, if she ever needs anything—that is, if I can help in any way…" His voice drifted off.

"Thank you Joshua. The fact that you hired me was quite enough. She and I both appreciate that very much."

"We've been happy to have you here."

Kristi tiptoed away from the office. She should not have eaves-dropped, but she'd been unable to tear herself away. Wilhelm's family had owned a gasthaus—a small hotel in Germany. His mother must have mismanaged it and then sold it against his wishes.

No wonder he didn't trust Kristi's judgment. He must shudder to see her coming along with a new idea. Still, they couldn't allow the Princess to stagnate. Doing things the way they always had, was not progress.

Maybe asking JT for support was the right way to go after all.

*

Traffic between the Princess and North Beach was light. She found a parking place and hurried to the restaurant, where Laura, Nicole, and Sam were already seated.

"*Buona sera*, Marco," she greeted their favorite waiter as he pulled out her chair.

"*Come stai, signorina?*"

"*Bene, grazie.*"

"*Vino?*"

"*Certo.*"

They had the same conversation every time. Marco insisted they at least begin the evening in Italian. He went to the bar to pour her favorite wine.

"Sorry I'm late, but it was worth it. Wait till you hear this." She told them about the conversation she had just overheard.

"So, JT hired him out of obligation," Nicole said. "And kindness."

"It sounded like it."

"Look," Sam said, using her I'm-being-completely-reasonable-here voice, "he's not going to like any of your ideas, especially the good ones. If they're bad, they reinforce his experience that women make bad business decisions. If they're good, he has to rethink his beliefs. What man is willing to do that?"

"You have to go around him," Nicole told her. "You can't allow his negativity to spoil this for everyone."

"Heather said..." Kristi began.

Nicole held up her hand. "We know what Heather said. You tried that. You talked to him first, and second, for that matter. There's no point in beating your head bloody."

Kristi closed her eyes, suddenly tired. Going around him was so unprofessional. Not to mention risky.

"Why are you so opposed to talking to JT about it?" Laura asked. "You know how much he likes you. I bet he'd support the Bridal Ball a hundred percent."

"*Signorina*," Marco said, putting a glass of wine in front of her.

"*Grazie*, Marco."

"*Prego*," he said, with a slight bow.

Kristi loved the man's old world manners and gave him a warm smile.

"You didn't answer my question," Laura said.

"I don't know."

But, Kristi knew exactly why.

Even excluding Wilhelm, there was another reason. A critical reason. Aligning herself with JT would put her in conflict with Josh. And that, she did not intend to do.

CHAPTER 18

Wilhelm sat behind his desk, the familiar condescending glare directed at Kristi. "What's on the schedule for this week?"

The Monday morning planning session with Wilhelm used to be torture. Since Tony had been attending, it was at least tolerable.

"We have the U.S. Chamber of Commerce all week," Kristi said. "They haven't made the final menu choices for the banquet. I gave them until three o'clock."

"Why would you do that? Tony has to order product." His voice dripped with distain, and made Kristi want to throw something.

"That's fine," Tony said. "I have till five o'clock to place orders." His voice was as placating as Wilhelm's was pedantic.

Thank you, Tony. I owe you, again.

"Good morning," JT said from the doorway.

"Good morning, Joshua. Would you like to join us?"

"No, thanks. But, I do have a question. I went fishing with Wyatt and his father yesterday and Wyatt mentioned something about a dance—well, not really a dance. He called it the Bridal Ball. Do you know anything about it?"

Kristi's heart took a giant leap, floundering and fighting to beat. While she struggled for the right words, Wilhelm had some ready.

"Yes. It's an idea Kristi and I have been kicking around."

Kristi's brain exploded. Rage raced through her, a speeding bullet on a rampage that lodged in her throat like a lump of lead. She fought to take a single breath.

"It sounds intriguing. I'd like to be in the loop. Include me in your next meeting."

"Of course," Wilhelm said. "We'd be happy to."

JT smiled at Kristi, but her mouth had frozen.

"Good. Then I'll see you later," JT said, and left.

Wilhelm's eyes lit on Kristi's face long enough to warn her against any objections.

Outrage choked her. Challenging him was imperative and impossible.

Wilhelm covered the remaining items on his agenda, then stood. "Unless one of you has a question, I need to meet with maintenance."

"I'm good," Tony said.

Say something, her brain bellowed.

"Thank you for being on time," Wilhelm told them, and with a final warning look her way, he left his office.

Tony's face was a mixture of amazement and amusement. "Wilhelm came up with the idea of a bridal ball? Seriously? What's going on, Kristi?"

"I'm not sure." She stood. "When I am, you'll be the second to know."

She walked to the dining room, sure that if she went into her office, she would close the door and kick holes in the wall. She poured herself coffee, sat at a table, and opened her notebook. She stared at the words on the page. Comprehension was beyond her.

It's an idea Kristi and I have been kicking around?
Kristi and I?
He wanted credit? After all the condescension and criticism and crap?
Did he expect her to go along with his lie?
She should confront him. Now.
Or, should she go to JT? Show him the website? Tell him Wilhelm had nothing to do with it whatsoever?
She heard Josh talking to the hostess. The last thing she wanted was to chat with him, but there was nowhere to disappear. She pulled out her best smile.
"Waiting for the salmon to come in?"
"Salmon sounds wonderful. A salmon omelet."
"Salmon Benedict?"
"Sold."
"I'll ask Tony to make them for us."
"I thought we were kidding."
"I wasn't. I'll be right back."
Maybe she should tell him.
Could be good; could be bad; could be a disaster.
Before she did something truly foolish, she wanted to talk to Heather.
Josh returned with a cup of coffee, sat across from her, and looked around the deserted room. "It's not the Ahwahnee, but it's regal in its own way."
He remembered. "It's a beautiful room. Your great-grandfather had a wonderful vision."
"He and the architect."
"They don't create buildings with grandeur anymore. Big, yes; flashy, yes. Grand? No."
"Where is mad King Ludwig when you need him?"
"Who?"
"King Ludwig of Bavaria. Wilhelm told me about him. Crazy as a loon, he ran down the country's coffers by constructing one elaborate castle after another. Wilhelm says

they're all spectacular. Disney used one of them as the model for Sleeping Beauty's castle."

"Sounds like the makings of a tour of Germany: See the mad King's castles," she said, but she was thinking about someone else who had ruined a family fortune. Interesting that of all the kings of Germany, Wilhelm had chosen to tell Josh about Ludwig.

Tony brought their meals to the table himself. "I'm not sure about the dill in the sauce. Let me know how it works, will you?"

Kristi tasted the Hollandaise with her finger. "I like it. It's delicate, but sweet and sharp."

"Enjoy," Tony said, a buttery smile on his face.

Kristi took another bite. "This really is delicious."

"But is it orgasmic?"

She wished she could hide the flush.

"Sorry, I couldn't resist."

"Do you think you could forget I said that?"

"I doubt it." He took a bite of the Benedict. "You're right. It isn't orgasmic. We'll have to work on that."

Anytime, she thought, before her better judgment jumped in and yelled, *Watch That Line!*

*

The minute she arrived home that night Kristi kicked off her heels, poured a glass of wine, and called Heather.

"I'm not sure how to handle it," she said after explaining the situation to Heather. "Do you think a jury would consider killing him justifiable homicide?"

"Murder is extreme. Maybe torture." Heather was quiet for a while. "He's put both of you in an untenable position. Calling him a phony is risky, particularly now that you know JT feels indebted to him."

"I just sat there; I didn't say a word; not one word!"

"It wouldn't have helped much to yell, 'Liar, liar, pants on fire'."

"No?"

"No. Nor would going to JT behind Wilhelm's back."

"I'm back to square one, then. I have to do something."

"I'd give it twenty-four hours. You'll cool off and Wilhelm will have to make a move. He has no access to the website, so his options are limited. He'll have to include you."

Kristi felt anger bubbling up like a fountain of poison. "I can't do nothing. I'm so mad at him I can barely stand to look at him."

"He knows that. He won't meet with you alone. He'll want a witness to keep you in line."

"To keep *me* in line?"

"To keep you from killing him."

"Still a tempting option." Kristi sipped her wine, considering Heather's advice.

"It will soon be clear whose idea it was. Wilhelm can't possibly contend it was his."

"I have to get something together. A presentation. If Wilhelm doesn't ask for one, I'll just tell JT I have it."

"Perfect. Smart, too. Wilhelm has to come to you for details; he has no other choice."

"It won't be hard to do. Heaven knows, I've put enough thought into it."

"Pitch it like you love it, like you believe in it, like you have a stake in it. Wilhelm can't do that. Make JT realize it's your creation."

"Own it."

"Exactly."

"That I can do." Her stomach began to settle.

"Strangely enough, Wilhelm's little charade may work in your favor. He can hardly bring it to the table and then undermine it."

Kristi immediately saw her point. "You're right. Heather, you're absolutely right."

"You figured it out. You just needed to bounce your ideas around a bit. Now, go trademark the website, if Nicole hasn't already done that. And stop worrying. The Bridal Ball is brilliant."

"Thanks, Heather."

"You're welcome. Call me after your meeting with JT. I'll be curious to hear how it goes."

A voice message from Wilhelm greeted Kristi the next morning. "Mr. Townsend has asked us to meet with him about the Bridal Ball on Thursday morning at ten. Be prepared to present the idea in full."

She would prepare so thoroughly that Wilhelm could never take credit.

She would tell JT the story of Laura's wedding, and her dream of giving her best friend the chance to dance in her wedding gown. She would show him the Bridal Ball website. She would give him one of the flyers, and the list of sponsors. She would read the post from the woman whose wedding gown survived a fire. Wilhelm would be no part of the presentation.

*

Ten minutes before the meeting on Thursday morning, Wilhelm came into Kristi's office. "Are you ready?"

"Yes."

"Good. Let's walk together."

He made it sound as if they were going on a date.

"I want to explain something to you," he said.

She listened as she collected the materials for her presentation.

"A concept such as the Bridal Ball is considered intellectual property. Since you worked for the Princess when you came up with the idea, legally it belongs to us."

Her head jerked up and her eyes fixed on his. Outrage consumed her; her heart kicked into overdrive, and her hands shook. "I had this idea long before I came to work here."

"Perhaps. But you didn't act on it. You didn't do that until you came to work for us." He gave her a smug smile. "So, whatever happens to you, the Bridal Ball will remain at The Princess."

You creep. You miserable louse. You can't have it! And you won't ruin it, you...

She refused to give him the satisfaction of a response. She moved out of her office and walked down the hall so quickly he was forced to run to keep up with her.

JT was in the conference room when they arrived.

"Good morning, Joshua," Wilhelm said. "I see you're ready for our presentation. I'm glad, because Kristi and I both think that the Bridal Ball is an exciting idea, and an opportunity for the Princess to answer the needs of an unnoticed and untapped clientele."

Kristi swallowed the anger that had caught in her throat. She set up her computer for the presentation, dimmed the lights, and showed the first slide—her favorite picture of Laura in her wedding dress.

"Please allow me to introduce you to my best friend, Laura Fisher. We've known each other since we were eleven, when Laura saved my life." JT and Wilhelm both turned to look at her.

So far, so good.

She related the story of her father's death, and her subsequent move to San Francisco.

"When Laura announced that I would be her best friend, my life went from miserable to manageable. Within months it had gone from manageable to marvelous. Laura made all the difference, at a time when I believed nothing would ever again matter.

"Laura's wedding reception was a catastrophe. A gas leak at the hotel forced an evacuation, and Laura never got to dance in her beautiful wedding gown. I've spent months trying to figure out a way for her to have the dance that never happened."

She switched screens to the home page of The Bridal Ball. Her enthusiasm bubbled as she moved from page to page, telling JT about the sponsors, the comments, and the stories women had shared about why they wanted another chance to wear their wedding gowns.

When she finished, she smiled at JT. "My dream is to have it here, in the Crown Ballroom."

Before JT had a chance to speak a word, Wilhelm said, "When Kristi came to me with the notion some months ago, I could see the potential. I encouraged her to flesh out the idea, and assured her we'd give it serious consideration."

"I like it, Kristi," JT said, ignoring Wilhelm. "I can easily envision it in the ballroom. This is precisely the sort of new idea I was hoping for when I stole you away from Heather."

JT's recognition and approval made Kristi's heart swell with pleasure.

Wilhelm's voice jumped into the silence. "Thank you, Joshua. I'm glad that you agree with my assessment."

"I'll need to speak to Josh, of course, but I think we should proceed with this. Our low season is in January; that would be the perfect time for the ball."

"I'll talk to Josh about it if you'd like," Wilhelm offered.

If she'd had a dagger, it would be sticking in his back. "I'd be happy to tell him about it."

"It might be better coming from me," JT looked at Kristi. "I'll want you to give him this same presentation."

"I'd be happy to."

JT stood. "Thank you both. I have a good feeling about this. I'll talk to you again after I've had a chance to speak to Josh."

Wilhelm stood. "There's something else I'd like to discuss, if you have a moment, Joshua."

"Of course."

The two men walked out together, leaving Kristi fuming. She closed her laptop and picked up the other materials. Wilhelm was going to do his best to take the credit.

Not happening.

The Bridal Ball was hers.

Not Wilhelm's. Not by any stretch. Not a chance in hell.

She waited all day, hoping to hear from JT. By the time she was ready to leave that evening, he hadn't called. She knew he, and Josh, and Wilhelm would be in meetings all the next day. She called and left a message on JT's phone. "I was wondering if you'd had a chance to speak to Josh about the ball. Let me know if I can help in any way."

A little past five o'clock on Friday afternoon, Josh walked into her office. "My dad is quite taken with your Bridal Ball idea," he said without preamble.

"And you?"

His face was non-committal. "It's not a bad idea. I think we'd be smart to give it a year or so, to do all we can to ensure a success."

"A year?" Her heart heaved a sigh so heavy that it stole her breath.

"Yes. It's one thing to post a story or a comment on a webpage, and another to plunk down eight or nine hundred dollars for a weekend at the Princess. We'll need time to market the idea, and educate prospective clientele so they don't suffer from sticker shock."

"The dinner dance wouldn't be all that expensive. We don't want to turn away couples who can't afford to stay the night."

"No. But the goal is to maximize revenue for the hotel, right?"

"My goal is to give my friend a chance to finally dance with her husband in her wedding gown."

"She can do that anywhere."

"Actually, she can't. A wedding dress is special. You can't just wear it anywhere. That's the whole problem. It has to be a special place."

"I can't argue that the Crown Ballroom is a special place. I just think we need to do more planning." His phone rang. "Yes?" He paused and then said, "I'll be right there." He hung up. "Sorry, I have to take care of a problem upstairs. We'll talk more about this next week."

*

Sam rarely had the girls over to her apartment. A studio on the top floor of a building in the Mission District, it was small, and Spartan, and stuffy. But, she had insisted that they have an evening there together before she left for China.

She managed to squeeze a table in, large enough for the four friends to sit down to eat.

"This is delicious," Nicole said, sampling one of the salads. "Where did you get this?"

"Whole Foods. Where else?" Sam said. "It's the only place to go for take-out."

"This is San Francisco, for heaven's sake," Nicole chided. "There are dozens of wonderful take-out restaurants."

"She's never home long enough to discover them," Laura said.

"I've been home a whole week." Sam helped herself to more eggplant.

"And you bought dinner how many times?" Laura asked.

"Please," Kristi pleaded, "let's not argue."

Nicole looked at her in surprise. "What's wrong?"

"Nothing is wrong. Sam is only here for one more day. Can't we have dinner in peace?"

An awkward silence fell over the room.

Once her plate was empty, Nicole picked up the container of beet salad. "Any progress on the ball? You know, at work?"

"No," Kristi said. She wasn't sure exactly what was happening, and she didn't want to explain the latest turn of events. Once JT had made a decision, she would tell the others.

"I've read the stories people have posted," Sam said. "Some of them are real tear jerkers."

"They're certainly more heart-wrenching than a gas leak," Laura agreed.

Kristi patted her arm. "Don't sell your story short. If it weren't for you, none of this would be happening. It's not a contest to find the most pathetic story. You had a huge disappointment on your wedding day."

Laura took a sip of wine. "It can't compare to a groom so hung over he couldn't stand up, or a father-in-law having a heart attack."

"Maybe we should give a prize for the saddest story," Nicole said.

"That sounds grim," Kristi said.

"We could have a drawing for a free night at the Princess." Nicole's face lit with expectation. "If enough couples threw in twenty dollars, it would pay for itself. It could be used any time, including for the next Bridal Ball."

"That's a terrific idea." Laura looked at Kristi. "Isn't it?"

"It is," Kristi said. "And, it beats the heck out of the Pitiful Polly prize."

Nicole picked up the container of orzo salad. "I have a question before I finish this."

"Shoot," Sam said.

"What's for dessert?"

"Chocolate eclairs," Sam told her.

Nicole spooned the remainder of the orzo onto her plate. "Slam dunk. I could eat twice this much and still find room for a chocolate éclair."

"You're so predictable," Kristi said.

"Now that really sounds grim," Nicole said.

*

Kristi called Heather on Sunday morning. "Did I wake you?"

"No. I was just finishing my second cup of coffee. How did the big meeting go?"

"Okay. Good, actually. JT liked the idea. Wilhelm did his best to insinuate that he'd been encouraging me all along, and that he thought the ball had real promise at the hotel."

"Try not to let him bother you. It'll be apparent that he had nothing to do with it. Be gracious. It'll pay off in the end."

"I hope so."

"Trust me."

"If you're wrong, can I have my old job back?"

"Are you looking to jump ship?"

"Not really. But I do miss you. Lexi, too. And our clients, for that matter." Kristi poured a cup of coffee, carried it to the living room, and opened the blinds.

"Perhaps you'll see some of them at the Bridal Ball."

"You haven't told them yet, have you?"

"No. But as soon as you set a date, I'll send out a priority email. I can name half a dozen women who would pay you today to be able to wear their wedding gowns again."

"That's what I'm counting on."

After they hung up, Kristi called Sam.

"I just buckled my seat belt," Sam said. "Thank heaven the flight attendant showed us how; otherwise I wouldn't have had a clue."

"I wanted to wish you bon voyage, safe travels, and warn you not to eat any blowfish."

"That's in Japan, sweetie."

"In that case, eat the most expensive caviar you can find."

"I'll definitely do that."

"How long will you stay in Russia?"

"I'm not sure. I'd like to do all the museums and palaces possible in Moscow. We'll see how quickly I run out of rubles."

"Safe travels, Sam."

"Absolutely. I gotta go. The flight attendant is giving me a look. *Do svidaniya*," Sam whispered, and she was gone.

*

JT saw Kristi as she came out of the stairwell the next morning, and waved her down. "How was your weekend?"

"Fine. Quiet, which was nice for a change."

"The Chamber banquet went very well. They've already booked for next year."

"So I heard. Queenie called me last night."

"She runs things like a pro," JT said.

"She is a pro."

He walked with her to her office. "I've run into some opposition to the Bridal Ball."

She put down her purse. "Josh."

"Yes."

"He doesn't like the idea." The weight of disappointment crashed down on her shoulders.

"He likes it, but not for this year. He thinks we should do more marketing to make sure it's a success the first time."

"I checked our banquet history last week. January is practically dead. There's rarely anything booked between New Year's and Valentine's Day. I don't see how we can lose, even if we only sell a few packages."

"Our reputation could be damaged if it's a bust. Making money isn't the only measure of success. If we advertise, and the press shows up to cover it, a bad turnout could make us look incompetent."

"If we tease people with the idea for months and months and never set a date, they may be so frustrated they don't attend when we do hold it."

"You make a good point. And between us, I agree. It isn't wise to raise expectations without awarding the prize."

Kristi sat down, her brain desperate for a solution. "We could set a drop-dead date. If we don't have enough paid registrations by then, we give everyone a full refund, and a priority number for signing up next year." She watched him contemplate the idea.

"That might work."

"Heather said that once we set a date, she'll send an email to all her clients, telling them about the ball."

"Did she? Well, we will certainly do the same. We've probably had enough brides here to fill the entire ballroom—twice."

"That's what I thought. Judging from the posts on our webpage, the majority of women think the Crown Ballroom would be the perfect setting. Once they know we're having it here, I'm sure reservations will start pouring in."

"I like your optimism." He was quiet for a while and then said, "Okay, you've convinced me."

Kristi wondered if he had made up his mind before he had even spoken. "What about Josh? Will he agree to the plan?"

"What plan?" Josh said, walking into her office. He looked at his father. "I had a feeling I'd find you here."

"Kristi and I were just discussing how best to ensure a successful Bridal Ball."

"And you didn't think that Wilhelm or I might want to be included in that discussion?"

"It was impromptu, Josh. I was walking past and it just happened."

Josh looked so frustrated that Kristi could feel his anger. "Would you like to share this new plan with me, or is it a secret?"

"The plan," JT said, "so far as it's gotten, is to determine a minimum number of paid registrations required to ensure breaking even, set a drop dead date, and make the announcement. If there are enough participants, we move ahead. If not, we cancel."

"And royally tick off a bunch of guests." Josh voice was so sour, it left a taste in Kristi's mouth.

"With any luck," his father said, "that won't be the case."

"It's going to take more than luck, Dad. It's going to take a colossal amount of work. That, and risking our reputation."

Kristi's stomach churned, seeing Josh's opposition. "Maybe we should take more time," she began, but JT stopped her.

"Josh, if I'm wrong this will be my swan song. I'll step aside, move out of the apartment, and leave you to run the Princess as you see fit."

Kristi watched the realization hit Josh at the exact same time it hit her: All he had to do was undermine the Bridal Ball, and he would have everything he wanted.

Josh contemplated the offer and smiled. "What if you're right?"

"Then we'll start planning the next one," JT said, winking at Kristi.

CHAPTER 19

JT gave Kristi a confident smile as the two men left her office. It did nothing to diminish her alarm. The Bridal Ball had just been offered up as a sacrificial lamb in a competition between father and son. More than anything, Josh wanted JT to hand over control of the Royal Princess. What would prevent him from sabotaging *her* dream?

The decision to *have* the Bridal Ball had put it in serious jeopardy.

Kristi saw little of Josh that week. He did not stop by her office to greet her in the morning; did not seek her out in the dining room at lunch; did not leave her any email or voice messages. What would happen to the ball if he, Wilhelm, and JT were making decisions without her?

As she prepared to leave on Friday evening, JT stopped at her office door. "We've pretty much decided on a date for the ball."

"Oh? When?"

"Saturday, February second. As you pointed out, we're not busy between New Year's and Valentine's Day, so it won't take revenue from any other event."

"I think that's the ideal time."

He came into her office, closed the door, and sat down. "I haven't abandoned you. Josh and I had to come to an agreement before we could take the plan any further."

"I hope I'm not going to be left out of the process."

"Not at all. Now that we've set the date, the real planning can begin. This is your vision. I see you taking the lead."

"I'm sad that Josh is opposed to it."

"Josh is opposed to failure. We simply have to make sure it's a success." He smiled. "A smashing success would be even better."

"I like the way that sounds."

"The four of us will meet at ten on Tuesday, and get a handle on a timeframe for marketing, prices for various packages, the vendors we'll want onsite that night, and so on. I've studied your website. You've got many of the details laid out already. It's very well done, incidentally."

"Thank you."

"We're going to make this work, Kristi. Trust me. Five years from now nobody will remember when we *didn't* have a Bridal Ball at the Princess."

"I hope you're right."

"I'm always right." He chuckled. "Well, mostly anyway. Have a good weekend, Kristi. And don't worry. It's going to turn out for the best."

Kristi couldn't help but wonder, the best for whom?

*

On Sunday morning, Kristi's cell phone rang before she was even out of bed. "Hi, Nicole. You're up early."

"I'm always up early. What are you doing today? Say you're not working."

"I'm not working."

"Really?"

"Really."

"Praise be! Miracles still happen. Listen, we've been planning to go to the Pops Concert at Stern Grove today. Blake has a huge project he insists he has to work on, although I bet if I wanted to go to a basketball game, he'd manage to find the time. Anyway, I thought maybe you'd like to go with me."

"I'd love to."

"Great. Everybody gets there early to find a good seat on the lawn. I'll bring lunch."

"*You'll* bring lunch?"

"I've been cooking all morning."

"*You've* been cooking?"

"Yeah, like that's going to happen. I ordered take-out from the deli on Chestnut. I'll pick it up on the way."

"What are we going to see?"

"Randy Newman is playing with a swing band."

"Sounds fun."

"Dress casually, and bring a hat. It may get hot."

Some days the fog in San Francisco burned off; some days it didn't. That day, it didn't.

"I'm freezing." Kristi rubbed her arms, trying to warm up. "I didn't realize you meant for me to bring a ski hat."

"Stop. Get up and do some jumping jacks." Nicole pulled out her phone and glanced at it. "It's sixty-four degrees. You'll live."

"Kristi?" a sweet voice said.

She turned. "Rebecca, hi. How nice to see you."

Had Rebecca Bailey managed to wrest control of her wedding from her parents since Kristi had seen her last?

The young woman spread out a blanket, and a young man put a small cooler on one corner.

"I don't think you've ever met Yancy," Rebecca said. "My fiancé."

"Hi, Yancy. This is my friend, Nicole."

Yancy nodded in greeting and began unpacking food from the cooler.

"Do you come to the free concerts often?" Rebecca asked.

Kristi shook her head. "Not any more. I used to come with my grandmother when I was a kid, but I haven't been in a long time."

"Yancy loves Randy Newman. When he heard he was playing, we had to come."

Yancy handed her a sandwich and a small bag of chips. "Beer or soda?"

"Soda."

"How are plans coming for the wedding?" Kristi asked.

Rebecca glanced at Yancy and then back at Kristi. "I wouldn't know. My mother has taken it over."

"Have you talked to her about what *you'd* like?"

"Why bother?"

Yancy leaned toward Kristi. "I don't understand how she has the guts to stick needles in screaming kids, but not enough nerve to argue with her parents."

"I told them what I wanted when we got engaged," Rebecca said. "They weren't interested."

"It's *our* wedding," Yancy said. "*We* should be planning it."

"Sounds reasonable to me," Nicole said, "not that anyone asked." She looked at Kristi. "Don't you agree?"

"I do. But weddings can be tricky. Parents often have strong opinions about what they want for their daughters. It's a struggle when the visions are vastly different."

"It's your wedding, for heaven's sake," Nicole said. "You'll only do it once. Do it the way *you* want."

Rebecca looked at Kristi. "What do you really think, Kristi?"

What would Heather say?

"It isn't my place to tell you what to do."

"I'm not asking what to do. I'm asking what you *think*. You see wedding receptions all the time. Which ones are the happiest?"

Kristi thought for a bit, and then said, "I have to admit the best receptions have been the ones where the bride has a dream, and she gets to make that dream come true." The minute she said it, she regretted it.

"You've heard it from the expert," Yancy said. "It should be our vision, not your parents."

Kristi could see it wasn't the first time they'd had this discussion.

"Couldn't you find a way to compromise?"

"I told you before what that means to my father."

Kristi knew she should stop; knew this was reckless. Still, she said, "There are things that are worth fighting for even if it's difficult or uncomfortable. I think your wedding is one. Maybe your mother could be persuaded, and then you could work on your father together."

The crowd began clapping as an announcer made his way to the microphone at the center of the stage.

"We'll talk more later," Kristi said.

But, the tension between the couple was oppressive, and the subject of their reception, however present, did not come up again.

Late that night, Kristi was still pondering their dilemma, and wishing she had been more impartial. Rebecca was the one who had to stand up to her parents if she wanted her dream wedding. Interfering was both unprofessional and unwise.

*

Wilhelm was waiting in the hallway for Kristi when she arrived at work the next morning. "I've just had a disturbing conversation with Dr. Bailey. Is it true that you told Rebecca she should refuse to have her wedding reception here?"

"Can we take this discussion to my office?" She walked down the hall toward her door, hoping to deflect his attack.

She had barely unlocked the door when Wilhelm said,

"Well?"

"No," she said evenly, moving behind her desk.

"Dr. Bailey said you spoke to Rebecca yesterday, and told her she should tell her parents she didn't want her reception here."

"I told her that she should be honest with them. It's her wedding reception. It seems reasonable that she have a say in the decisions."

"Really."

"Yes. She and Yancy want a small beach wedding, without the people and panoply her parents have planned."

"So, you told her to go against her parents' wishes."

"I suggested she should try to compromise—to talk to them and see if they can't work out their differences."

Wilhelm leaned on her desk; his eyes narrowed to sinister slits. "You are an event planner, not a therapist. Your job is to sell the product. They came to the Princess for a reception, and that is what we will provide. You will not give advice, or opinions, or suggestions unless they support an event we are hosting here. Is that clear?"

"Yes," she said as evenly as she could. Her tone held none of the terrible turmoil in her stomach; a roiling reminder that Wilhelm was her boss, and she had little recourse if she wasn't willing to go over his head.

"Fine. I'll be handling this event from now on; you are clearly not qualified. I suggest you consider whether you want to continue at the Princess. You may have turned away clients at Current Events, but we don't do that here."

If he was expecting a response, he could wait all morning.

When she said nothing, he turned to leave. He stopped at the doorway. "If you can't perform your job, it doesn't matter how much Mr. Townsend likes you. The Princess cannot afford to support incompetence."

Kristi called Heather that evening, and told her about Wilhelm's attack.

"Try not to let him bother you. He feels threatened. He's building himself up by tearing you down."

"He's such a bully. There's no reasoning with him."

"Kristi, you said exactly the right thing to the girl. If she has strong feelings about her own wedding, she should be fighting for it."

"Even if her parents are paying?"

"It sounds to me like the wedding Rebecca wants would cost very little. She could probably pay for it without any help from them. Why doesn't she have an intimate beach wedding with family, and a big reception at a later date if they feel so strongly about it?"

"That would be the perfect solution. I should have thought of it."

"You'd be smart to stay out of it."

"I feel bad. I not only let her down, I made things worse."

"Let it go, Kristi. Wilhelm is enjoying lording this over you. He took a bullet over the Bridal Ball, and he's making you bleed. Stay under the radar a while. The whole thing will blow over."

"I hope you're right."

"Not always; but about this, I believe I am."

Later, Kristi called Nicole and asked her about the upcoming planning meeting. "Any thoughts?"

"Don't let Wilhelm intimidate you," Nicole said. "Figure out as much as you can: possible packages, services that might be available, costs, sponsors who want to be involved. Wilhelm has no doubt studied our website by now, and he will have ideas to offer. Make sure you get your say first. Explain how you and Laura and I have done it on our own, without any advice or support from anyone."

"I'll do my best. He can be pushy. I don't want to look like a power-hungry bitch."

"You're a competent business woman."

"Sometimes men have trouble telling the difference."

"You'll do fine. Call me tomorrow night; I want all the details."

"Will do."

*

When she walked into the conference room the following morning, Kristi handed folders to Wilhelm, Josh, and JT. Inside were screen shots from each page of the Bridal Ball website; a list of possible packages for the weekend of the ball; a list of every sponsor's name, address, phone number, and website; a proposed budget; suggestions from the comments section of the site; and three of the most touching stories women had posted about why they wanted to wear their bridal gowns again.

Wilhelm looked through his quickly and said, "Well done, Kristi. I knew if I asked for an overview, it would be complete."

"Thank you. This has been my dream for a long time. It wasn't difficult to put it all together."

"This is terrific." JT's compliment pleased her and boosted her confidence.

"You didn't price out the packages." Wilhelm's voice carried an overdose of aspartame.

"I thought it best to leave that to you and Josh. You both know better than I do, the percentage of mark-up on rooms. I can calculate food costs once we decide on a menu, of course, but I knew you'd want all of us to discuss that."

He gave her a look that said she was pushing her limit. She sat back, wondering what he would say next.

"What have you got for us, Wilhelm?" JT asked.

"I've studied the website," Wilhelm said. "There isn't anything complicated about it. We should be able to take it over without any problems."

Kristi's stomach plunged. "Take it over?"

"Of course. If we're going to have the ball here, we

should manage the website," Wilhelm smiled at her, obviously enjoying her misery.

"I thought it was copyrighted," JT said.

"It is," Kristi said. "And we applied for a trademark."

"Then we can't take it over," Josh said.

"I assumed they would want us to," Wilhelm said, "to maximize our chance of success."

"My friend Nicole put it together and she's done a fine job of managing it thus far."

"She certainly has," JT agreed. "A very fine job."

"All we need is a link to the Princess website that says Register Here," Josh said. "Our site will publish the particulars on pricing and deadlines for payment."

"We'll want to make a big deal of announcing that we've chosen the venue for the ball," Kristi said. "On both websites, naturally."

"Yes," Josh said. "I'll have IT coordinate with Nicole."

"Have you contacted any of these vendors about prices, Kristi?" Wilhelm asked, guiding the conversation away from one he wasn't dominating.

"No. I wanted a complete list first. I think you'll agree there's no point in doing it twice. I knew you must have a list of vendors we've used in the past."

He winced.

I could learn to like this.

"We need to decide on a drop-dead date, and a minimum number of paid reservations before we make any announcements," Josh said. "I don't intend to risk losing a fortune or ruining our reputation on an unproven venture."

If he'd yelled at her, the message couldn't have been louder or clearer.

"Perhaps you could get us some suggestions on that, Josh," JT said.

"Once we make the announcement," Kristi said, "Heather will email her client list to tell them about the Bridal Ball."

Wilhelm sat up straighter. "Just a minute. We have our own clients to consider."

Kristi smiled to herself. *Zing*!

"Yes, of course," JT said. "We'll email our clients at the same time we make the announcement. I'm sure Heather will understand if we ask her to wait a day."

"As soon as we determine prices, I'll make up a new flyer for the shops sponsoring the website," Kristi said.

"I know a few businessmen who might like to be involved," JT said. "I'll make some calls and let you know."

"Thank you," Kristi told him.

"Anything else?" JT asked.

"I'll put prices together for the various packages," Josh said. "Wilhelm, I'd like you to determine a drop-dead date. Kristi, could you put Nicole in touch with IT, so they can coordinate the links? Dad, you can ask around to see what other businesses would like to sponsor the ball."

"If Wilhelm will give me a list of orchestras, emcees, and photographers we've used in the past," Kristi said, "I'll make a price comparison spreadsheet."

Before Wilhelm could object, JT said, "Good idea. Thank you, Kristi. Let's plan to meet again next Tuesday."

Kristi walked out of the meeting unsure of who was in charge, but convinced it was *not* Wilhelm. From the look he gave her, he knew it, too.

*

Kristi's mom called to her when she unlocked the door to her apartment later that week. "Got a minute, sweetheart?"

"Sure. Let me put my stuff upstairs."

Her mother led the way into her studio, where a huge painting sat on the easel. The scene, a French sidewalk café, drew Kristi over like a familiar friend. Black tables and chairs sat among potted plants, under a crimson awning, beckoning the viewer to sit down and relax.

Kristi put her arm around her mother and hugged her. "I love it, Mom. It's wonderful, and it's perfect for my office. It's exactly the feeling I want for clients: Come in, sit down, let's talk."

"That's what I was trying for."

"Is it dry?"

"Yes. It's ready to go to its new home."

"I'll take it tomorrow. Do you have pictures of it?" Her mother kept a photographic record of all her paintings.

"Of course."

"We should celebrate. Let's go get Chinese."

"Dim sum?"

"Yum. Want me to drive?"

"It's beautiful outside. Let's walk."

Kristi took one more look at the painting. "Too bad we can't go *there* for dinner."

"All it would take is a flight to Paris. This is from a photo I saw on a travel website."

"Is that legal?"

"As long as I don't sell it. I'm not worried."

"You know, if you go to jail, they won't let you paint your cell."

"Talk about cruel and unusual punishment—four gray walls." She shuddered.

"*Three* gray walls; one would be bars."

Kristi called the maintenance department when she arrived at the hotel the next morning.

"I'll have Pete meet you at your car, Kristi," the clerk told her.

Pete brought the bulky painting to her office, and half an hour later, it hung on the wall behind her desk. "I don't think I'd put it there," Pete said as he packed up his tools.

"Why not?"

"You'll never see it. It's behind you."

"True. But, it's not really for me. It's for our clients. It sets a mood."

He picked up his toolbox. "Give me a call if you want me to move it."

Ten minutes later Josh stopped at the doorway. "Nice," he said, nodding toward the new painting.

"You like it?"

"Very much. It changes the whole feel of your office: it draws you right in."

Good.

"Has Dad seen it?"

"Not yet."

"I'll send him down. Gran, too. As I recall, she wanted to see what your mom would create."

Kristi had visitors all day long, curious to see the new painting. At nearly four feet square, it was a sizable presence in her office. JT brought his mother by that afternoon.

"I knew I'd love it," she said. "Your mom has such talent. I visited one of the galleries where she's displaying work. In fact, I'm considering a piece for my living room."

"Really?" Pride pulled at the corners of her mouth. She wished her father had lived long enough to see her mother's success. To see the proof that a woman's creative life could be as valuable as money.

"Yes. I'll be sure to tell you if I decide to buy it. In fact, I'll have you over for tea."

"Thank you." Kristi admired the older woman's spunk. She must be in her mid-eighties and she was still buying art. "We would both love that."

"We'd better let Kristi get back to work," JT said.

"Come by any time," Kristi told her as they left.

Josh's grandmother's visit left Kristi feeling melancholy about her own grandparents. Josh was fortunate to have his father *and* his grandmother.

Strange. Josh's mother had deserted him; Wilhelm's mother had disappointed him. Both men had good reason to distrust women. Was that why neither appeared to be in a relationship?

A relationship with Josh might not be possible, but there must be a way to prove to him that he could trust her. She wouldn't give up on that.

And, if he did learn to trust her, maybe...

*

Nicole called her on the weekend. "I thought you were going to let me know about your big meeting."

"I'm sorry, Nicky. It's been a crazy week."

"How did it go?"

"Really well. Josh wasn't as negative as I expected. In fact, he was pretty supportive. Of course, his father was there, and Josh might have felt like he had no choice. I think he was surprised by the extent of detail in the folder. I know Wilhelm was."

"Sweet."

"And how about this: Wilhelm wanted to take over our website."

"What?"

"Not to worry. Josh had already seen it was copyrighted, and knew it belonged to us. But, I gave IT your phone number and email address. They'll be contacting you about the links."

Nicole's voice had returned to near normal by the time she said, "That's fine. Links are good. But no takeover."

"No takeover."

"Have you read any of the comments lately?"

"Not in the past few days. I've been swamped."

"Women are starting to use the sponsors' services, and leaving reviews. So far, every one has been positive."

"I would hope so. They were hand selected."

"Some people complain no matter what. We're lucky we haven't heard from anyone who is impossible to please."

"Let's hope our luck holds." She knew it was more than luck. They'd put their hearts into this venture. For Kristi, it meant the world.

"I'm asking users for their email address. I won't give away or sell the information; it's only for updates about the ball. I'll also keep a list of all the couples who attend. If we ever part ways with the Princess, we'll have our own data base. I noticed that some of our followers are interacting with Laura on the blog."

"I'm sure she's enjoying that," Kristi said, "especially when you consider most of her daily interactions are with Chloe."

"Speaking of interactions, any news with regard to the concierge?"

She wished. "Not a thing. If he's interested, he's keeping it a secret. Maybe the whole Bridal Ball thing has ruined any chance I might have had for a relationship. That, and the pesky fact that he's my boss."

"A fact he apparently overlooked when you were in Yosemite."

"But has remembered ever since."

"You need to go on another trip with him."

"Wouldn't that be nice?"

"Well, don't give up hope. Sometimes working on a successful project can bring people together."

"Except when one of them benefits from it failing."

"Let's not think that way. It's going to be a success; I'm convinced of it. And somehow, he'll be a winner just like us. I don't know how, but I honestly believe that."

"Okay, Pollyanna, you keep that winning attitude. I'll call you when I need a fix."

When she hung up, Kristi was anything but convinced. Josh was making all the right moves, but, the only way he would get what *he* wanted was for the Bridal Ball to fail.

She had to stay vigilant to protect her dream.

She knew one thing. If it came to a choice between Josh and the Bridal Ball, there was no hope for them as a couple.

Kristi would choose the ball.

CHAPTER 20

Josh and Kristi had lunch together on Tuesday afternoon. As they walked back to her office he said, "Nice job on that spreadsheet."

"Thanks." She was tempted to tell him that Wilhelm had resisted giving her the information she had asked for, but thought better of it. Best to let the man hang himself, even if the process was slow. "We have plenty of choices, and that's good. One thing I know—the orchestra is key. A DJ won't provide the ambience the ball requires. "

"It adds a huge cost, Kristi. We'd be wise to consider a DJ."

"Once you've danced to live music, you're spoiled. That's the secret to making folks book again next year."

"Prices hinge on that one factor, and so does our margin."

"Serve a less expensive cut of meat with a dynamite sauce. Dinner lasts half an hour; the ball lasts four."

"People never forget bad food."

"There's no such thing at the Princess. Besides, once they experience the magic, they'll come back for more."

"We're probably not going to agree on this." He looked

past her to the new painting. "Did your mom do that from experience, imagination, or a photograph?"

"A purloined picture. But, she says since she didn't sell it to me, she didn't break any laws."

"I really like it. I feel as though I could walk right into it and sit down." He looked back at her. "Do you have a lot of her paintings in your house?"

"I do. What about you? What's on your walls?"

His look was innocence piled on embarrassment. "Paint." When she laughed, he said, "I don't like to rush these things. However, my gran bought one of your mom's paintings. A still life. Not my style, but she loves it."

"I'm glad she's happy. Your gran is a real lady."

"She's a firecracker. When you get to know her, you'll find that she's not much of a lady. Her father was a stevedore, and she grew up on the docks. Tick her off and you'll hear language unknown even to sailors. We can dress her up, but we have to be careful where we take her. She can bring an entire party to its knees with a few choice words."

"I love it. I'll invite her for our next Girls' Night Out."

"She'd put you all under the table."

"I'd like to see that."

"I should let you get back to work."

Not yet. Not when they'd just laughed together. "When do you think we can start advertising?"

"I'm aiming for next week. I still have to factor the photographer, the music, and the emcee into the prices."

"I'm grateful for all the support you've given me, Josh. I know you don't think it's a good idea."

She watched him struggle with a response. "It's not a bad idea; just bad timing."

The laughter disappeared. Deep down, he wanted the ball to fail, and she knew it.

Kristi called Nicole a few days later. "Are you ready to go with the hotel link?"

"Sure am. Is Heather ready?"

"Yes. She has an email set to go out Wednesday, with links to our site and the hotel page."

"Are you excited?" Nicole asked.

"What do you think?"

"I'd say you're driving yourself nuts with second guesses."

"I'd say you're right." Friends who knew you well were a treasure.

"Laura has rewritten her blog post half a dozen times. If it isn't perfect at this point, it never will be. Oh, I've been meaning to ask—how many brides do you think they're emailing from the Princess?"

"JT decided to do a general email: *all* of our former clients will get the notice, which means hundreds of letters will go out. He said if there's one thing he's good at, it's turning over stones."

"So, midnight tonight?"

"Yep."

"Are you going to stay up?"

"Nope." She got little enough sleep.

Nicole laughed.

"You said we wouldn't know much for several days."

"And we probably won't. Your IT department will be tracking visitors, and they will ping me every time someone registers with a payment. I'll be tracking each click-through, so we'll know how many came from us, and how many came from the Princess's site."

"I hope you're getting a percentage."

"I hope so, too."

"GNO this Friday night?"

"Yes. Laura wanted to do Korean."

"Fine by me. Let me know where to meet you."

"Talk to you tomorrow," Nicole said. "Sleep tight."

By noon the next day, the hotel had two paid registrants for the first annual Bridal Ball: Laura Fisher and Georgia Warren.

"No surprise," Josh told Kristi, when she saw him in the dining room. "Georgia said she wanted to be the first."

"So did Laura."

"I'll be getting a report of all registrants every evening," Josh said. "Do you want one, too?"

"Absolutely. I want to ask you about the band I found. They require a nonrefundable deposit now, and full payment by December first."

He shrugged. "I still think we should go with a DJ, but get me an invoice, and I'll take care of it. What about the emcee and photographer?"

"Pretty much the same thing."

"It's only fair. We reserve a date—they turn down other jobs—we cancel—they're out of luck."

"Like any other business."

Josh's phone rang. He looked at the screen. "Hey, Mrs. Warren, what's up?"

He listened for a minute, then put his hand up to tell Kristi to wait a minute. "I see your point. Thanks. No, I'll call IT right now." He paused, listening. "I appreciate your help, Georgia. Talk to you soon." He hung up. "Georgia says we need to add the words *Formal Attire Only* to the reservation form. It seems obvious to me, but she says these days, people show up in all sorts of inappropriate outfits."

"I've seen guests in the dining room who look like they came directly from the gym."

"They probably did."

"My grandmother would have a fit."

"Mine often does."

"It's a shame people don't recognize the beauty of a room as old and stately as this, and show respect. Casual is fine for every day, but the Princess Dining Room is an institution. It deserves deference. I don't care what anyone says: you feel different when you're nicely dressed."

"You're quite the traditionalist."

"Yes, well, I'll get down now, and take my soapbox

back to my office."

"On this, I agree with you. I like going out in a tux now and then, but I can't deny that I'm more comfortable in jeans."

She almost blurted, *I love your jeans.* Instead, she said, "Special places demand more effort. Though I imagine some women put a *lot* of effort into pulling on their skinny jeans."

"I'd better get to IT before Georgia checks the site again."

"See you." She watched him walk away, imagining him in jeans.

*

Laura's voice was muffled when she answered her phone late that night. Kristi had called to give her the latest information on paid registrations. "Only four?" Disappointment dripped from her voice like sour milk.

"It's completely new," Kristi said. "Don't get discouraged. Our drop-dead date isn't until December."

"I know, but all those women who posted stories and comments—why aren't they signing up?"

"Most of them haven't seen the announcement yet. It hasn't even been twenty-four hours, Laura. And even if they have, they need to talk to their husbands about it, and be ready to make a substantial commitment for something six months from now."

"So, tomorrow will be better?"

"Right. We'll probably be sold out by noon."

By Friday, Kristi was as discouraged as Laura. Only seven couples had registered and paid the deposit. Traffic on both sites had increased, and several more stories had been posted. But, the meager number of commitments left Kristi doubting herself and her idea.

Wilhelm stopped in her doorway, and she had to force a smile.

"Not exactly a stellar start for your dance's debut," he said.

Nastiness budded in her brain; she stifled the urge to sling a caustic remark. "I'm not concerned. It'd take time for people to register even if it were a well-established event. It's brand new. I'm sure you're aware of how these things go, with all your experience. If you have any advice that would improve sales, I'm sure Josh would appreciate it."

He narrowed his gaze. "There isn't much one can offer to fix an idea that was so ill-advised."

"I believe that's what they told Edison, the Wright Brothers, and Steve Jobs. No matter. I'm sure the ball will be a grand event, with or without your support."

"Good luck with that." He left, taking with him her bravado.

She wasn't sure if he could ruin the ball, but she was foolish to provoke him. She had to watch herself when he baited her, ignore his negativity, and not let it demoralize her.

Later, she was so engrossed in her thoughts that she nearly ran into JT, who was standing by the door to the stairwell.

"Not a bad start for registrations," he said.

"Seven?"

"Our first week? I think seven is remarkable."

"You do?"

"Yes. We're looking at a demographic who are either working or have small children. Most of them don't check email until the weekend, especially when the email comes from a hotel."

"Oh."

"You weren't discouraged, were you?"

"Well..."

"You're discouraged after four days? Come on now, have a little faith. This is your dream. If you don't believe in it, how can you expect anyone else to?" He patted her arm.

"It's going to be fine, Kristi. Give it some time."

"Thank you, Mr. Townsend. I sincerely appreciate your confidence and your support."

"You're more than welcome, Kristi. And, thank you, for a terrific idea."

*

Kristi was the first one at the restaurant, and sat looking at the menu without seeing it.

Nicole and Laura came in together, and slid into the booth. "This is a first," Nicole said. "Did you get fired?"

"No. I quit."

"What?" Laura's eyes registered shock.

"She'd never quit before the ball," Nicole said.

"If there's going to be a ball." Kristi blurted, unable to hold it in another moment.

"What's up, buttercup? Bad day?" Nicole looked up at the waitress who had stopped at their table. "We'd like three glasses of chardonnay, please." She turned back to Kristi. "Now, please don't tell me you're discouraged already."

"Seven registrations. Seven."

"I will not join your downer dance. Let's see what the weekend brings before we give up all hope. Geez, Kristi, it's four days in, not four days *out*. Give me a break."

"I expected…"

"It's going to take time. Even Laura isn't discouraged."

"Not at all," Laura said. "I'm getting to know these women. They want to go to the ball, and they'll do whatever it takes. But, it may require some saving, some finagling, and some planning." She reached over and squeezed Kristi's arm. The gesture was so familiar that Kristi had to blink back tears. "It's going to be great. Be patient."

"See?" Nicole said. "Optimism reigns supreme."

The waitress put down their drinks. "Are you ready to order?"

"I am," Laura said, pointing to one of the items on the list. "I don't know what it is, but Ethan promised me I'd like it."

After they ordered, Laura said, "Have you guys been reading the stories on the site?"

"No," Nicole admitted. "Not this week."

"Me either," Kristi said.

"I'm glad I brought this, then." She opened a sheet of paper and began reading. *"My husband is a volunteer fire captain in a small town in northern California. We had a beautiful wedding, with nearly the entire town there. Just as we finished the third dance at our reception, the fire bells started ringing. My husband and all the groomsmen raced across the street to the firehouse, pulled on their uniforms, and tore off to fight a fire that was burning in a house six blocks away.*

"Hours later, he came home, filthy and apologetic. They'd had no choice, of course, so I wasn't mad. I tried to hide my disappointment, but he knew how unhappy I was. I'd planned our wedding day so carefully; the only thing I couldn't figure in was a fire.

"I would absolutely love the chance to spend an entire evening dancing with my husband, in my wedding gown—especially if we're nowhere near a firehouse." Laura smiled. "Isn't that a great story?"

"You know what we could do?" Nicole said. "We could print some of these stories in the program we give out the evening of the ball."

"Not without written permission," Kristi said.

"Of course. But, do you like the idea?"

"Some people might not want their stories made public," Laura said.

"They posted them on a website. How much more public can you get?"

"It's something to consider," Kristi said.

The server brought their meals and conversation waned

while they sampled each dish.

"Yum," Nicole said. "Good choice."

"Did you hire an orchestra?" Laura asked. "Last I heard you hadn't made up your mind."

"Josh likes the sound of the dance band. I wanted strings, but Wilhelm agreed with Josh. I found a twelve-piece band, with a singer. We'll use the photographer I recruited from the Sunset. His price was the best, and it seemed only fair given he was one of our first supporters."

"Some of the other sponsors might want to have representatives at the ball, as well," Nicole said. "The travel agency, for instance, and the jeweler. Maybe the cleaners. Oh, has anyone signed up for the dance lessons?"

"Not yet. But, I don't expect that to catch on until closer to the date."

"What does the concierge have to say for himself?" Laura asked.

Kristi considered the question. "He says the right things, but I know he wants JT to be wrong, the ball to be a failure, and his father to give him control of the Princess."

"That's bleak. Does JT realize that?" Nicole asked.

"Probably more than anyone."

"Isn't there some way to turn it into a win-win?" Nicole asked.

"I keep asking myself the same thing," Kristi said, "but I haven't been able to figure it out."

"If JT retires, will you leave, too?" Nicole asked.

The thought hadn't even occurred to her.

"If the ball is a flop, Wilhelm might be intolerable to deal with. I have a feeling that without JT there, unless Josh steps up, your life could be miserable."

Laura gave Nicole a warning glance. "Don't you think she has enough to worry about? Let's not borrow trouble." She lifted her wine glass. "Here's to a beautiful, successful Bridal Ball."

Kristi and Nicole touched glasses with Laura's, and

drank a toast of optimism.

But, a fresh kernel of doubt took root in the fertile soil of Kristi's imagination, and it immediately began to germinate.

*

Two weeks later, there were only ten additional paid reservations. JT said not to worry; Wilhelm smiled at her with perverse pleasure; Josh was unreadable. By the end of the month, only twenty-six couples had registered. Kristi was unable to tolerate Wilhelm's haughty condescension, and avoided him whenever possible.

The morning after Labor Day, Georgia stopped by Kristi's office to say hello. "Got time for coffee?"

"Sure."

They walked to the dining room and ordered coffee and cheese Danish.

"How's married life?" Kristi asked.

"Truthfully, not much has changed. We're both so busy we hardly see each other. We don't even bother to have date nights any more, which is sad."

"Not much of an argument for marriage."

"It should get better soon. Kids are going back to school, and folks are less inclined to put houses on the market. I've been so busy these past three months, I've barely had time to think. My last place closed on Friday, and I'm going to take a couple of days off."

"Congrats on the deal."

"Thanks. I've wanted to call and ask how sales are going. For the Bridal Ball, I mean."

Kristi's face told the story. "Not all that well, unfortunately. I'm disappointed it hasn't caught on the way I'd anticipated."

"That's terrible. I was sure it would be the talk of women's circles all over the Bay Area."

"Apparently not."

"Well, we're going to have to change that."

"I've been racking my brain, but with no luck."

"There's no luck involved. It's all strategy." Georgia pulled out her phone and looked up the website. "Do you have new flyers with the date, the package prices, and a picture of the ballroom?"

"We have all the information, but no picture."

"The picture is the clincher. The Crown Ballroom is an extraordinary venue; it sells itself. Send me the artwork, and I'll update it. I love doing that sort of thing." She gave Kristi a conspiratorial smile. "Did I ever mention I was a design major at Cal?"

"No, you didn't."

"We need to get this ball rolling," she said, then laughed at her own pun. "I meant to get involved before now, but I've been swamped at work."

"I'd appreciate anything you can do." Kristi was touched. Georgia had said she wanted them to be friends, and here she was, offering to help make Kristi's dream a reality. Men liked to take control; women rolled up their sleeves and helped friends get the job done.

Georgia took a bite of her Danish and followed it with a sip of coffee. "I'll start by calling all the women whose receptions I know were at the Princess. We need to get them on board. We couldn't *buy* better ambassadors."

Kristi's spirits rose with Georgia's infectious enthusiasm.

"Right. Now, what else?" she said, almost to herself. "I belong to a group called Cal Women In Business. It isn't just Berkeley grads, it's women from all over California. We meet monthly. It's a large group, probably about four hundred in all. I'll put a notice in our newsletter and get a link on the website. Considering you and Nicole and Laura put together the Bridal Ball idea, I reckon you qualify as Women in Business."

"Isn't that stretching it a bit?"

"Not at all. The Bridal Ball was entirely your concept; all the Princess is adding to the mix is the ballroom."

"Don't say that too loudly."

Georgia smiled. "Credit where credit is due, Kristi. It's a wonderful idea, and we're duty-bound to get the word out. There are thousands of beautiful wedding gowns out there, swathed in acid-free paper, suffocating in zippered garment bags. They were created to waltz around a beautiful room. It's our moral obligation to set them free."

"Hey, Georgia." Josh bent down for a kiss.

Kristi had not seen him, and hoped he hadn't heard what they'd just said.

Georgia pushed out a chair with her foot. "We were talking about the Bridal Ball. Join us."

He checked his watch. "I only have a couple of minutes."

Georgia waved at the waitress and mouthed the words, "Coffee, please?" pointing to Josh.

"What new ideas have you two come up with?"

"Marketing, mostly," Georgia said. "I'm going to rework the flyer, get it in the newsletter for California Women in Business, and make some calls to a few Princess brides."

Josh's face was a noncommittal mask.

"You know this is a great idea, Josh. The only reason sales are so paltry is that not enough women have heard about it."

He took a sip of coffee. "It's been a month."

"By this time next year, the next ball will be sold out."

"Can I hold you to that?" Kristi asked.

Josh looked at Kristi with sudden tenderness. "We should be able to grow it into a successful event."

Her heart squeezed. "I just hope women will want to attend more than once."

"Women will want to come as long as they can fit into

their wedding gowns." Georgia gave Kristi a knowing grin. "We have a special relationship with our bridal gowns. It's almost magical the way we're transformed when we slip into them." She looked back at Josh. "You wouldn't understand. But, I'm sure you would understand that if someone spends three or four thousand dollars on a dress, she'd like to get some mileage out of it."

"That part I get," he said.

"The truth is, you're providing an invaluable service to the women of the Bay Area."

"I'm a saint," Josh said.

"Don't get carried away. But seriously, this is a need that has never been addressed before. It's a brilliant idea."

"I'm a pioneer," he said.

"No, you're not. Kristi is." She finished the last bite of her Danish. "I should get going." She turned to Kristi. "Can you give me a copy of the flyer? I'd like to start working on it."

"Sure. And, I'll send the PDF."

Josh walked with them to Kristi's office.

"Say," Georgia said to Josh as Kristi found the stack of flyers in her briefcase, "didn't you mention something about the Dragon Boat races?"

Josh hesitated, his look unreadable. "Kristi's friend Sam says there's no point in attending unless you're in China."

"Nonsense. It's the first thing Wyatt has been interested in all year." She glanced over and gave Kristi a huge grin. "Probably because it involves the word *boat*."

Kristi handed her half a dozen flyers.

"Thanks. I'll email you a copy of my ideas this afternoon." She looked back at Josh. "Anyway, the races. We want to go. With you two, I mean."

Josh looked like he'd been ambushed.

"I don't know…" Kristi began.

"We're going. The only question is Saturday or Sunday. Check your schedule here, and figure out what day is best.

We'll do the races and then dinner."

"Okay." Josh brightened, and looked back at Kristi. "You in?"

"Sure," she said, though she wished it had been his idea.

*

"At least *somebody* had the idea," Laura said when Kristi talked to her later that week.

"It felt like Georgia put him in a corner, and he had no way out other than to agree."

"He's a big boy, Kristi. He could have said he was busy that weekend."

"She didn't say what weekend it was."

"You can go one of two ways with this, Kristi. You can say 'woohoo,' embrace it, and have a great time; or you can make excuses, second guess it, and have a lousy time. Which one is it going to be?"

Kristi thought a moment and then said, "I'm leaning toward door number two."

"You're impossible."

"It's hard to go out with someone when his hands are tied behind his back."

"You've had fun with him other times. Why is this so different?"

Kristi only had to think a moment. "Georgia railroaded him into it."

"He could have said no. He didn't, so roll with it. Relax. Have a good time. Maybe you'll have so much fun he'll ask you out again."

"Which, of course, is a very bad idea."

"Oh dear, I think I hear Chloe crying. It's so much easier to cope with a screaming baby than to deal with you."

"Okay, okay. Point taken."

"So, stop."

"Done."

There was a long silence.

"Any luck?" Laura asked.

"Yes. I'm cured. I can't wait to go out with Josh."

"Children's Theater was *so* lost on you."

"It would be nice being together away from the hotel."

"That's the spirit. I think there may be a future for you, though I doubt it will be in acting."

CHAPTER 21

"Have you seen the visitor count on our website?" Nicole asked Kristi two weeks after she'd had coffee with Georgia.

Kristi had just left her office, and was walking downstairs to the garage, talking to Nicole on the phone. "No. We've been so busy I haven't had time. Tell me."

"Someone opened the floodgates. The site is hot. We've had hundreds of hits the last four days, and many have clicked through to the Princess."

"Sales must not be up, or JT would have told me. How disappointing."

"They're coming to us in droves, Kristi; *some* of them are going to attend the ball."

"I hope they hurry up and register. We're already in the middle of September. If one hundred and fifty couples haven't signed up by December first, it's all for naught. At this point, we're not even close."

"I wonder where all the interest is coming from."

"Georgia had some marketing ideas she wanted to try: a couple of women's groups she belongs to, and a favor or two that people owed her. She and Wyatt have a lot of contacts."

"If that's the only thing that's changed, she must be the answer. We need to clone Georgia."

Kristi unlocked her car and turned on Bluetooth. "I'm afraid that she's one of a kind."

"Is she still spearheading your date for the Dragon Boat races next weekend?"

"Yes."

"You don't sound all that enthusiastic."

Kristi pulled out of the driveway and onto the busy street. "It feels like Josh was forced into the whole thing. It's awkward."

"Relax and enjoy it. You like him; apparently Georgia thinks that's a good thing."

"I guess."

"Perk up. What's wrong with you today?"

"I'm tired. It's late, it's been a rough week, and this weekend is going to be brutal."

"Sorry I asked." Nicole was quiet for a moment and then said, "What can I do to help?"

"Get a hundred couples to register for the ball."

"That's easy. What else?"

"That's it. Thanks. 'Bye."

Nicole's laugher spilled from the speaker into Kristi's car. "Want to come by for a glass of wine?"

"I can't, Nicky. I'm beat, and I have to be at work at six."

"I wouldn't have your job for the world."

"Funny, I was thinking that same thing earlier."

"About *my* job?"

"No. About mine."

She had the same thought more than once that weekend. By Sunday night, she wasn't sure she had the energy to drive home. She sat in her office, put her head down on her folded arms, and promptly fell asleep.

"Kristi," she heard from a soft distance. "Kristi, are you okay?"

She opened her eyes, squinting in the light.

Josh stood beside her desk, his eyes dark with worry. "Are you sick?"

"What time is it?"

"Twelve-thirty."

She struggled to stand up. "I need to go home."

"You look exhausted; maybe you should stay here tonight. I'm sure we have a vacant room."

"No, thanks, I should go home."

"Well, let's at least get you some coffee."

She would have preferred to leave. It was bad enough that he'd found her sleeping; making conversation when she was exhausted was impossible. But, she could see the concern in his eyes, so she followed him to the bar, where they sat, and ordered coffee.

"I want you to stay home tomorrow. This isn't healthy. You need some rest."

"But Wilhelm…"

"Leave Wilhelm to me; I don't want you getting sick."

"I'm fine, Josh. I don't need a day off."

"I say you do. Are you seriously going to argue?"

She was far too tired for an argument. "No." Besides, it felt good knowing he was concerned.

"There's been a dramatic increase in traffic on our Bridal Ball page."

The word *our* touched her. "Yes. I think Georgia has called in all her markers. It's the only possible explanation."

"Whatever she did, it's working. The site is getting lots of new visitors."

"Now if it will only translate into sales."

She drank the steaming coffee as fast as she dared, wanting more than anything else, to get home and get into bed. "I need to go," she said when she'd drained the cup.

"I'm going to follow you."

"You don't need to."

"I'll sleep better tonight if I'm not worried that you got pulled over for a DWD."

"What's that?"

"Driving while dozing."

If she hadn't been so tired she could have stifled the groan.

"It's late. What can I say?"

She was soon pulling up in front of her house, with Josh close behind her. She gathered her purse, her jacket, and her briefcase, and opened the car door.

"Is that everything?" he asked.

She jumped, not realizing he was already standing next to the car.

"I didn't mean to startle you." He put his arm around her waist. "You really do need a break. I'm serious about you staying home tomorrow."

He walked her to the door, where she fumbled with her keys.

"Let me," he said, taking them from her.

Once the door was open, they stood awkwardly, looking at each other. She wanted to invite him in, but an unwanted yawn betrayed her.

"Sorry," she said, covering her mouth.

He leaned down and kissed her gently.

Kristi's heart gave a giant kerthunk.

"Get some rest," he said, turning her toward the living room. "I'll see you on Tuesday."

Ten minutes later she collapsed into bed, the soft kiss lingering on her lips.

*

Wilhelm would make her pay for the day off. Even with JT's approval, Wilhelm would not allow her the pleasure of a free day without doing his best to spoil it.

JT escorted her to the weekly meeting with Wilhelm on Tuesday morning. "She looks better after some rest," JT said to him. "Don't you agree?"

"All of us would look better with a day or two off during the week," Wilhelm said, the kind voice in no way disguising his displeasure.

"All of us didn't work the last eleven days straight," JT said, leaving Wilhelm no room for comment. He smiled at Kristi. "I'll see you later."

As he walked out of the office, Kristi braced herself. Wilhelm said nothing. She sat waiting as he busied himself on his computer.

Finally he looked up. "Do you need something?"

"Aren't we having a meeting?"

"About what?"

"This week's schedule?"

"Aren't you able to run things on your own *yet*?"

He was as unpredictable as a flash flood: Kristi never knew what was coming, where it would hit, or how to prepare.

"I'm perfectly capable." *As I have been since the day I was hired.*

"Then, get to work."

Wilhelm's version of a blessing, she thought as she walked back to her office.

Josh found her in the dining room, having a late lunch. "May I join you?"

"Of course."

He put down a plate that held a sandwich and a handful of chips. "Dad is worried about you. He's afraid we're working you too hard."

"I was tired the other night, that's all. It was a mistake to put my head down, even for a minute. If you hadn't come by so late, he never would have known."

"He has an uncanny way of knowing everything. He's just so present—so *here*—all the time."

"You have no idea how lucky you are."

His eyes clouded with remorse. "I'm sorry. You're right, of course. I shouldn't complain."

"I'm sure it's a challenge, both of you working here, but..." She paused, knowing she shouldn't get personal. But, she'd already started and temptation pulled her over The Line. "You'll never regret appreciating him. You might, if you don't."

"You miss your father."

She wiped at the renegade tear on her cheek. "Every day."

"Sorry. I didn't mean to upset you."

His voice brought more tears. *Don't be nice. Change the subject.*

"So," he said, as if her plea had eclipsed the space between them, "the Dragon Boat races. I checked the website; we can take a shuttle from Chinatown, or try to find parking on Treasure Island. The thing is, Georgia wants to go out for dinner afterward in Berkeley."

"Which means we'll be driving back and forth in a shuttle, and then driving back and forth again later, or, driving around looking for parking on T.I."

"It doesn't start until eleven-thirty. From what I've heard, the restaurants there have few recommendations. I say we leave early, take breakfast, find a place to park, and eat on the beach."

She wondered if the plan had been his, or Georgia's. "Sounds good to me. Do you want me to fix something?"

"I'll ask Tony to whip up a quiche or a frittata that we can eat cold."

"Why don't I bring O.J. and coffee?"

"Perfect. I'll pick you up at eight, if that's okay."

"I could meet you here, if you'd rather."

"I live in the Haight. You're practically next door."

"Okay, if you don't mind."

"Not at all."

He didn't sound like it was an obligation. She hoped he hadn't proposed it because Georgia told him to.

He picked up his empty plate. "Get some rest this week if you can. I understand the races can be exhausting."

"Why?"

"Didn't I tell you? Georgia signed us up to paddle." He walked off, chuckling to himself.

Kristi strained to hear the delicious rumble for as long as possible.

Laura called her Thursday night. "You're spending the weekend with the concierge, right?"

"Right."

"Both nights?"

"Yeah. I think I'll move in with him."

"Smart apple. You're going to have to sleep with him eventually."

"Oh really? Did he tell you that?"

"No, Nicole did."

"Even if I were tempted, which I am," she admitted aloud for the first time, "sleeping with the boss is not in my job description. I know. I checked."

"It wouldn't be a job. Speaking as one who's seen him, it would be pure pleasure."

"Can we not go there, please?"

"*I* can't, that's for sure."

"Did you call for a special reason?"

"Yes. I wanted to read you a story that was posted on our site today."

"About the drunken groomsman who spilled red wine all down the front of the bride's gown?"

"You already saw it."

"There is more than one of that same story; kind of awful when you think about it."

"I would have killed him."

"Which is why we'll be serving colorless cocktails."

"To prevent stained dresses?"

"No. To prevent murder."

*

Kristi was up early Saturday morning, baking orange-cranberry bread. She filled a Thermos with coffee, and put cups and juice, along with napkins and the warm bread, into a picnic basket. She covered it with a brightly colored kitchen towel, and was downstairs by the curb, checking email on her phone when Josh pulled up in front.

"Good morning," he said, and she rejoiced. He had on jeans and boots.

He put the basket in the trunk, and opened the car door for her. "I just spoke to Georgia. They're meeting us for breakfast. Good thing I told Tony to make extra."

"I made bread. We've got coffee and O.J."

"Georgia said she'd bring fruit. I guess we'll have enough."

"Were you worried?"

"The classic fear of every hotelier."

"That, and whether the salmon will come in."

When he laughed, her chest contracted with delight.

It was going to be a good day.

*

"Did you get it?" Josh asked, helping Kristi down from a cement retaining wall near the beach.

"I think so." She shaded the screen on her phone and scrolled through the pictures she had just taken. "There," she said, showing him a photo.

"Good one. Really good."

"Did you get close enough, Kristi?" Georgia asked, coming up beside them. "Nobody in this crowd is willing to move an inch."

"She got a great shot," Josh said, "just as that dignitary was painting the eyes on our dragon."

"*Our* dragon?" Kristi showed Georgia the photo.

"That *is* good," Georgia said.

"Yes," Josh said. "Our dragon. We have to root for one of the teams. That dragon came alive right in front of our eyes. He wants our support; he begged for our support."

"What's that word when you give human attributes to inanimate objects?" Georgia asked.

Wyatt put his arm around Josh's shoulders. "Crazy?"

"I'm serious," Josh said. "That dragon looked right at me. He wants us on his team."

"Did you put any mystery ingredients in that bread, Kristi?" Wyatt asked.

"And feed it to my boss. I think not."

They walked along the crowded, rocky beach until they found a place large enough for all of them to sit together. They cheered on the boat Josh had chosen, and were not the least disheartened when it came in last.

"They'll do better next time," Josh assured them.

Georgia stood and brushed sand off her legs. "Kristi and I are going to take a walk through the craft fair." She slipped her arm through Kristi's. "Come on. The races will go for hours. Let's check out the booths for something fun to remember the day."

"Okay." The last thing Kristi wanted was to be dragged away. But, since declining would be awkward, she went.

As soon as they were out of earshot, Georgia said, "Are you having fun?"

"I am."

"Josh is a great guy."

"He is." Kristi was unsure where the conversation was headed.

"At the risk of sounding ridiculous, do you like him?"

"He's nice." Where was this going?

"I probably should have chosen a better time for this, but I thought you might want to know. Josh likes you. It's unlikely he'll ever say it himself. Wyatt told me that he couldn't stop talking about you the entire week after you were in Yosemite. That was when they went on their annual fishing trip, remember?"

"I remember." Kristi tried to take in what Georgia was saying.

Georgia stopped at a booth long enough to pick up a bracelet. "Nice," she said to the artist.

"Thank you," the woman replied.

They continued walking, Georgia back to their conversation. "Apparently he went on and on about how terrific you are, and what a great time you had together."

"I never would have guessed."

"That's why we invited you to our Fourth of July party."

"Did he ask you to invite me?"

"No. Wyatt and I decided on our own. But, he was pleased to see you, right?"

"We had a nice evening, later, watching fireworks from the hotel. But, he didn't..." She struggled for words that didn't sound juvenile. "...he didn't act especially interested."

"Like most of us, he's had some crash and then crash again relationships. And, like most men, he's a chicken. He told Wyatt he's wary about making himself vulnerable again."

"Why are you telling me all this? I can't imagine he asked you to."

"Lord, no. He'd kill me if he knew. I thought if you were interested, you might want to encourage him."

"There's the small problem of his being my boss."

"It wouldn't be the first time an employer dated an employee."

"For obvious reasons, it can be tricky."

"No doubt about it. But, as I said before, he's a great guy. I think he's worth the risk."

"I'm not willing to throw myself at him. That's not me."

"Inez has tried that. It's not him, either."

"Yes. I noticed that at your party."

"Poor girl. She's had a crush on him for ages."

"I'm glad you told me what Wyatt said. I had fun in Yosemite, too. It was a great weekend."

"Then all you have to do now is figure out how to let him know you're interested, too."

"Right."

"We'll do our part." Georgia put her arm around Kristi's waist.

"What does that mean, exactly?"

"Before the evening is over, we'll have plans to go to the Big Game together. Josh told Wyatt you've never been."

"It's true. I haven't." She'd never been to the Dragon Boat races either, but they didn't need to know that.

Georgia gave her a quick hug. "This is fun. I haven't played matchmaker in ages."

"I don't want you to railroad him into anything."

"You saw him handle Inez. He can get out of any situation he wants to, trust me. He's a master escape artist."

"Okay." Kristi was far less reluctant than she sounded. She could barely contain the joy she felt over Georgia's revelation. He'd talked about her all week. A master escape artist and a master at hiding his feelings. He sure was. He'd fooled her.

"Look," Georgia said, pointing at a display of jade bracelets. She tried one on. "I need to buy something, or Josh will see right through this little shopping trip."

*

Georgia had made a reservation at Alice Waters' award-winning café, Chez Panisse. Kristi had heard a lot about the restaurant, and was not disappointed by the rustic setting and innovative menu.

She read the offerings with difficulty. Between each item, her heart tripped and fell back on Georgia's words. Could she have been wrong? Josh hadn't made a single move, either at the races or in the car on the way to dinner.

Kristi wanted to believe it, but was that wise? She didn't want to make herself look like a complete fool.

"What looks good?" Josh asked, tapping Kristi's menu.

"What doesn't?" Georgia said.

"I don't suppose much can compare with the salmon," Josh said, his voice just loud enough for Kristi to hear.

"Some things are beyond comparison. That salmon was one."

"I'm sure their chef will do his best."

"We've never had a disappointing meal here," Wyatt said.

Georgia made a face at him. "Faint praise, darling. I've been delighted every time we've eaten here." She pointed to the menu. "I'm going to have the lobster bisque and saffron fettuccini." She looked up. "What about you guys?"

Wyatt chose the grilled lamb; Josh, the roasted pork loin. The three sat looking at Kristi, whose mind was still tripping over Georgia's words.

"I think I'll have the sea bass with couscous," she said at last. She couldn't imagine how she'd eat, with butterflies having a field day in her stomach.

"How are plans going for your Bridal Ball, Kristi?" Wyatt asked. "Georgia tells me she's been out with the bush beaters, flushing out every bride we've ever met."

"We've had far more activity on our websites recently, so kudos to your wife," Kristi said. "Unfortunately, traffic hasn't translated into increased sales."

"Yet," Georgia said. "I know they're coming. Women have to make arrangements for baby sitters and such. After all, it isn't just an evening out; it's the better part of a weekend."

"I appreciate your optimism, Georgia, but I'm afraid we may have jumped into this venture entirely too quickly," Josh said.

Kristi's stomach clenched, scattering butterflies everywhere. "You're not canceling it, are you?"

"Not yet, although ultimately, we may have to."

He sounded regretful. Was that for her benefit, or Georgia's?

"Can't you cut costs, so you can have it even if there aren't as many couples as you'd like?" Wyatt looked from Kristi to Josh. "What's your biggest expense?"

"Besides food? The band."

"Don't have a band. Have a DJ. That would reduce costs, wouldn't it?"

"Absolutely," Josh said.

"We can't do it with a DJ," Kristi said. "The band is key. Dancing to live music is central to the elegance of the ball."

"Music is music," Wyatt insisted. "What difference does it make?"

It felt to Kristi like an attack, like the ball was being stripped of its essence. "It's the difference between ordinary and extraordinary. The difference between a house band and the Philharmonic. The difference between Justin Bieber and Pavarotti. We're trying to create a peak experience. Women can dance to recorded music in their living rooms."

She couldn't read Josh's look. Was it pity, or embarrassment?

"I agree," Georgia said. "The majesty of the Crown Ballroom *demands* live music. It's only fitting in that glorious space."

"But, if it's the difference between having the ball and not having it?" Wyatt asked.

"I'd rather not have it," Kristi said.

"Which is what I was just saying," Josh told her.

Their meals arrived, but Kristi's appetite was gone. She forced down what she could, enjoying it not at all. Had Josh put Wyatt up to it? Asked him to play devil's advocate?

You're being paranoid. Eat your dinner. It's beautiful and delicious.

But she couldn't shake the thought that Josh was trying to warn her what was to come. Would she really rather cancel the ball than have a DJ?

How could she disappoint Laura after all this? Not to mention the other brides who had already registered?

They finished their entrees; the wait staff cleared their plates and poured coffee for everyone.

"I can't possibly eat dessert," Kristi said. The server had packed most of her meal into a take-out carrier.

"It comes with the meal," Georgia said. "It's small."

"I'm stuffed," she said, though she knew the tightness in her stomach wasn't from food; she had hardly eaten.

"Someone will eat it," Wyatt assured her.

Kristi excused herself to go to the restroom, thinking a splash of cold water might help bring her out of the funk. She had barely turned on the water when Georgia followed her into the ladies' lounge.

"Kristi, you mustn't let Wyatt discourage you. I can see what he said about the music was upsetting. Ignore him. What does he know about what you're trying to create?" Their gazes met in the mirror.

"It's just that…"

"You don't have to explain. I understand completely. It's Cinderella—really—it's the magic ball, the whole package. It *has* to be live music. I agree. Don't let them talk you out of it." She leaned on the counter next to Kristi. "I mean it."

"It sounds infantile. A magic ball. Really? Are we six years old?"

"The dream is planted when we're young, planted in all of us. Well, most of us. We want the dream. If we can have it a second time, why wouldn't we? If we never had the dream, if it was interrupted, or ruined, or beyond reach, we keep on wanting it. Not on the outside, where others can see it, but hidden deep down, in secret."

"Do men ever understand?"

"Probably not. But, who cares if they do?"

Kristi's laugh was hollow. "I do, especially when they can make or break that dream."

"The most important thing right now is for you to keep your momentum. Keep your belief about what the ball should be, paramount. Don't let anyone talk you into compromising."

"I'm fighting all of them."

"No, you're not. JT thinks it will be a wonderful event." Georgia smiled. "And so do I. And so do dozens of others."

"I hope they hurry up and register. If they don't, this dream is going to turn into a nightmare."

"Take a deep breath, Kristi. You can't do a thing about it right now. Instead, we're going back to the table and have dessert. And, talk about Big Game."

"Big Game?"

"Yes. That's the next item on our social agenda, and we have to make sure Josh realizes he's taking you."

"I don't want you to manipulate him, Georgia. It's uncomfortable."

"I'm not manipulating, I'm facilitating."

"Whatever. I want it to be *his* idea."

"Are you kidding? He talked to Wyatt about it for an hour. He couldn't believe you'd grown up in the Bay Area and never gone to Big Game."

"Then why hasn't he asked me?"

"He probably has some antiquated reservation about being your boss."

"He's right. Let's wait and see if he invites me himself."

"I don't have the time or patience for that. Come on," she said, and she pushed Kristi out of the lounge and into the restaurant.

CHAPTER 22

"Sorry about Georgia," Josh said as he guided the car through the heavy traffic onto the Bay Bridge. "Sometimes she gets pushy like that. She gets an idea in her head and won't let go."

"It didn't bother me at all."

"I don't want you to feel pressured to go to Big Game if you don't want to."

"It sounds like fun."

"It is fun." He was quiet for a bit and then said, "So, does that mean you're interested?"

"Yeah, I am." Was that enough encouragement?

"It's a long day, what with the tailgate and all."

Was he trying to talk her out of going? "Do you want me to go?"

"Yes!"

"Okay then, it's a deal." She almost blurted, "It's a date." She wasn't sure what it was, but if it wasn't his idea, how could it be a date?

He turned on the radio and switched the station from big band music to show tunes. Soon, they were both humming along to the theme from "Breaking Dawn." The decorative LED lights on the Bay Bridge sparkled, rippled, and danced, in perfect time to the music, a ballet on the cables that spanned the bridge.

Kristi craned her neck to see out the window. "It's prettier than the Golden Gate."

"Some think so. Myself, I prefer that iconic, hulking, red landmark across the bay. I loved walking there when I was a kid. Sometimes my mom would pack a picnic lunch; we'd park and eat near one of the military batteries, and then walk across the bridge and back. Seeing the ships pass underneath was amazing."

"I was there the day the Queen Mary II came in. She was so tall that they had to bring her in at low tide. News helicopters were filming it, hovering at eye level with the pedestrians. One popped up right in front of me and scared me to death. I thought we were being attacked."

"Your Children's Theater is showing."

"I'm not exaggerating."

His eyes lit on her with butterfly wings, then darted back to the highway.

"Do you think I'm kidding?"

"No. I think you have a vivid imagination."

They entered the city, where the streetlights were as bright as daylight. Josh drove slowly along the Embarcadero; ships of every size and shape sat in dock, waiting for departure.

"Have you ever wanted to go on a round-the-world cruise?" Josh asked.

"Actually, no."

"Really?"

"I'm perfectly content right where I am. My friend Sam, by comparison, has been to every state in our Union, every country in the European Union, and every continent on earth."

"What's next? The moon?"

"If it were possible—read here affordable—Sam would be the first in line."

"A regular nomad."

"An adventurer, always chasing something new and different."

"Unlike you."

"Unlike me."

As they approached the Sunset District, Kristi decided to take Georgia's advice. They pulled up in front of her house, and she said, "Would you like to come in for a drink?" It sounded so lame, she felt her face flush.

"I don't need a drink, but I'd like to see your mom's paintings."

Kristi took a mental inventory of her apartment. She had seven of her mother's paintings; one was in the bedroom. Was the room a mess? "Sure," she said, hoping she hadn't left stray underwear on the bed.

He followed her upstairs, where she fumbled with the temperamental lock on her front door. She flipped on the hallway light, and then a lamp in the living room.

One of her mother's paintings hung over the narrow fireplace, a picture of an old, gray clapboard house, its trim a dusty white. "My mom painted that from a photo I took when I went up to visit my brothers in Seattle. It was a rainy afternoon. I loved the way the light reflected in the wet street." Her breath caught, as it often did when she looked closely at the house. "The upstairs window, the one on the right, was my bedroom."

"You lived there?"

"Until my father died."

"Doesn't it make you sad to see it every day?"

"No. To be honest, most of the time I don't see it at all." She looked up at him and grinned, an urge to needle her boss overwhelming. "I suppose I spend way too much time at work." She was quiet a moment and then said, "I read somewhere that if you really want to see artwork, keep it fresh, you should move it around periodically."

"Do you do that?"

"No. But I think about it, periodically."

Pulling his laugher out of him, made her giddy with pleasure.

"This is my mom's, too." She pointed to a much smaller painting, which sat on a miniature easel on the bookshelf.

He examined the delicate beach scene, with fawn-colored dunes, and glistening aqua waves. "Is this near here?"

"I'm not sure. She works from photographs a lot. Some she takes herself, some I take, and some she downloads from the net. A few websites allow use of their photos for free."

"I like it. I can almost smell the salt in the air."

"She'd love hearing that."

"Do you have any others?"

"If you're looking for something for your house, you'll have to check the galleries. I'm not parting with any of mine."

"I might want to commission a piece. Have you ever asked her to paint something special for you?"

"Just our old house."

"Do you suppose that was difficult?"

"Not long ago, she told me it was a catharsis. I was reluctant to ask her, but my brothers both encouraged me."

Kristi showed him all the paintings, relieved she had put away her underwear, and pulled up the covers on her bed.

"That's it," she said, pointing to the last picture.

"They're all great; and they're all unique. She certainly is talented. You must be proud."

"I am." She glanced at the painting over the fireplace. "It's sad. I don't remember that my father was. What I mean is, he never really thought much of her painting. To him, it was something to keep her occupied at home. She didn't get the respect she deserved until she was on her own."

"Apparently neither of our fathers gave their wives the appreciation they wanted, or needed."

"I wonder why it was so hard for them?"

"I don't know about your father, but mine was so involved with the hotel he had no time for anything else; better said, he took no time. Not for my mom, and not for me. I have few childhood memories with him. If I have kids, I intend to live very differently."

"If?"

He sounded unsure of himself, something Kristi had never heard before.

"When, I guess. I've never been serious enough about anyone to see myself having kids." She felt his eyes on her. "What about you?"

"I definitely want kids, but with the hours I work, it's hard to find time for a relationship, much less a baby."

"Our business doesn't lend itself well to successful relationships. Between late nights and weekend events, there isn't time for much else."

"Maybe I should quit and get a nine to five job."

"Please don't." He put his arms around her. "I'd miss seeing you every day." He leaned down and kissed her. "I'd miss you a lot."

When he kissed her again, Kristi's heart tripped and tumbled and toppled into heaven.

*

On Monday morning, Kristi had barely turned on her computer when Josh stopped by her office. "Good morning."

She smiled at his greeting, which carried new meaning since they'd last said good night.

"Good morning."

"I was wondering, have you ever been to the Oktoberfest at Pier Forty-eight?"

"That would be the one that's not in Munich?"

"That's the one."

Sam would never approve. "I haven't."

"It's this coming weekend. I thought it might be fun."

"We don't have to create a burger for the event, do we?"

"No. They do sausages; lots of sausages; all kinds of sausages."

"And sauerkraut?" Her screwed up face felt like a five-year-old's.

"You don't like sauerkraut?"

"Not my favorite thing."

"The entrance fee doubles if you refuse the sauerkraut."

"Why?"

"Too much left over sauerkraut."

"I'll pay."

He leaned against the door jamb. "Is that a yes?"

"Yes."

"Good. Saturday is best. Queenie can do the dinner that night. I'll come by at five. Wear your dirndl."

"My dirndl?"

"You don't have a dirndl?"

"No. Do you have lederhosen?"

"Yes. My grandparents bought them for me when I was about five. But, since you don't have a dirndl, I'll wear jeans."

Works for me.

*

They left Josh's car at the hotel and took a taxi to the Oktoberfest. When the driver dropped them off, the entrance line stretched halfway down the pier; hundreds of revelers, many in lederhosen and dirndls, already in party mode.

Kristi and Josh had barely joined the throng when they heard a familiar voice. "There you are." Georgia came up behind them, hugged Kristi, and gave Josh a quick kiss.

"Surprise! Wyatt said you were coming tonight. I hope you don't mind us joining you."

"Not at all," Josh said. "Where's Wyatt?"

"Up at Will Call. We ordered our tickets in advance."

"I should have done that, too," Josh said. "We'll be waiting here all night."

"The line should move quickly once they open. We'll save you a place."

The fest hall smelled of beer, roasted nuts, and grilled sausage. Kristi and Josh found Georgia and Wyatt at a long table, along with several others, all singing "Sweet Caroline" with the band.

Wyatt greeted them. "I didn't think you'd object to us tagging along."

"Of course not," Josh said.

"I know you like to dance," Wyatt said to Kristi, "being the creator of the Bridal Ball."

"You're right, I love to dance."

"Get out there on the floor, you two," he said. "Show us your moves."

"It's not break dancing, Wyatt." Georgia hugged her husband.

"All I can do is the Chicken Dance," Josh said.

Kristi turned to him. "Liar. You're a wonderful dancer."

The band started playing a polka, and several couples hurried to the dance floor.

"Look at that," Josh said, pointing at his feet, "I didn't wear my dancing shoes."

Kristi took his hand. "Boots are better. Let's dance."

"Oh my gosh," Georgia cried, "they're yodeling! I thought that was a Swiss thing."

"Swiss and Bavarian," Josh said.

Georgia clapped her hands. "I love yodeling. There was the most adorable girl on one of those talent programs a few years ago, who could yodel like a pro. I think she won the competition."

THE BRIDAL BALL

"Do you suppose any of those guys are from Germany?" Kristi asked.

"No; they're all Americans," said a tall, bearded man behind them. His lederhosen, checked blue shirt, and green hat implied he just might know.

"Are you a friend of theirs?" Wyatt asked.

"I'm one of their roadies. There's not a native German in the bunch."

"Which one is Chico?" Kristi asked him.

The roadie laughed. "Common mistake. Actually, they met at Chico State University; they were all music majors. Forty years later, they're still together. Great story, don't you think?"

"I do." Kristi looked from the roadie to a big, bearded musician on the stage. "Is that your brother playing the tuba?"

"Brother from another mother, as we like to say."

"Jeff!" someone yelled, and the roadie turned. "Give us a hand over here."

"*Auf wiedersehen*," he said to Kristi, and headed off.

As the evening wore on, Josh told Kristi how impressed he was with the variety of music the band played. "We should have hired these guys to play for the ball."

"A polka band? That's not exactly the mood I was aiming for. I love the lederhosen, but I was after something a skosh more formal."

"Long lederhosen?"

"Yeah. No."

He hugged her, laughing, then kissed her. "Let's go get some sauerkraut."

They ate sausages, warm potato salad, and drank beer in mugs the size of wading pools. They danced waltzes, polkas, tangos and the chicken dance. Josh's arm lingered protectively around her waist, keeping her safe from a crowd that grew increasingly intoxicated.

By eleven o'clock, the room was vibrating with thousands of people, all moving and talking at once. "The fest ends in half an hour," Josh said.

Kristi strained to hear him over the din.

"We'd be smart to get out of here now, and avoid the mass exodus."

"I agree. It's getting crazy." Kristi leaned away from a group of six, burly men, dancing on the table next to them. "We probably should have taken off when Georgia and Wyatt left."

They walked out to the front of the building, where a long, rowdy line waited for taxis.

"Let's walk over to the Embarcadero. We'll get a cab faster there."

They headed toward the great hulk of AT&T Park, which stood across from Pier 48. As they neared the Third Street Bridge, Kristi saw a couple arguing in the shadows.

"Come on, you little shit," the man said, "The car is the other way." He yanked on her arm, and she tried to pull away.

"You're drunk," she said. "We need to take a cab."

"To where?"

"To my house."

"You stupid twit, that'd cost a fortune."

She struggled out of his grasp and moved toward the bridge. "I'm not getting in the car with you."

"The hell you're not." He grabbed her by the hair.

She screamed, twisted, lost her balance, and fell on the sidewalk.

"Get up!" He kicked her leg, and she cried out.

Kristi's body stiffened, feeling the blow.

Josh tensed, and dropped his arm from around her waist. "That's enough, buddy."

His harsh tone made Kristi's breath catch in her chest.

The man whirled, and Kristi saw how young he was. He glowered at Josh. "Piss off, *buddy*."

THE BRIDAL BALL

Kristi helped the young woman to her feet, both of them trembling.

"Your friend is right," Josh said. "You shouldn't be driving. Be smart; go find a cab."

The man reached for the woman, but she pulled away. "You little…" he began, but Josh pushed between them.

"That's enough!"

Without warning, the man leveled a punch directly at Josh's face. Josh ducked, but the man's fist grazed his head with a crack. Josh grabbed his arm, twisted it behind his back, and whirled him around. "See those policemen?" He nodded at the knot of uniformed men outside the fest.

The man swore at him.

"You have two choices. You can go find a cab, or we're going to go meet a policeman."

"And then what?"

"And then I'll press charges for assault."

Only then did Kristi notice the blood dripping down Josh's cheek. Her heart jumped into her throat.

"If she wants to take a cab, she's welcome to it," the man said. "I'm outta here."

Josh let him go, and he lurched back toward the fest hall.

"Let's go find you a cab," Josh said to the young woman.

She began to cry. "I can't. I don't have any money."

"Where do you live?"

"San Jose."

Josh thought only a moment before saying, "You're going with us."

She stumbled along between them, Josh looking back several times to make sure they weren't being followed.

"You're hurt, Josh," Kristi said.

He touched his cheek, looked at the blood, and wiped it on his jeans. "I'll be fine."

Kristi winced as more blood appeared. "Josh…"

"I'm fine. Don't worry."

His voice had a touch of Yosemite in it, talking down another danger. Being a protector. Ready to pay the price for his decisions. Kristi felt pride replace the fear that had gripped her. She was in good hands.

She was sure the young woman was in no shape to remember, but Josh introduced themselves to her. "We're taking you to a safe place," he said, wiping the blood again.

They hailed a cab, and squeezed into the back seat. When they reached the hotel, Josh paid the cabbie, and helped the girl out.

"You're going to spend the night here," he said.

She looked up at the wrought iron gate work at the entrance to the Princess. "I couldn't afford this in a million years."

"There won't be a bill," he said, putting his arm around her to escort her in.

She pulled away. "I'm not a prostitute!"

Kristi took the girl's hand. "You're perfectly safe. Josh's family owns this hotel, and I'm the event coordinator here. He's not going to hurt you. You need somewhere to spend the night. You can't stay on the street."

The girl looked around, taking in where she was. "I don't have to pay?"

"No," Kristi and Josh said at the same time.

"And no kinky stuff?"

"Absolutely not," Josh said.

She looked up and down the street again. "Okay." Her hesitation was clear, but she let them guide her inside.

"May I help you?" the desk clerk asked, and then she gasped. "Mr. Townsend, you're bleeding! What happened?"

"I'm fine. This young lady needs a room for the night. It's on me. She can have room service for breakfast."

"Room service?" The girl sounded as though he'd offered to buy her a month's groceries.

"A single?" the clerk asked, already keying the information into the computer.

"Yes. And have a bellman escort her to the room, please."

"Of course, sir."

Josh looked at the girl. "Can someone come get you tomorrow?"

"Yes."

"Good. You should think about dating a guy who treats you better than that…uh…jerk."

"Thank you for helping me."

"You're welcome." He turned to Kristi. "Shall we go?"

"Don't you want to clean up?"

"I'll do it at home."

Once in the car, Kristi handed Josh several napkins she found in the glove compartment.

He pressed them to the side of his head. "That bum was wearing a ring; he made sure he got me with it."

Kristi still felt shaky. "I can't believe what just happened. That was…"

"Nothing compared to the bear. If that mama had attacked us, we'd both be in shreds."

"It's no joke, Josh. He could have really hurt you. What if he'd had a knife, or a gun?"

"You don't think shouting 'Go, go, go,' would have done the trick?"

"It's not funny."

"What would you have me do, walk off while he beat the crap out of her?"

She flushed, guilty. He was prepared to pay the price. "No."

He started the car. "I'm fine. You're fine. And for tonight, she's fine."

"Do you suppose she'll go out with him again?"

"Who knows? With luck, she'll wake up in the morning and take a good look at her future. If she keeps seeing him, I'm afraid there won't be a happy ending."

"I have to admit I was impressed by how you handled him."

He turned slightly in his seat. "I certainly hope so. I wouldn't want all this blood to go to waste."

He walked her up to her door, where she stood on her tiptoes and kissed the unbloodied cheek. "Thank you for another memorable occasion. I'll never forget tonight."

"That's what I was aiming for."

"Aim a little lower next time. A forgettable evening would be a relief."

"I'll plan something boring that doesn't involve bears or blood."

"I accept in advance."

"I'll call you," he said as she slipped in through the open door.

When she changed into her PJ's, she realized there was blood on her shirt. It struck her again how seriously Josh could have been hurt. He was a hero, in a way.

Her hero, anyway.

*

Kristi called Laura the next morning. "You won't believe what happened to us last night." She told her about the fest, the fight, and the finale.

"He attacked Josh?"

"He hit him. But, Josh got him under control."

"And, saved the damsel in distress."

"You could say that."

"I *am* saying that. He's a prince, Kristi. With a terrific castle, I might add."

"Don't get carried away."

"I'm telling you, Prince Charming has turned up in your life. Pay attention. You don't want him to ride off into the sunset with someone else."

"I'm doing my best." She padded into the kitchen and poured herself another cup of coffee.

"Have you asked him over for dinner?"

"No."

"What's the hold-up?"

"The last time I saw him he was bleeding. Food was not on my mind."

"Call your wounded warrior, and see how he's doing. He might have a concussion. You should probably go check on him in person."

"You're right, I should check on him."

"That's more like it. Call me later, preferably with news of some progress."

Kristi hung up and called Josh. Her heart stammered when she heard his drugged voice. "Are you okay?"

"I'm fine. I was watching football. I guess I fell asleep."

"Okay. I don't suppose you'd like to come for dinner."

"I've got a killer headache. Can I take a raincheck?"

"Sure. Do you need anything?"

"Just some rest. Thanks for the invite. See you tomorrow?"

"I'll be there."

She sat in the living room, drinking coffee and considering Georgia's advice.

And Laura's advice.

Josh was worth fighting for. He was a man who could take care of himself. Who could take care of a woman. Who could dance!

No more eggshells. Tomorrow, she'd make her move.

CHAPTER 23

A terse message from Josh greeted Kristi when she arrived at work. "Please see me as soon as you get in."

Something was wrong, but what? She grabbed her laptop and hurried to his office, where she found him talking to his father.

"Kristi, you're here. Good. Please come in," Josh said.

She looked at him as closely as she dared. A small bandage on his temple covered the cut. "Are you okay?"

"I'm fine."

JT gave Kristi his chair, and poured her a cup of coffee.

"Wilhelm had an urgent call from Germany last night," Josh said. "His mother was in a serious car accident yesterday, and was critically injured. They have no other relatives there, so Wilhelm is leaving for Munich this morning. We have no idea how long he'll be gone."

"How awful. I'm so sorry." Kristi wouldn't wish ill on anyone, not even Wilhelm.

"Needless to say, we'll have to divide up his responsibilities."

"How can I help?" Kristi asked.

"I'll be taking the bulk of the work," Josh said. "Dad will

take over some of my duties. Anything related to events or catering, we'll pass on to you. Until Wilhelm returns, you'll report directly to me."

That could be fun. Or awkward.

"He's going to email a complete list of projects," Josh continued. "I'll sort through them, and get the appropriate info to each of you. If you have any questions, see me right away."

"Okay." Kristi watched the prospect of dinner disappear down the drain.

"I think that's it. Dad?"

"Nothing now. I have no doubt we can manage this. It shouldn't be for too long. Wilhelm's mother is as stubborn as he is; she'll be up and running the hospital in no time. He might be back by the end of the week."

But Wilhelm was not back at the end of that week, or the next. After working fourteen days straight, Kristi was exhausted. The only things that kept her going were the regular meals Tony prepared for her, and her daily meetings with Josh. One evening, they shared a quick supper in her office, and twice, they had lunch together.

But mostly, they worked.

"You can look forward to a handsome bonus at Christmas," JT told her one morning as he met her coming out of her meeting with Josh. "Provided you survive that long. Can you get away early tonight? You look beat."

"We've got a banquet."

"For how many?"

"Forty."

"Queenie can handle it. She had the weekend off. You need a break."

"Are you sure?"

"Absolutely. I'll talk to her and Josh. I want you to leave no later than four."

"Thank you. A break would be wonderful."

She could feel the tension in her body melt away as she walked to her office. A night off. Absolute heaven. The afternoon couldn't pass quickly enough.

By three-thirty, she was thinking little about work and a great deal about a simple supper and a very hot bath.

"Hey," Josh said from her doorway. "Dad says you're off early today."

"Is that a problem?" Her body stiffened at the thought of losing JT's largesse.

"Not at all. In fact, I think I'll do the same. Queenie is set for the banquet. She can probably run it better than all of us put together."

"No doubt."

He ambled into her office. "So, what's on your agenda, a glass of wine and a hot shower?"

"Close."

"What about if I make dinner for you?"

Her stomach churned up a cocktail of hesitation and anticipation. "Seriously?"

"Yes. You've done a great job these past weeks. I'd like to thank you with a nice meal."

"Really?"

"Yes."

"I'm no dummy. I won't turn down a home-cooked meal."

"What time is good for you?"

"Whatever you say."

"How about I pick you up at six."

"I'll be ready."

She'd be ready at five.

*

His apartment was not at all the young-bachelor-does-San-Francisco-place she'd expected. It was big, it was open, and it was stunning: arched doorways, soaring tray ceilings, decorative moldings, and a state-of-the-art kitchen with granite counters, stainless-steel appliances, and a Sub-Zero refrigerator.

"It's beautiful," Kristi said after he'd given her a tour. "How long have you been here?"

"About six years. I managed to get in when the market was low, at least such as it ever gets in San Francisco. I've done nothing since I moved in. It was in pristine condition, and I haven't touched a single thing."

"Why would you? Although you could use one or two pictures on the walls."

"I knew you'd say that. It's easy for you. There are no artists in my family. I wouldn't know where to begin."

"You start by deciding what you like, deciding whether you can afford it, and if not, deciding on a good substitute."

"You make it sound easy. And, logical."

"It's actually more emotional. The right thing on the wall can change your mood. It can brighten a gloomy afternoon, or give you a boost of enthusiasm."

"It sounds more like an energy drink than a painting."

Josh poured wine, and indicated for her to sit on one of the two stools at the kitchen island. He'd already set the table in the dining room, so she knew they'd be eating; but she noticed that nothing was cooking.

"Hope you like steak." He opened the refrigerator and pulled out a large bundle wrapped in brown butcher paper. From a lower shelf, he lifted a bowl of colorful greens and fresh vegetables. He found a bag of sliced brown mushrooms in a drawer, and set it all on the counter. "It won't be fancy, but I promise you won't go hungry."

"Looks wonderful to me."

When the steaks were ready, Josh cut thick slices of the traditional Fisherman's Wharf sourdough bread. "More wine?"

"A little. I don't want to fall asleep before I finish this lovely meal."

"I got a report just before I left the office. We've made our numbers for the ball. It looks like it's a go." He raised his glass to her. "Congratulations."

"Really? Josh, that's fantastic." She waited for him to say he was pleased, too. Then she remembered: if she got what she wanted, he didn't.

They ate in silence, until Josh got up and turned on the sound system. Big band music blasted so loud that Kristi jumped.

"Sorry." He turned it down.

"Your dad won't stay there forever, Josh. He knows you want to take the reins. I'm sure he'll retire soon."

"I wish I shared your confidence. With Wilhelm gone, he's enjoying the extra responsibility way too much. I had no choice. I had to ask him to step in. But, I knew when I did it I was creating a problem."

Kristi's appetite shrank; she wasn't sure if it was the size of the steak or the depth of Josh's despair. His unhappiness was painful; the joy she'd felt about the ball was evaporating. She wanted to call Laura and Nicole, and share the news, but, that was impossible in front of Josh.

"Full already?" he asked.

She nodded.

"That's no good. We've got dessert."

"I couldn't possibly."

"Maybe later. I got a movie for us to watch. You know, in case my scintillating conversational skills were too much for you."

She started to protest, then decided against it. She was there; she may as well enjoy herself. She might not get this chance again soon—or ever, for that matter.

"What movie?"

"I got *Les Miserables*. I know it's dark, and you said you

don't like dark musicals; but, everyone I talked to said it's outstanding."

He remembered what she liked, even if he picked what she didn't.

"I've heard it was good, too."

She started to clear the dishes, but he pushed her into the living room. "Relax. This is your night off."

He soon joined her, and was setting up the movie. "I've got popcorn, if you want."

"Are you kidding? I'm stuffed."

He sat down next to her on the couch just as the opening scene began. "Hugh Jackman looks like a scarecrow," he said when the actor appeared.

"Who knew Russell Crowe could really sing?"

"He has a band, doesn't he?"

"Hardly a prerequisite."

When the priest handed Jean Valjcan the silver candlesticks, tears puddled in Kristi's eyes. She wiped them away with a quick swipe.

Josh patted her arm, and handed her a box of tissue. "I wondered if you might need these."

"Thanks. You couldn't have rented *La La Land* or *Beauty and the Beast*?"

"This movie was groundbreaking. The vocal parts were all recorded live, something that's never been done before."

Kristi looked at the dark image on the screen. "That's because it was so depressing, the actors refused to do it more than once."

"Want me to turn it off?"

"No. I'm teasing you. Sort of."

But, the sad story seeped from the screen, across the room, and into Kristi's heart. When Fantine sang "I Dreamed a Dream," she wept. Josh put his arm around her shoulder and pulled her close.

"It's going to get better."

"Not for her."

She closed her eyes, trying to keep the sordid saga at bay. It crept in despite her efforts, and laid a heavy hand on her heart.

Halfway through the movie, Josh switched it off. He turned on the radio, and found show tunes.

"You didn't have to do that."

"I think you're right. Musicals shouldn't be so dreary. Let's cheer up. Let's have dessert."

She noticed the pungent aroma of coffee and followed him into the kitchen, where he served cheesecake and coffee.

Kristi took her first bite and moaned.

"Is it orgasmic?"

"Not quite; but close."

"I'll have to keep working on it."

If only.

"I suppose I should get you home," he said when they'd finished eating. "It's past ten, and you're supposed to be catching up on your rest."

"Tonight was restful. Being waited on is very restful."

"Sorry about the movie. I should have listened to you."

"Maybe I should choose the next one."

"Good idea. Just one caveat."

"What's that?"

"I don't like dark musicals."

When they reached her house, he walked her up the stairs to her apartment. She unlocked the door, and switched off the glaring hall light. A glow from the small living room lamp cast warm, gentle shadows on them.

Josh put his arms around her. "Sorry again about the movie."

"Don't worry. I'll get my revenge."

"I'm going to have to watch *Annie*?"

"Twice."

"And when will this revenge take place?"

"I've heard it's most effective to punish someone as soon as possible after the offense is committed."

He glanced toward the living room. "You have *Annie*?"

"No. But I have streaming."

"Okay. But, don't blame me if I fall asleep."

"That's not happening. You have to sing along."

"The sun'll come out, tomorrow," he sang in a smooth, rich bass.

"Nice."

"Glad you liked it." He leaned down and kissed her. He pulled back, looking at her with curiosity.

"I liked that, too."

He kissed her again, his hands slipping slowly up her back, and then, gently, into her hair. His lips were sweet with the taste of cheesecake.

Pleasure swept over and through her; pleasure so complete it stole her breath. He leaned close to her ear and whispered, "There's nobody else in your life, is there? Someone you haven't mentioned?"

"No."

"Good."

By the time he left, The Line was a misty memory.

The new challenge was navigating a relationship with her boss. She fell asleep suspended somewhere between delight and dilemma.

*

Her phone rang moments after she sat down at her desk the next morning. On the other end of the line was a frustrated band leader.

"I thought we'd agreed on the initial payment no later than September first. I can't hold on to this date any longer."

"What?"

"I've waited long enough. You should have at called me

if the event was cancelled."

"What are you talking about? The event has not been cancelled. We made our minimum last week."

"If you want us to play for your ball, I need a check today."

"Give me a chance to find out what happened, at least," she pleaded. "You've played here before. You know we're good for it."

"I thought you were. This has made me wonder."

"I'll call you back after I speak to Accounting."

"Fine. But, no more stalling."

"I'm not stalling. There's been a mix-up. Let me find out why. I'll call you within the hour."

She punched in the number for the accounting department, and asked to speak to the payables manager. "What happened with the check request for the musicians we hired for the Bridal Ball? It was submitted weeks ago."

"Let me look," she said. "Hang on." She came back on the line moments later. "It looks like Josh put a hold on it."

The words were a sharp slap in the face. She thought a moment and then said, "Can you pay it on my authority? They're insisting on a check today."

The clerk hesitated. "I'd prefer to hear it from Josh. I don't want to get into trouble."

"I understand. I'll get back to you."

Josh put a hold on it? Why? So the ball would be a failure? So his father would leave?

The thought pierced like a poison dart.

"Good morning."

She looked up to JT standing at her office door. "Good morning, sir."

"You look rested."

"I feel rested, thank you." She made a snap decision, the kind Heather always cautioned her against. "There's been a hold-up on the check for the band. Could you do me a favor and ask Accounting to cut it right away? The leader says if we don't pay him today, he'll cancel."

"Of course." He pulled out his phone. "I wonder what happened."

"I have no idea. Whatever it was, I'll need to hand deliver it, so there's no more question. I don't want to take a chance of losing them; the music is more important than anything."

JT made the arrangements for the check, and told the clerk Kristi would pick it up at ten o'clock. "Would you like me to speak to the fellow?"

"No. I told him I'd call him back."

"Fine. You take care of it. And, congratulations on the ball. We've got our minimum." He gave her a mysterious smile. "No one will be more pleased than my mother." He hesitated a moment and then said, "Can I tell you a secret?"

What was he going to say that she'd regret hearing? "If you'd like."

"My mother and I are going to the ball. She's having her wedding gown altered; it was a bit too snug."

She felt happy for the first time that morning. "Really?"

"Yes. She's as excited as a schoolgirl before her first prom. We haven't registered yet. She wants to surprise Josh."

"I'm sure he'll be pleased." She smiled, barely registering the conversation. Her mind was stuck on Josh's duplicity. Last night's pleasure was gone. In its place sat a lump of cold betrayal.

"Kristi?" JT said.

"I'm sorry, what?"

"I asked if you needed anything else."

"No. Thanks for getting the check straightened out."

Before she left with the check, she called JT. "Nicole has some free time, and wanted to go over the updates on the Bridal Ball site. I'll be at her place. I can work remotely."

"No problem."

"Thank you, sir. I'll see you tomorrow."

"Do you want me to tell Josh?"

She knew it would make him angry. "Yes."

"See you tomorrow, then."

She dropped off the check, apologized again to the band leader, and then went to Nicole's. She decided not to tell her anything about her evening with Josh, or the check fiasco. There would be time enough for that after Kristi decided what to do.

"There was a wonderful story posted this morning," Nicole told her. "Have you read it?"

"I haven't been on today."

Nicole pulled it up. "Look."

Kristi sat in a chair beside the desk. "Read it to me." She had no energy for it, but Nicole was obviously excited.

"I am writing on behalf of my five brothers and sisters, and for all of us I would like to say thank you. Our parents were married fifty years ago—three weeks before our father was sent to Vietnam. It was a small gathering at a wedding chapel in Las Vegas. The only photograph taken on the occasion shows my parents, dressed in casual clothes, looking ecstatic. Although they've been very happy and have raised six successful children, I know my mother feels she missed out not having a real wedding.

"Thanks to you, my parents will have a second chance to celebrate. For their fiftieth anniversary, my siblings and I are giving them tickets to the Bridal Ball. The girls will take Mom shopping for a wedding gown; the boys will take Dad to get a tux. If it's possible, we'd all like to join them for brunch on Sunday morning.

"We offered them the option of renewing their vows, but they both declined. Dad said, 'We don't need to do it again; it took the first time.'

"We are all so excited, and wanted you to know how much we appreciate you creating this wonderful event."

Nicole looked over at Kristi. "Is that beautiful or what?"

"It's beautiful. I never considered older couples wanting to come."

"From what I've seen, it's appealing to all ages. Women aren't giving their ages, but they are saying how long they've been married. Unless they got hitched when they were ten, some of them are in their sixties."

"And they can still fit into their wedding dresses?"

"The ones who can't are having them altered. A few are buying new ones."

"A new one? The ball is supposed to give them a chance to wear the original one again."

"Maybe that dress wasn't special enough; maybe there was a divorce; maybe they couldn't afford a beautiful dress the first time around. We don't want to discriminate against a new dress, do we?"

"Of course not. JT told me that he's taking his mother to the ball. Josh doesn't know; she wants to surprise him."

"Is the hunk showing any more enthusiasm these days?"

"He was happy we met our minimum already," she lied. He was not happy about it at all.

"It's about time," Nicole said.

"Yes, it is."

"I've got the update finished, if you want to take a look at it."

"Sure, pull it up."

The two friends worked on the site for two hours, carefully wording the news, and encouraging couples still on the fence to solidify their plans to attend the ball.

"It's a fine line," Nicole said. "We can't say we're almost sold out. Still, it'd be helpful to have a final count sooner rather than later."

"Five percent won't commit until the last minute."

"If we know that, we can plan for it, right?"

"Right."

"Have you figured out what to put in the goody bags?"

"I've thought about it, but I haven't talked to any of our vendors yet. Now that I know it's on for sure, I can make inquiries about donations."

"And, don't forget the raffle for a night at the Princess. Did you talk to Josh about that?"

"Not yet."

"Let's get on it, Miss Creator of the Ball. Are you losing interest?"

"No, of course not. Have you talked to Laura?" she asked, changing the subject.

"I called her last night when I realized we'd hit our mark."

"I'll bet she was ecstatic."

"Nearly busted my eardrum."

Nicole's phone rang, and she checked the screen. "It's a client. I have to take it."

"I'm gone," Kristi said. "See you soon."

Kristi drove home, her mind once again fixed on Josh's effort to undermine the ball. *How will I face him? What am I going to say?*

She didn't realize until she'd parked and climbed out of her car that Josh's car was sitting across the street.

He walked over, took off his dark glasses, and glared down at her. "What the hell is going on?"

CHAPTER 24

He was mad? *He* was mad? Kristi was Orville Redenbacher in a microwave.

She wrapped her words in anger and slung them at him. "You screwed me."

Shock shrouded his blue eyes. "Screwed you?"

Kristi didn't want the entire neighborhood to witness their argument. "Let's go inside," she said, and led him up to her apartment.

She tossed her purse, her jacket, and her laptop on the dining room table, and turned to face him. "The band leader called me this morning. He still hadn't received the deposit that was due last month. I called Accounting. They told me you'd put a hold on it."

"Why didn't you come to me?"

"I wanted a check, not a fight."

"So you went to my father."

He sounded like she'd gone to the devil. "He came by my office, and I asked him to help."

"Because he's more dependable that I am?"

"No."

"Because he's unable to say no to you?"

"No."

"Because he's the one in charge?"

"No!"

"Then why go to him? If I did it, why not ask me to fix it?"

"I asked him because—because he wants the ball to succeed." Her voice had reached a shrill peak. She dialed down the volume. "You don't."

"You actually think I stopped the check so we'd lose the band?"

"Yes."

"Purposely? Even though I know how important the music is to you?"

"Yes."

"So the ball will fail, and my father will retire."

She nodded, pushing tears every which way except down her cheeks.

He stepped back, recoiling from her. "I'm not that desperate, Kristi."

"Then why did you do it?"

"I didn't."

"Accounting said you did."

"You didn't stick around long enough to discover the truth. You ran, like women do." His voice was hurt and harsh, scarred by an old wound.

"Then tell me. What happened?"

His blue eyes were flat, lifeless, silent. The sparkle that normally lived there, had vacated. Instead, she saw a deep pain, a pain that grabbed her breath and wrung it from her lungs. "Why couldn't you have come to my office and asked me that eight hours ago? Why did it have to take an entire day to sort this out?"

"It isn't sorted out."

"I signed the check requests, and gave them to Wilhelm to process. We talked about the cost of the band, and I told him I was concerned how that one item could ruin the event. I was convinced we should use a DJ."

"Wilhelm?"

"Yes. After you refused to answer my calls, I spoke to Dad. He told me about the check. I went to Accounting, and found out that when Wilhelm turned in the requests, he told them I said to hold the band deposit."

"Wilhelm." Anger and relief collided like bumper cars in her head.

"If only you'd come to me—trusted me—all this could have been avoided."

She closed her eyes. Being wrong never felt good. Being a fool felt worse.

"I can handle almost anything, but I can't handle you running away."

"I was hurt, Josh. I couldn't have faced you. Not then. I thought you'd done it on purpose and I had to figure out how to deal with that betrayal."

"I'm committed to the Bridal Ball, Kristi. I don't have the emotional connection that you have, but I want it to succeed. I still think it's too soon, and I still think a DJ would work. But, undermining a great idea is stupid."

"A great idea? You've never said that before."

"I haven't? Well, I should have." The life that had left his eyes was back. "Georgia thinks it's brilliant. I'm not willing to go that far."

"I love Georgia. She's been all-in since the minute I told her."

"And I'm all-in now."

"I'm sorry. About earlier, I mean."

"I've been in a lot of relationships, mostly unsuccessful. One thing seems clear—running away never solves a problem. Talking is the only thing that works."

"If I had gone to talk to you, I might have killed you."

He put his arms around her—arms that meant more than words. "I faced down a bear. Do you really think you could scare me?"

"I'm a pretty bad mama."

"I'll take your word." He pulled her close and kissed her; soft, slow, and sweet. The taste lingered on her lips like honey.

Kristi felt the sweet contentment of the previous night invade her heart again.

"This is nice. I'd like to stay. Do you have anything we can fix for supper?"

"I'm sure I can find something."

"I'll help."

She glanced into the darkening night, and noticed his car. "How long were you waiting for me?"

He held her close, his breath a slow, easy rhythm. "My whole life."

*

She made a simple dinner: linguini con vongole (with packaged noodles and canned clams), grilled tomato on a bed of romaine (with a tired beefsteak and a piece of wilted lettuce revived in a cold water bath), and toasted garlic bread (using a sourdough roll she had in the freezer). Heather had coached her on how to make gourmet something out of practically nothing.

He sat, drinking wine, watching her move around her kitchen. "Do you like to cook?"

"I do. I love trying new recipes. That's why I'm always curious when Tony puts something different on the menu."

Outside, the night had turned cold. Inside, Kristi started a fire, lit candles on the table, and finished dishing up.

Josh took his first bite of pasta. "This is delicious." He looked up at her with a you-know-I'm-never-going-to-forget grin. "Maybe not the best by your unique rating system, but I think it's great. The next time Tony is out sick, you can take over in the kitchen."

"I have several signature dishes."

"I want to try them all."

"That can be arranged." She sipped her wine. "You never told me how long you were outside."

"A couple of hours. I had my laptop. I sat there and worked, and waited for you to show up."

"You knew I wasn't going back to the hotel?"

"Dad told me."

"So, you left work in the middle of the day. How did you explain that?"

"I told him I was going to go sort things out with my girlfriend."

"Uh…" She began, and tried again. "What did he say?"

"He said to make sure you're back to work tomorrow. Things don't feel right around there when you're gone."

"I'd like to keep this to ourselves. For the time being, I'd prefer to keep things professional at work."

"No trysts in your office?"

"No."

"Furtive kisses in the stairwell?"

"No."

"Stopping the elevator between floors for a little…"

"Cut it out."

His laughter brightened the room. "Don't worry, I won't fire you if you turn down my advances."

"I'm serious. Workplace romances are packed with problems. There's always someone who notices, someone who's resentful, or jealous, or spiteful. Let's keep it between us."

"You know people are going to find out."

"Eventually. But not right away, please."

"Whatever you want."

Kristi could tell he disagreed. But she'd seen office romances crash and burn, and the results affected not only the couple, but everyone around them. Employees spent weeks navigating the charred remains of a love affair gone bad, trying not to say something that would set off one party or the other, or send someone into a crying jag.

"I don't have to call you Ms. Peyton-Scott, do I?"

"No. You can stick with Ma'am."

*

The next two weeks flew by, and still no Wilhelm. Reservations for the ball continued at a steady pace; comments on the website were now from excited women, promising to meet at the hotel.

JT agreed with Kristi that her relationship with Josh be kept private, so things changed little at work. But evenings, when they weren't working, they spent together at one home or the other, learning about important matters like their favorite authors, shows, and restaurants.

"I love all the discoveries," Kristi said one night. She was snuggled under his arm like a chick under its mom's wing. "I love finding out if you've read my favorite book, or seen my favorite movie, or like my favorite dish."

They were sitting on his couch, having just finished Chinese take-out from his favorite restaurant down the block.

"There are quizzes online that can tell us if we're compatible," he said, "if that's what you want."

"That's cheating. Besides, if I read your favorite book, maybe I'll like it better than mine. Maybe your favorite movie is extraordinary, or your favorite dish is…"

"Orgasmic?"

"Yes. I love learning things about you that I wouldn't have suspected. I have so much energy when we're together that I swear I could stay up talking all night."

"It's adrenaline."

She kissed him. "It's more than that."

"You could stay over."
"I don't think so."
"Why not?"
"I can't stand the way you roll the toothpaste."

*

Kristi suspected more than one person at work had figured it out. Queenie knew; Kristi was sure. The woman had known Josh for years. She was observant and perceptive, and often gave Kristi a conspiratorial smile. Tony knew. They were always asking him to make dinners for two.

Josh had told his grandmother. When she came by Kristi's office to see the new painting, she told Kristi how pleased she was that he finally had a nice girlfriend.

JT knew, and although he'd never said a word to her about it, Kristi knew he was pleased. His subtle suggestions, such as "You two go ahead and leave early," were often not so subtle.

Of course, Wilhelm didn't know.

Kristi worried about what would happen when he returned.

*

Nicole called Kristi the following weekend. "GNO is on Halloween. We're meeting at Laura's."

Kristi was ready for bed, and had already turned off the heat. She pulled an afghan around her shoulders. "Okay. Is Sam back?"

"Yes. She's coming dressed as the Queen of Sheba."

"We have to dress?"

"We dress every year. What's wrong with you?"

"Nothing. I'm tired is all."

"If you'd sleep with that man instead of talking all night, you wouldn't be so tired."

"Not happening. Not yet, anyway."

"You know, Kristi, every fruit has the perfect time for plucking."

"Are you referring to me, or to him?"

"I'm not sure."

"I'll see you at Laura's on Wednesday. Six o'clock, right?"

"Right."

It rained all night on the thirtieth. On Halloween morning, water cascaded down the windshield of Kristi's car, and blurred her view. She gave silent thanks that she could park under the hotel, and wasn't forced to walk blocks in the downpour.

"Wouldn't you know?" she said to Debby as they were both getting coffee. "We're in a drought for years, and we get our first decent storm on Halloween."

"If it doesn't let up, there will be a whole lot of disappointed kids in the city," Debby said.

"And a whole bunch of parents with three thousand bars of the same candy."

Josh was waiting in her office. He greeted her with a quick kiss. "I just spoke to the chairman of the California Democratic Party. They're planning a huge fundraiser next year, and they want to hold it here."

"Really?"

"Ten thousand dollars a plate."

"Oh my gosh, that's fantastic, Josh. When?"

"February second."

Her head snapped around as if jerked by a chain. "And…"

"And I told him we'd love to do it for them…"

Her heart took a single, painful beat.

"…any night but that one."

Tension drained out of her as quickly as it had appeared.

"Did you think, even for a second, that I'd cancel your ball?"

"Everything has a price."

"That's pretty cynical."

"Sorry. I still have trouble believing it's really going to happen. I keep waiting for some invisible shoe to drop."

"Have faith. Nothing is going to go wrong."

CHAPTER 25

"Trick or treat!" Kristi cried when Laura opened her front door.

Laura laughed, tugging at the sleeve of Kristi's raincoat. "You look just like Paddington Bear."

Kristi shook each of her bright red boots before stepping onto Laura's pristine hardwood floors. "These are so tight, I've got to take them off."

"No, wait! I want a picture first."

Sam swirled into the room swathed in layers of turquoise organza and jangling bracelets.

"Can you eat with that veil over your face?" Kristi asked.

Sam pulled the veil aside, smiling angelically. "I could eat with a bucket over my face."

"Stand right there," Laura instructed. "Nicole! Get out here."

Nicole, dressed in a pink poodle skirt, saddle oxfords, and bobby sox, joined them, licking her fingers.

"Stand in the middle," Laura said.

"What about one of all of us?" Sam asked.

"Ethan," Laura called. "Come help."

THE BRIDAL BALL

"We could do a selfie," Nicole said.

"Those always look so awkward," Laura said. "Let Ethan take it."

Ethan came in holding Chloe, who was dressed in a green pea costume, complete with dangling tendrils. He handed her to Laura and took the camera.

Kristi reached out to the baby. "Hello, sweet pea." The child lunged toward Kristi, nearly knocking her over.

"Smile," Ethan said.

"Wait till we're ready, for heaven's sake," Laura said, trying to arrange the group.

Chloe pulled on Kristi's hat, which dripped water down the little one's outfit.

"You'd better take it fast," Nicole said.

"Smile," Ethan said again. He took the picture and Chloe began to cry.

"She's hungry." Laura took the fussy baby from Kristi.

"Who can blame her?" Nicole said. "Let's eat."

*

The four friends sat in the living room, drinking wine and talking, long after Chloe had gone to bed.

"It sounds like the Bridal Ball is going to be a big hit," Sam said.

"I sure hope so," Kristi said.

"Ten years from now it will be considered one of the highlights of the San Francisco social season," Nicole said. "Too bad you won't be in town, Sam."

"I don't have a wedding dress anyway," Sam said.

Nicole shrugged. "Neither does Kristi."

"Soon? Maybe?" Laura asked.

Kristi made a face at her.

"What *are* you going to wear that night?"

"A navy blue business suit."

"You're not!" Laura cried. "You have to wear a gown."

"I'll be working."

"That's not fair. I want you and Josh to dance, too."

"I'll take my bridesmaid's dress. If I get a chance, I'll change after dinner."

"Is your baker friend really going to make wedding cakes for dessert?" Sam asked.

"Just one wedding cake, which we'll display in the ballroom. The rest will be sheet cakes," Kristi told her.

"Oh," Laura said, "there's a story that was posted early this morning that really tore me up."

"The woman who's been sick?" Nicole asked.

"Yes." She looked from Kristi to Sam. "Did you guys see it?"

Neither one had.

"I have to read it to you." She went in the other room, and came back a bit later with a single sheet of paper.

"Get out the tissue," Nicole said.

"Hush," Laura told her. She sat down on the couch, swallowed hard and began to read. *"Dear Friends: I've been reading the stories here for three months, and now I'm finally ready to share mine. Last year, I was diagnosed with breast cancer. I had surgery, which was considered successful, and then a course of chemotherapy. I was very sick throughout the six-month treatment, and was devastated, last spring, when my oncologist recommended a second round. I resisted, but he convinced me it was crucial.*

"Treatment began in April, and although I couldn't imagine it was possible, I was even sicker than I was the first time. By the middle of the summer, I was so depressed that I didn't care whether I lived or not.

"One day, when I was so weak I couldn't get out of bed, my husband sat down next to me holding his tablet. 'I found something I want us to do together,' he told me, and he put the tablet on the pillow. I barely had the strength to turn my head, but when I did, I saw the Bridal Ball homepage.

"His request was unimaginable. I couldn't even stand, much less dance.

"'When?' I didn't have the energy to say much else.

"They haven't set a date yet. But whenever it is, we're going to be there.'

"He propped me up enough to page through the site, which was more beautiful to me than anything I'd seen in months. The idea of dancing again in my wedding dress gave me hope when little else could.

"After that, I took his tablet with me to every treatment. He uploaded a picture of me in my wedding dress as the wallpaper, and our wedding video for me to watch during my treatment. Every session, I'd watch that video, and dream of being well and strong and dancing with him again.

"I've visited your site every day since my husband first showed it to me. You could say that the Bridal Ball pulled me through the most difficult days of my life.

"My chemo is finished; there is no sign of cancer; and best of all, we have registered for the ball. I tried on my gown last week; I looked like a ten-year-old playing dress-up. I'm trying to gain weight, but will probably have it altered for the ball.

"I wanted to thank you for helping me; for giving me hope and strength when I needed it most; for creating an event that has reached so many women's hearts. I hope I'll have the opportunity to thank you in person."

"That's quite a testimony." Sam looked from one woman to another. "You guys have created something bigger than you realized."

Kristi was stunned. "I never imagined that the ball would actually *help* women."

Laura reached over and squeezed her hand.

"You need to have something ready to say the night of the ball," Nicole said.

"You mean a speech?"

"It doesn't have to be long. Just a few words about why you created the ball, and how touched we've been reading the stories. Besides, people will undoubtedly want to thank you."

"I hate giving speeches. The story is on the website."

"You need to do it, Kristi. And, you have to introduce Laura. The women will want to see the bride who started it all."

"In that case," Kristi said to Nicole, "they'll want to know who's behind the beautiful website. We'll do it together. The Three Musketeers."

"I'll be out of town," Sam said. "Another perk of my job."

"Where will you be?" Laura asked.

"Anywhere other than in front of a room full of strangers."

*

When Kristi got into bed that night, she called Josh to say good night.

"How was GNO?"

"Lovely. Chloe was adorable. The girls had some ideas about the ball. I'll tell you tomorrow."

"I have some news too."

She didn't like the way he sounded. "What?"

"Wilhelm called late today. He's asked for a three-month leave of absence."

Kristi did the math; he'd be back at the end of January, just in time for the ball. "Is his mother worse?"

"No. But, the doctor said it'll be two months before she can be alone. Wilhelm needs to take care of her until then."

He was the last person Kristi would want taking care of her. "Are you worried about handling the holidays without him?"

"We've done fine this far; I'm sure we'll manage."

"I have to confess, I don't miss him in the least."

"I know."

She waited for him to agree, but he didn't. "Do you?"

"Yes. I prefer doing my own job, instead of his on top of mine."

"Sorry."

"You know who else I miss?"

"Who?"

"You. This place feels empty when you're not here."

"I know how to fix that." Her voice vibrated, low and sultry.

"How?"

"Quit rolling the toothpaste wrong."

She fell asleep, the sound of his laughter singing in her ears.

*

The rain pounded even heavier the next morning. Kristi fought her way across town, dodging drivers who seemed particularly crazy that day.

Josh pulled into the parking space next to her just as Kristi got out of her car. "Good morning." He kissed her lightly. "How are you?"

"Better now. I swear, everybody on the streets this morning has forgotten how to drive in the rain."

"Some of them weren't old enough to drive the last time it rained."

He opened the door to the stairwell, and followed her in. He kissed her again, without the risk of prying eyes. "Let's have soup tonight. With sourdough bread, in front of the fire, while we listen to the rain."

"Sounds like a perfect evening."

*

It rained every day between Halloween and Big Game Day. The break in the weather was hailed by football fans as a good omen for the Cal Bears. Kristi and Josh met Georgia and Wyatt, and the rest of their group, to tailgate before the game.

Kristi and Georgia sat huddled next to each other, trying to keep warm.

"Did you get a gown for the ball?" Georgia rubbed her hands together then stuck them under her jacket.

"No. I'll be working."

"You can change after dinner. There's no reason you can't join us once the cake is served."

"It's not the same; I don't have a wedding gown. I suppose I could use my bridesmaid's dress."

"Bridesmaid's dresses are designed especially so that the bride looks beautiful by comparison. Forget the bridesmaid's dress. You need a new gown. Oh, and I messaged the hotel to reserve places for you at our table."

"I don't know, Georgia. It's a big event. I want to be sure it runs perfectly."

"You know I'm going to get my way, Kristi, so don't even bother to argue."

Josh brought Kristi a steaming cup of coffee.

"Are you wearing a tux to the ball?" Georgia asked him.

He looked at Kristi. "I don't know, am I?"

"She's wearing a long dress. You need a tux."

"You already bought a dress?" he asked.

"Not yet," Georgia said. "I'm taking her shopping."

"Get something black," Josh said.

"In that ocean of white?" Kristi asked. "I don't think so."

"Not to worry," Georgia told him. "We'll find something you'll like."

Once they were seated in the stands, Kristi was grateful for the crowd. She was squished between Josh and Georgia and was warm for the first time that day.

Ten minutes before the end of the game, Wyatt said, "Stanford doesn't have a chance of catching us, and I don't want to sit in traffic half the night. We're going to take off."

"I'll call you," Georgia told Kristi. "There's a shopping trip in our future."

"Okay," Kristi said. Objections were pointless.

Cal won, 46 to 17. Kristi's throat felt like it had been scraped with a serrated knife. She looked in her purse for a lozenge, but found only one renegade Rolaid. She popped it in her mouth, hoping for the best.

They left the stands for the field, where spectators, players, and band members milled like ants at a picnic.

"Zeb!" Josh yelled to the band director.

The man waved. "Wait a sec." After talking to several uniformed musicians, Zeb joined them.

Josh introduced Kristi.

"Nice to meet you," Zeb said. "You've got a good man here. I hope you're taking care of him."

"I'm doing my best."

"The band sounds fabulous," Josh said.

"They're amazing. They can sight-read *anything*."

"Unlike my rag-tag group."

"I've had better bands, but never a better student." He grasped Josh's arm. "I wish I could have a dozen more like you."

"You only say that because I'm gone."

"You might be right."

"This wasn't the best Big Game I've ever been to," Josh said. "I like it when it's close through all four quarters, and then the Bears pull it out right at the end."

"Those games are hard on the medics."

"More injuries?"

"No. More heart attacks in the stands."

Two band members approached. "Hey, Doc, do you want us to hang around?" one asked.

"No. Go ahead. I'll meet you at the restaurant." He turned to Josh. "A little post mortem on the half-time performance. Care to join us?"

"Thanks, but I think we'll head back across the Bay. We're still on for the game next Sunday?"

"Wouldn't miss it," Zeb said. "Nice meeting you, Kristi. I hope next time we'll get a chance to talk."

"That would be wonderful. Josh says you were a huge influence in his life. I'd like to hear more about that."

"Join us next Sunday."

"Uh…" Josh began.

"Sorry, Kristi," Zeb said. "I almost forgot; these get-togethers are for guys only."

"BNO," Kristi said, her brief disappointment quelled. She smiled at Josh. "Boys night out. It's only fair."

As they walked out of the stadium, Josh said, "How about a little stroll down memory lane? I'll show you all my old haunts."

"And introduce me to all your skeletons?" His laughter thrilled her, as it always did. She cuddled closer.

"Where have you been all my life?" he whispered in her ear.

"Getting ready."

CHAPTER 26

Kristi and Laura walked around huge, grungy puddles the best they could, as they made their way to the theater to see *The Nutcracker*.

"Oh, dang." Kristi extracted her left foot from ankle deep water. "These boots are going to be ruined."

"No complaints." Laura pulled her toward the curb. "You said you wanted rain."

"Not every day for six weeks. Enough is enough."

They hurried into the building, and collapsed their umbrellas.

"Oh, look!" Laura said, pointing to two little girls in tutus. "What fun—going to the ballet in costume."

"They must be freezing."

"They're so excited they don't even know it's cold."

They were ushered to their seats, settled themselves, stowed their umbrellas under their seats, and opened their playbills.

"Thanks again for lunch," Laura said.

"You know they don't charge me anything at the hotel. You don't owe me any thanks."

"Tell Josh, then. And, tell him for me that the dining room looks spectacular. That Christmas tree right in the middle is wonderful. It's so big. How long does it take to decorate?"

"Hours and hours. They do it in the middle of the night."

"Too bad it won't be there for the ball."

"We're going to use twinkle lights wrapped in white tulle for the backdrop. I think it will be lovely."

"Have you figured out the program yet?"

"Pretty much. We'll feature our sponsors, of course. We decided against printing any of the brides' stories. People can read them online. We'll have a prize for the longest-married couple. We'll give info about the band, the singer, the door prizes, and the raffle for next year's ball."

"What about introducing the women?"

"JT is calling it the Parade of Brides. We'll call up one table at a time, so we don't have the entire crowd lined up around the room. Nicole says it will be ideal for the women who have met each other on the site. They can hardly say, 'I'll be the one in the bridal gown.' Nametags were not even a consideration."

"Have you decided on your dress?"

"I've narrowed it down to two. Georgia thinks I should get the black one, but I think that's too much, with most women in white. I don't want to stand out that much."

"You think aqua blue would be better?"

"I do."

"I vote for the black," Laura said.

"You've never even seen it."

"You'd be the black swan."

"You've got ballet fever."

*

"Got time for coffee?"

THE BRIDAL BALL

Kristi looked up from her desk.

Georgia stood in her doorway, dressed in a beautiful cranberry wool suit. "I don't have to meet my client until nine."

"Sure. You look gorgeous. Why so early?"

"I thought the traffic would be worse, considering all the rain. People must be using mass transit."

They walked to the dining room, and sat at a table near the Christmas tree.

"What are you doing for Christmas?" Georgia asked.

"Everybody will be at Mom's on Christmas Eve. My brothers and their families were going to drive down from Seattle, but the weather has been so awful, they've reconsidered. I told Mom she should fly up there, but I don't think she wants to leave me alone."

"You'd hardly be alone. So then, who is everybody?"

"Josh, JT, and Josh's grandmother, Laura, her husband, and Chloe. Laura has celebrated Christmas Eve with us for years."

"That's lovely. I want to establish traditions like that, too." Georgia stirred cream into her coffee. "What are you giving Josh for Christmas, if you don't mind me asking?"

"I can't decide. He has plenty of clothes, never wears jewelry, has a watch he loves, and doesn't ever mention anything that he wants."

"Get him a day at a spa."

"A what?"

"A spa day: massage, manicure, pedicure, facial."

"He's a pretty manly kinda guy. I don't see him sitting in a pedicure chair."

Georgia smiled, her eyes bright with mischief. "Exactly. It's way out of his comfort zone: someone else in complete charge. It'd be good for him."

"It's supposed to be a gift, not a gauntlet."

"I think he'd like it. Once he got over the shock." She laughed. "Poor Josh. I've been tormenting him ever since Cal."

"He doesn't act like he's suffering."

"Josh prefers to suffer in silence."

"What do you mean?"

"He doesn't talk about what bothers him. If he ever tells you about his mom, you'll know more than any of us. Even Wyatt isn't sure what happened."

"Wow."

"Well, I like the spa idea. There are a plethora of them in the city. What about New Year's? Surely he's dreamed up something special."

"I have no idea what he's got planned. He said he wanted to surprise me. I figured you and Wyatt would be involved."

"We're not. Wyatt insisted that we go up to Heavenly Valley to ski. I think it's going to be a madhouse, but at least it doesn't involve boats." She pulled out her phone and checked the time. "I'd better run. If I don't see you before then, have a Merry Christmas, and a fabulous New Year."

"You, too," Kristi said, hugging her. "And drive carefully in that rain."

Kristi went shopping at Stonestown Galleria that night, walking through store after store, trying to find a gift for Josh. Nothing seemed right. She had no idea what he might give her, but she wanted something special for him. By the end of the evening, she was completely discouraged.

Since Starbucks wasn't crowded, she decided to get a hot chocolate for the road. It hadn't been raining when she arrived, but judging by the many people carrying dripping umbrellas, it was now. She placed her order and stood to the side to wait.

"Kristi?"

She turned to a young woman at the table behind her. "Rebecca. How are you?"

"I'm okay," she said, pushing aside an empty mug.

"What's wrong?"

"Nothing. How are you?"

"I'm fine."

The barista called out, "Kristi."

"That's mine." She picked up the cup and returned to Rebecca's table. "Okay, now tell me what's wrong."

"It's the same thing it always is. Yancy and I had another argument about our wedding. It seems like that's all we do. I'm afraid Christmas is going to be ruined."

Kristi took a sip of the chocolate, and instantly regretted it. She put the cup down on the table and removed the lid. "Way too hot."

"Are you ready for Christmas?"

"I'm not. I can't figure out what to get my boyfriend."

"What does he like?"

"Everything."

"What does he need?"

"Nothing."

"Nice for him. Tough for you. Can you think of anything he's never done before? You know, an adventure of some kind?"

Kristi thought of Georgia's suggestion.

"Maybe he's never been sky diving."

"I don't think I'm prepared to watch him jump out of an airplane."

"There's always paragliding, or a ride in a glider."

"Have you done all those things?"

Rebecca laughed. "No. It's stuff Yancy wants to do."

"Outdoor things."

"Yes."

"And you really want to get married outdoors."

Tears filled the girl's bloodshot eyes.

"I know I shouldn't say this, but honestly, Rebecca, if I were you, I'd fight for the wedding I wanted."

"Yancy would be so happy if I tried again."

"Do it together. Go to your parents. Be kind and respectful. But, you can do that and also be honest. I believe you have the right to live your dream."

"Can I quote you?"

"I wish you wouldn't. This isn't exactly the hotel policy."

"I understand. I don't want you to get in trouble either."

"Thanks. Let me know how it turns out."

"I will. And good luck on your shopping."

She drove home, knowing she'd made a rash decision. But, she'd seen Rebecca miserable so many times, she simply had to say it: you only get married once; do it the way you want.

*

On Christmas Eve, JT carved the turkey Victoria had roasted, while Josh mashed potatoes, Kristi made gravy, and Rose poured wine.

"I've never had so much help in my kitchen in all my life," Victoria said.

"You've never had so many people in your kitchen in all your life," Kristi told her.

"And three of us are missing," Victoria said. "I'm disappointed that Chloe is so sick. Poor little pumpkin."

"Laura just didn't want to bring her out in the rain. She'll be fine when she realizes she gets to open all the gifts under their tree," Kristi said.

They lingered over dinner, sharing stories of Christmases past. Rose told them about her favorite grandchild with the skill of a standup comic. Kristi noticed that not one of the stories involved his mother.

At eleven o'clock, Rose tapped JT's arm, and said, "It's time for me to get my beauty rest, JT. I think the rain has let up, so let's scoot home before it starts again."

Kristi and Josh escorted them to the car, and watched them drive off.

"Can I come back in for a minute?" Josh asked.

"Of course. Do you want another glass of wine?"

"No. I'm not going to stay long. But, I wanted to give you your present."

They sat on the couch and Josh pulled a carefully wrapped box out of his pocket. "Don't panic. It's not a ring. Gran said to be sure to tell you that." He kissed her cheek. "I hope you like it."

She slowly unwrapped the small package. The leather-covered box inside looked old and tired, and Kristi's heart swelled with sweet surprise. An antique. When she opened the box, she found a beautiful gold, Art Nouveau pendant necklace.

Two intertwined hearts, the large one encircling the smaller, cradled an aquamarine gemstone. At the bottom of the large heart, a stylized gold tulip held a smaller stone.

She lifted it carefully from the box and looked more closely at the intricate work.

"It's a lavalier. It was made in Germany the same year the Princess was built. My grandmother helped me choose it. She said it would match your eyes."

She undid the clasp. "Would you help me?"

He took the necklace and fastened it around her neck.

She walked to the hall mirror; the woman looking back at her had tears in her eyes. "I love it, Josh. Thank you so much."

He slipped his arm around her waist. "I was hoping you'd wear it on New Year's Eve."

"I'd love to. Here's the thing—your gift isn't finished yet."

He cocked his head and sniffed. "Why? Is it still in the oven?"

"I'm not telling. You'll have to be patient."

"You know patience isn't my best quality."

"This will give you some practice."

"I practice patience every time we're together." He wrapped her in loving arms.

"It'll be worth the wait," she said, and fell into the familiar comfort of his embrace.

*

The rains continued, constant, relentless, day after day. Streets flowed like streams, streams flowed like rivers, rivers crested and flooded, creating cascades of mud. Getting around the city was difficult, whether by car or by foot.

Kristi heard the water drumming on the roof as she dressed on New Year's Eve. She stepped into a low-cut black gown with long sleeves, chosen to deflect the damp city air. She'd borrowed a full-length black cape from Nicole, and prayed her umbrella would be big enough to keep them both from ruination.

"You look stunning," Josh said when he arrived.

Her hand went to the lavalier. "It's perfect with this dress, don't you think?"

"I do."

They drove across town to a small French restaurant, and then to Davies Symphony Hall downtown. Huge banners hung in the windows of the hall, advertising the program: "A Night in Old Vienna". That was when she realized why he'd insisted on the long dress. They were going to dance.

To a full orchestra!

"Oh, Josh." She swallowed salty tears. "This is a perfect way to spend New Year's." Her chest heaved, making room for an invasion of joy.

Inside, Kristi delighted in the old world charm of women in long, romantic evening gowns. Several people stopped to compliment her on the cape, which had survived the storm brilliantly.

"Do we have to take our seats right away?" Kristi asked.

"Why?"

"I want to stand here and take it all in. I want to see every outfit. It's so rare to see people dressed formally."

"Someone will show up in jeans. Georgia guaranteed it."

"Georgia knew we were coming to the symphony?"

"Not until this morning. I didn't trust her."

The first half of the concert featured European masterworks, marches, and romantic ballads. The audience applauded appreciatively after each piece. During the intermission, the stage was reconfigured to accommodate a dance floor. Members of the audience were invited on stage, to dance to a selection of Strauss waltzes.

Josh twirled Kristi around, careful not to collide with any of the other couples.

After three dances, Kristi's face flamed. "I never would have worn long sleeves if I'd known we'd be dancing."

"Maybe I should have told you the plan."

She shook her head. "Surprises are romantic."

The orchestra paused momentarily, and then the strains of "The Blue Danube Waltz" floated into the air.

Josh's arms encircled her waist and they waltzed around the floor. Kristi felt delight explode with each step. "I hope all the brides at the ball will be as happy as I am tonight."

"How could they not be? I've read those stories. The Bridal Ball is going to send women over the moon."

*

She invited him in when they returned to her apartment.

"Light the fire," she said. "I'm going to open some champagne."

She brought glasses out to the living room, and joined him on the couch.

He raised his glass. "Here's to the Bridal Ball." He sealed the toast with a tender kiss.

"It was a wonderful surprise, Josh. Dancing to an orchestra, the symphony of all things. Nothing could compare. Thank you so much."

"My pleasure."

"I have a surprise for you too. Your Christmas gift is finally finished."

He sniffed. "Strange, I don't smell anything."

"I'm going to get it, but you have to close your eyes."

Moments later she said, "Ready?"

"I am."

"Open!"

She stood across the room, holding a painting of Sather Tower, the Campanile on the Berkeley campus. Fully lit in the early evening sunset, it dominated the left side of the painting, and dwarfed the glittering city and bay behind. Muted tones of pale blue, pink, lavender, orange, and crimson highlighted the tower. The light in the belfry shone brightly, beckoning a boy in his bedroom across the bay.

A smile flickered across Josh's face and then, unexpectedly, tears. He wiped them away with a swipe of his hand. "My God, Kristi, it's beautiful. Absolutely spectacular. Your mother's, of course."

"Of course."

"I'm a kid in my room, looking out, seeing that light. It's calling me." He paused and then added, "Until now, that was the happiest time of my life."

Tears softly streaked down her cheeks.

He took two long strides and gathered her into his arms. "I've never had a gift that meant more to me. It's…" But he couldn't finish.

She wiped his tears and kissed him.

"I love you, Kristi," he whispered.

With four small words, her heart, and her world, fell into place.

*

They stood together in his living room the next afternoon, the Rose Bowl game on the TV, and the painting propped on a chair.

"I want the perfect place for it," Josh said.

She looked around the bare walls, one room opening into another, with wide, arched doorways. "You have plenty of choices."

"I want to see it every day. I want to remember that time in my life, like you seeing your old house." He was quiet for a long while. Then, in a cracked, bleeding voice he said, "If I'd known she was going to leave, I would have appreciated her more—enjoyed her more—spent more time…" His words stopped as if the sentence had been hacked in half.

Kristi saw herself telling her father she didn't want to go to the market with him. The memory had haunted her for years. If only she'd known. "You were young. You couldn't have anticipated or changed what happened."

He turned and gazed out the window.

"Why did she leave?"

His answer stuck in his throat, and he coughed. "She met someone; someone who had more time for her, who took more time for her. My father was always working, even when he was at home, he was at work. I loved living at the hotel. My mother hated it. She begged him to move, but he wouldn't. Couldn't, maybe."

"Where is she now?"

"New York."

"Do you ever see her?"

"Occasionally. If I go there. She hates San Francisco; she says it's full of bad memories."

A silence spun of shared sadness hung suspended between them.

"Being with her there is strange. She's a different person now. I suppose I am too. It's awkward. I look forward to it, and then I'm always disappointed. I'm not sure what I expect, but whatever it is, it never happens. It would be easier if she had died."

"No, it wouldn't."

His face twisted. "Oh, God, of course it wouldn't. I'm so sorry, Kristi. What an asinine thing to say."

"It may be hard, but it isn't impossible. Maybe you could meet halfway, in Chicago or Dallas. You'd both be out of your element; you'd only have each other. Nothing familiar."

"I never thought…"

"Would she do that?"

"I don't know. But you're right, I could try."

"There's the difference. When they die, you don't get to try anymore."

"Does it ever stop hurting?"

"It gets better. But I never stop missing him. There's a sadness about every special occasion—the realization that I'm missing something most people take for granted. He and I will never share so many important events."

"Like a piece forever missing from a puzzle."

She leaned her head against his shoulder. "My mom is wonderful. She's done a great job—she's always there for me. But she can't replace him."

"Same for me. Dad tries …"

"But he can't fill her shoes."

He laughed, as she hoped he would. "No, she took them all with her. You don't leave a pair of Jimmy Choo's behind."

"She liked Jimmy Choo?" She remembered Georgia telling her that the designer was Inez's signature.

"It was all she wore. Money was never short—only time." He looked back at the painting. "Let's get this hung so we can enjoy it."

"Where?"

"Over the buffet in the dining room. We can see it from the entry, the hallway, the living room, and while we're eating. Prime real estate, as Georgia would say."

They sat together on the couch after they'd hung the painting, appreciating their decision.

"Your gift couldn't be any more perfect," Josh said. "For here, or for me." He cupped her face in his hands. "I love it. And, I love you." His tender voice brought tears to her eyes.

Her own voice was barely a whisper when she said, "I love you too, Josh."

He kissed the tears from her cheek.

If her heart were any fuller it would have burst. Joy pushed against her ribs and her breath came in a short gasp. "I love you more than I can say."

They sat holding each other, savoring the magical moment.

"It's scary to be so happy." Kristi said.

"If we keep it to ourselves, the gods might be angry."

"I read somewhere that sharing pain cuts it in half; sharing joy doubles it," Kristi told him.

"We should have a party."

"Yes. A dinner party."

"We'll ask your mom. We'll show her how perfect the painting is. Maybe we'll ask Dad, and Gran too."

"My mom would love that."

"Before or after the ball?"

"Let's do it before."

"Okay, then, what should we serve?" he asked, settling back, his arm around her shoulders.

Just like an old, married couple, Kristi thought.

*

Josh poured a glass of rosé for his grandmother, then sat down at the table next to Kristi.

"Did Tony help with the menu?" Rose asked. She took a bite of the salmon. "This sauce is as light and delicate as any I've ever tasted."

"I agree," Victoria said.

"Kristi and I did it, Gran," Josh said.

She tasted the sauce again. "Well," she said, drawing out the word as if it had two long syllables, "if you ever get tired of the hotel, you could open a restaurant."

"I'll never get tired of the hotel, Gran."

"That's a relief," JT said. "Mom, no more career counseling, please."

She smiled, her mischievous eyes twinkling at Josh. "Just trying to be helpful."

They sat in the living room later, drinking coffee and eating tiramisu.

"It's lovely that you can see your painting from so many places," Rose said. "Victoria, I like this one almost as much as mine."

"Thank you." Victoria beamed at the compliment.

"You can't have it, Gran," Josh told her. He leaned over and kissed her cheek. "But you can come by to see it anytime you want."

"Keep making meals like that one, and I'll be moving in."

Lightning flashed outside; in less than three seconds, thunder boomed, and the electricity blinked off and then on again.

"Are you about ready, Mom?" JT asked. "We should get going before Josh loses power." He looked at Victoria. "Can we drop you?"

"No. I drove."

Josh helped the women with their coats. He gave Kristi's mom a hug and said, "Thank you again. The painting means more to me than you'll ever know."

"I'm glad, Josh. Kristi was hoping it would suit you."

He took Kristi's hand. "Like nothing ever has before."

*

Wilhelm returned a week earlier than expected. He came by Kristi's office on his first day back. "Joshua tells me you did a fine job while I was gone. I appreciate your taking over so many of my duties."

"You're welcome. I'm happy your mother is doing so much better."

"Thank you. There was a message from Dr. Bailey in my voicemail. He's coming by to meet with me at ten. I'd like you to be there."

"I'm sure it's because…" she began, but he stopped her.

"No matter. We'll sort it out when he arrives."

Dr. and Mrs. Bailey were both in Wilhelm's office when Kristi walked in an hour later. She greeted them and sat in the only vacant chair. Her stomach churned as though she'd swallowed a bowl of molten lava.

"Now," Wilhelm said, looking at Rebecca's father, "tell me the problem."

"This young lady," Dr. Bailey said, nodding toward Kristi, "has been working behind our backs, trying to convince Rebecca to have her wedding on a *beach*." He said the word as if he were spitting sand.

"Is that right, Kristi?"

"Not exactly. She asked me for an opinion, and I gave it to her."

"What was that opinion?"

"That I personally would fight for the kind of wedding and reception that I wanted, if it were different from my parents' vision."

Wilhelm looked at Dr. Bailey. "Seems reasonable to me. Why do you find that objectionable?"

Kristi's jaw dropped like a heavy anchor had caught the corner of her mouth. Had she heard him correctly?

"We want the reception here, as you well know," Bailey said.

"Rebecca's been telling you for more than six months that she doesn't want it here, Philip. Isn't it about time you listened?"

Bailey looked incredulous. "Are you telling me we can't have it here?"

"No. I'm telling you that it's Rebecca's wedding. Let her decide what suits her best. She's not a child, Philip."

Bailey stood, nearly knocking over his chair. "Wilhelm, I'm afraid the Princess has just lost a valuable client."

Wilhelm stood, sighing with the effort. "Better we lose a client, than you lose a daughter," he said, with more emotion than Kristi thought he possessed.

It was clear from his shocked look, that nobody had ever spoken to Dr. Bailey so candidly. He stormed out, his wife trailing him like a duckling.

Kristi stood, dumbfounded. "I don't understand."

Wilhelm shuffled some papers on his desk. Without looking up he said, "I had a good deal of spare time while I was in Germany. Distance can give one perspective, don't you agree?"

He peered up and gave her an awkward smile. "No matter. I think we won't see much more of the Baileys." He pointed to the chair. "If you have time, I'd like to hear more about the Bridal Ball."

CHAPTER 27

Kristi set her champagne glass down on Josh's coffee table and snuggled up next to him on the couch. Lightning blazed outside, splashing across the living room and rattling the windows. "That was close."

Josh held her tightly. "No worries. This apartment is guaranteed to withstand a category three hurricane."

"What happens in a four?"

He leaned close to her ear. "All hands abandon ship."

"I should have listened to mom. She warned me to wear my galoshes. At this rate, we may have to swim to work tomorrow."

"How did your meeting go with Wilhelm?"

"It was strange. First, he agreed with me about the Bailey reception. The doctor had a complete meltdown and stormed out. Then, as if nothing unusual had happened, Wilhelm asked me about the Bridal Ball. He wanted every detail. After all that resistance. I don't get it."

"Dad talked to him last night. Apparently seeing his mother so close to death had a profound effect. Dad called it an epiphany. Pretty prosaic for my father. Oh, and Dad told him about us. He thought it would be best to have that on the table. Anyway, Dad thinks life with Wilhelm will be much easier in the future."

"Ah. That explains it."

"What?"

"He insisted that *he'd* work the event. He said I should enjoy the evening, since I'd worked so hard to create it."

Rain pounded on the windows, cascading in endless sheets from a heavenly faucet. Kristi lifted her champagne glass toward Josh, and with as much optimism as she could muster, said, "Here's to a dry Bridal Ball."

"With any luck."

Kristi prayed Wilhelm's transformation was genuine, and not a way for him to ruin the evening he'd opposed so completely. Though not superstitious, Kristi couldn't shake the notion that something would still go wrong.

They'd paid little attention to the TV show they'd turned on, but a strident Sig Alert, and the words "Special Report" pierced their contentment.

Kristi felt her stomach tighten. "Oh, Lord. What's happened now?"

A somber-faced newscaster stood in front of a map of the California coastline. "Highway One north of Big Sur has been closed due to a massive mudslide. Alternate routes are necessary for travel in both directions." The map showed a broad swath of land that had been affected. "Emergency crews are on the scene. No injuries have been reported. The Highway Patrol has warned drivers to avoid the area."

"If this rain doesn't stop, half of California will end up in the ocean," Josh said.

"If it doesn't stop, the ball will be a soggy disaster; half of our brides will be arriving in their gowns."

The next day, reports of vast destruction dominated the news. The entire west coast was under attack by the weather front; stories from Los Angeles to Seattle told of devastating loss. Unfortunately, the rain was not expected to stop before the weekend. Kristi clung to the hope that there would be a break on Saturday night.

Late in the afternoon, her phone rang. She recognized the band leader's name on the display.

"Hi, Robert. What's up?"

"Kristi, I'm afraid I have some bad news."

She braced herself for words she'd been dreading. "What's wrong?"

"We're up in Oregon, at Crater Lake. We played for a big event here over the weekend."

He paused, and Kristi knew the shoe was about to drop.

"We're snowed in, Kristi. There's no way the bus can get us out. The storm is predicted to last through Saturday. We're stuck."

It took a few seconds for it to register. "Stuck?"

"We can't get out. I'm so sorry, Kristi. I've called every band leader I know; nobody is available. It's too late to book anyone for this weekend." He was quiet, and when she didn't reply, he said, "I'm really am sorry."

"You couldn't…"

"There's no way for us to leave. I talked to the local and state authorities. They all agree: we'll have to stay put until it's over, and even then, they'll have to dig us out."

Her mind swirled, and then crashed in despair. "Okay. Well, I guess we'll have to make do somehow."

"I'll send you a full refund, of course."

"Yes, thank you." She paused and then added, "Take care of yourselves."

"We will. I really am sorry, Kristi."

"I am, too."

She hung up, and stood.

Then she sat down again.

She pulled up the file of bands they had considered at the outset, and called every one.

None were available.

Not one.

She walked down the hall to Josh's office, her feet dragging in deep sea diver's boots.

He looked up from his computer. "Hi. What's up?"

The tears she'd barely been able to control, broke free.

"Kristi? What's wrong?" Josh rushed around to her. "What is it? Tell me."

For a moment, she couldn't speak. Then, with extraordinary effort she said, "The band is in Oregon, snowed in. They can't get out—they won't be here for the ball."

Josh reached back and pushed his office door closed. He pulled her to her feet, and wrapped his arms around her. "It's okay. Don't cry. There are other bands. We'll find someone who can play."

"No, we won't. I've called. Nobody is available. It's too late."

Despair wrapped around her lungs and squeezed. All this work, all this planning, all this preparation, all in ruins. The rain would ruin the ball. The beauty of live music, the music she'd fought so hard for, would not happen.

"It'll be okay, Kristi. I'll call around. Someone will know someone who'll be able to play."

She was desperate to believe him. "Do you think so?"

"Yes."

But, even Josh's optimism could not alter reality. Hiring a band four days before an event was impossible.

On Wednesday, he came to her office with a list in his hand. "These are the DJs Wilhelm says we've used in the past. Do you want to take a look?"

She shook her head.

"Do you want me to choose one?"

"If any of them can do it at this point, we'll be lucky."

"I'll check them out."

"Thank you," she said, her voice stripped of life.

After he left, Kristi faced the reality: Josh had wanted to use a DJ from the start, and it had come to that in the end.

Irony sucked.

She called Nicole to tell her. "Do you think we should announce it on the site?"

"No. We can explain the change that night. There's nothing we can do about it, so why make it a big deal?"

"It is a big deal, Nicole. A really big deal."

"People losing their houses in mudslides is a big deal, Kristi. Cars shoved over cliffs is a big deal. People separated from their families or work is a big deal. This is a disappointment, not a tragedy. Everyone will still have a delicious dinner, meet new friends, and dance all night, just as we planned. Everything will be fine."

Fine—but not magical.

Not wonderful.

Not the way she'd intended—just fine.

By Thursday, Kristi had put thoughts of the ball out of her mind. Thinking about it only made her miserable. Josh said he'd taken care of the music, and he thought she'd be pleased. Kristi doubted it, and wondered if couples would bother registering for the next year, if the first Bridal Ball were not an unparalleled event.

Nicole had been right; it wasn't a disaster. But, the Bridal Ball she'd envisioned was a Viennese ball, not a high school prom. As grand as love, as eternal as memory. Without the band…

*

JT called her on Friday afternoon. "The new programs are finally here. Do you want to see them?"

"Is everything correct?"

"Seems to be."

"I don't need to see them. Would you let Queenie know, so she has them for setup tomorrow?"

"Of course. We have quite a turnout for the dance class. Twenty-two couples."

"I hope they're fast learners."

He laughed, but it did nothing to lift her spirits.

"I've called the vendors who will have booths tomorrow night, and everyone is set. They'll unload at the dock and come up the service elevator."

"I think you've covered every possible contingency."

"Let's hope nothing else goes wrong."

"Nothing is going wrong, Kristi; it's just going differently."

He sounded just like Nicole. Of course, they were both right. "I know."

"The ball is going to be every bit as wonderful as you've imagined. I promise. You need to sit back and enjoy it."

"I appreciate that, sir. I'm sure you're right."

She and Josh had a quiet dinner on Fisherman's Wharf that night. Restaurant spotlights highlighted the heavy rain that pelted the water, splashing like hundreds of brilliant diamonds jumping into the sea.

"I heard the weather report earlier," Josh said.

"Tell me."

"There's a possibility of a break in the storm tomorrow afternoon."

"If there is, it'll restore my faith in miracles."

"We'll put up the runway tent anyway. The women will be covered from the moment they get out of their cars."

"What about the men?"

"They're on their own."

"Maybe we should have baskets of hairdryers in the men's rooms."

"You know, I have a feeling that the rain is going to stop, just for us."

""From your lips to the Lord's ears," Kristi said, then followed it with a silent, *Please*.

CHAPTER 28

Kristi prepared to step into her gown the next evening, and realized that there was no noise outside. No patter, no thunder, and no lightning. She peered out the window at a crescent moon floating in a crystal clear sky.

She almost started crying. *Thank you, Lord.*

After she dressed, she went downstairs to her mother's apartment. Victoria had attached her camera to a tripod, ready to take photos before Kristi and Josh left for the ball.

"You look beautiful, darling," her mother said, kissing her on the cheek. "You're right about the gown. It's perfect. And your up-do really shows off the lavalier."

Kristi had been uncertain about the dress. The one-shoulder, beaded bodice seemed too bare for midwinter. But the bouffant skirt was a heavy taffeta, and the soft rustling when she moved had charmed her. A matching, heavily lined stole would keep her warm when they weren't dancing. The color convinced her in the end—it matched the aquamarine stones in the necklace as if it had been designed for it.

She glanced at the camera. "You really need a tripod?"

"I haven't had any formal pictures of you since college. I thought it would be nice to take a few. Besides, I wanted an excuse to try out my new lens." She took several shots of Kristi perched on the arm of the couch. She scrolled through the pictures. "Josh might want one of these. They're lovely."

A car pulled up in front of the house and stopped.

"That'll be Josh." Butterflies fluttered in Kristi's stomach exactly like the night of her senior prom.

"I'd like three or four shots of you together," her mother said, taking the camera from the tripod, "but I need a different lens. I'll be back in a minute."

"Thanks." Her mother was giving her time to greet Josh privately.

She buzzed him in, and then opened the front door.

He stopped in the entry, holding her away from himself while he took in every detail. "You look stunning. Beautiful. Perfect."

She pulled him into the living room. "Stop. I can only take so much."

"The gown is dynamite. It was made for the lavalier. We have to get a picture so I can show Gran."

"She'll see…" Kristi caught herself. "…plenty of pictures. My mom practically has an album."

"I do not," her mother said from behind her. "But now that you mention it, let's see how many more I can take before you get annoyed."

Half an hour later, they pulled up in front of the hotel, the car's windshield miraculously dry.

"Aren't you going to park in the garage?" Kristi asked.

"You don't enter the Princess in that gown from the garage. The valet can park it."

Kristi wrapped the shawl around her shoulders as Josh got out of the car. She noticed him sending a text as he walked around to her door. What was that about?

The valet opened the door. "Good evening." He helped her out. "Have a nice time, Kristi," he said as she took Josh's arm.

THE BRIDAL BALL

When they entered the hotel, everyone in the grand foyer turned to look at them. Kristi counted eleven brides in various shades of white; she was the only one wearing a colorful gown.

Josh escorted her toward the ballroom, and Kristi heard music. Not a recording. Real music. They walked through the arched doorway and a singer began to croon, "The Way You Look Tonight."

Kristi's mouth dropped open and her heart exploded in bliss.

Two rows of musicians from the Cal Band sat on a stage at the far end of the room, dressed in black slacks, white tux shirts, and blue cummerbunds, the stands in front of them laden with sheet music. Zeb turned briefly, smiled, and waved.

"Oh Josh…" was all Kristi could manage. Her throat constricted and tears, like warm raindrops, splashed on her shawl.

He pulled her close, his arm warm and loving. "I told you everything would be fine."

"You did. You made it happen."

Music filled the room and happiness filled her heart.

"Thank you, Josh."

"My pleasure."

From behind Kristi heard, "Good evening."

They turned to JT and Rose, resplendent in a tux and wedding gown.

"Gran!" Josh cried. "Look at you." He hugged her.

JT said, "Kristi, you look beautiful tonight."

"Yes," Rose agreed. "That gown is just what the lavalier needed. You look lovely, my dear."

"So do you," Kristi said. "Your wedding dress is beautiful." Typical of the late fifties, the long, lace-covered gown was modest—full skirted, with a sweetheart neckline, and long sleeves that tapered to delicate points on her hands.

"I'll have to be careful I don't fall and break my neck," Rose confided to Kristi. "I was not only taller when I got married, I was wearing heels."

"Don't worry, Mom," JT said, "we'll pass on the Bunny Hop."

"Kristi!"

She turned again. "Hi, Georgia; hi, Wyatt."

"Hey there, Georgie girl," Josh said, "nice to see you can still fit into your dress."

Georgia gave him a look and a short shove. "Come along. Laura and Nicole are already at the table."

"We're all together?"

"Of course." Georgia leaned close to Kristi, making no attempt to lower her voice. "I have some pull with the owner."

Georgia led them through a sea of black and white, to the table nearest the band. Pristine white tablecloths draped gracefully to the floor, accented by deep crimson napkins, and floral arrangements like bridal bouquets, in crimson and white chrysanthemums.

Hundreds of twinkle lights wrapped in white tulle hung behind the band; 5' wide light curtains had been placed around the ballroom at even intervals, infusing the room with a soft glow.

"Since you'll be speaking, it made sense to be in front," Georgia told her.

Laura jumped up when Kristi reached the table. "Oh Kris, that gown is beautiful."

Kristi hugged her. "You look as lovely as you did on your wedding day."

"Thank you for this. I can't tell you how happy I am."

"I'm glad."

Nicole looked her up and down, smiled, and said, "Perfect."

"How about some champagne?" Wyatt asked.

"I'd love it," Kristi said.

The men left for the bar, and Kristi took time to look around the room. Four tables had complete wedding parties: one bride and women in colorful matching gowns.

She noticed an Asian woman in a beautiful, bright red gown trimmed in gold, and remembered reading that one registrant planned to wear a traditional Chinese dress.

When they each had a glass of champagne, Josh raised his and said, "Here's to my sweetheart's brilliant idea—the Bridal Ball."

"The Bridal Ball," the others said.

Laura looked at Kristi, tears pooling in her eyes. "Thank you. You made my dream come true."

*

After the cake had been served, Zeb took the microphone, and within moments, Kristi knew he was the perfect Master of Ceremonies.

"Welcome, ladies and gentlemen, to what we hope will be the first annual Bridal Ball. You've seen the website, you've read the stories, and tonight, you'll meet the principals—three women whose vision and passion have created this incredible event. It is my pleasure to introduce you to Kristi Peyton-Scott, Laura Fisher, and Nicole Jackson."

Kristi, Laura, and Nicole, walked to the bandstand.

"Congratulations, on this brilliant evening," Zeb said.

Kristi swallowed the tears that threatened to steal her voice. "Thank you, Zeb."

He handed her the microphone, and applause erupted. "Good evening, everyone. First, I'd like to thank you all for coming tonight. Without you, The Bridal Ball wouldn't be happening. Second, none of us would be here if it weren't for my friend, Laura. I'm sure you've all read her story, and know that's why we created this event."

Laura's shy smile reminded Kristi of the young girl, at her front door, demanding that they be best friends.

"And last, I am grateful for the ingenuity and creativity of our friend, Nicole, who designed the beautiful Bridal Ball website. All three of us have been touched by your posts, and we thank you for your willingness to share your stories. My hope is that this evening is so successful that we'll all meet again next year."

The room exploded in applause and shouts of, "Yes, yes."

Kristi handed the mic back to Zeb, and the three friends returned to their table, arm in arm.

"And now," Zeb said, "it's time for the Parade of Brides. You'll be invited to line up by table. Bring your introduction cards, and I'll do my best not to butcher any names."

It was a fashion show of bridal dresses through the ages: bouffant, straight, high-necked, low-cut, loose-flowing, princess, fit-and-flare; every imaginable style and shade of white was worn by someone in the parade.

Every bride handed her card to Zeb, who read her name and then, "escorted by," and her husband's name. Then, they proceeded across the dance floor, so everyone could appreciate each unique gown. Kristi recognized some names, but couldn't connect them with any of the stories.

I should've made a cheat sheet of every bride's story. Next year…

A few of the women stopped at their table to thank Kristi personally. Three had tears in their eyes and could barely croak out their thanks.

"Do you realize how amazing this is?" Georgia asked Kristi. "These women are in heaven. In giving Laura this gift, you've given it to all these other women as well.

"And," Wyatt said, "You've tapped an enormous market."

"I never imagined," Kristi said.

"I did," Nicole said. "It'll be even bigger next year."

Josh looked around the ballroom. "We can't accommodate too many more."

"You might have to hold two balls," Nicole said. "One in January and one in July."

Josh looked at Kristi. "Might have to," he said with a nod. "Might just have to."

When the last bride had crossed the room, Zeb said, "And now, the dance you've all been waiting for—the *first* dance. I'd like Laura Fisher and her husband, Ethan, to take the floor. Laura selected the song; it's the one they *would* have danced to on their wedding day."

"Our Love is Here to Stay," brought fresh tears to Kristi eyes. She never heard the song without thinking of the sad end to Laura's reception. Now, at last, the spell was broken.

"He can dance," Nicole whispered. "When did that happen?"

"He must have known the pressure would be on," Kristi said.

When the song was over, many in the ballroom applauded. Laura curtsied gracefully, and the two returned to their table. Kristi thought Laura might break into tears, but instead, she looked up at Ethan and said, "The bucket list is busted."

"Ladies and gentlemen," Zeb said, "I'm going to invite couples to the dance floor by the year they were married. We'll begin with Mrs. Townsend, who was married in nineteen fifty-eight. She chose the song, 'Unforgettable.'"

JT escorted Rose to the floor, put his arm around her waist, and kissed her forehead. "Ready?"

"I'm always ready to dance," she said.

And she was.

The crowd clapped as JT and Rose moved around the floor, a mother and son clearly accustomed to dancing together.

"Well done, Dad," Josh said as his father and grandmother danced by their table.

"All those married during the sixties," Zeb said, "are now invited to the floor."

Three couples joined JT and Rose.

"The seventies," Zeb said after a bit.

He continued until all the bridal couples were dancing.

It looked like a flurry of snowflakes, swirling, spiraling, spinning—each unique, each beautiful, each bride special in her own way. Kristi was touched by the myriad of smiles. The dream had come true. The brides were dancing. Her heart filled with such happiness she thought it might split open her chest.

"I trust the rest of us will get to dance sometime tonight," Josh said. "Giving Zeb a mic may have been a mistake."

"He's perfect," Kristi said. "Nobody could have done this better. Do you think he'll agree to play next year?"

"As long as it isn't during football season."

"The dance floor is now open to everyone," Zeb announced.

Josh took Kristi's hand. "Shall we?"

He escorted her to the dance floor, and put his arms around her. "I'm so proud of you. You were right. This was a fantastic idea."

She didn't hear any regret, and her last doubt dissolved. "I know you thought it was too soon. I know if you hadn't stepped in, we wouldn't have a band. Without the band…" Tears came to her eyes and she blinked them back. "The music was so important; everything hinged on that. I can't thank you enough for making it happen, Josh."

"You and I make a good team."

Sheer pleasure swept through her as they danced, skating around the room, an aqua blue ribbon weaving in and out through white eyelet.

She caught Laura's eye and saw tears.

"Thank you," Laura mouthed.

When the band took a break, Josh went to get them another glass of champagne.

A good-looking young man approached their table. "Excuse me, Miss Peyton-Scott?"

"Kristi. Please, call me Kristi."

"My wife would love to talk to you if you have a minute."

"Of course. Where is she?"

"We're sitting in the back. We danced a couple of times, but she doesn't have much stamina. She had chemo last year, and she's still getting back her strength."

"She wrote her story on our website."

"Yes."

"I'm so happy you were able to come. I was hoping I'd get to meet you."

She followed him to a table near the ballroom entrance, where a pale, thin young woman sat drinking hot tea. "Kristi, this is my wife, Allison." He touched her shoulder with tenderness. "I'll let you two talk."

Kristi pulled a chair close to her. "I'm so glad to meet you."

"Me, too. I wanted to thank you in person. What you did, what you gave me, I will always be grateful." Tears slid down her cheeks, and her voice stumbled. "You—you and your friends—got me through it."

"You chose a way to get yourself through, Allison. You're stronger than you realize. Your story touched us, and inspired so many other women. Everyone is impressed by your courage."

The woman was clearly exhausted. Kristi took her hand, which was thin and cold, but returned a firm grasp. "I hope we'll see you next year."

"We're coming. By then, I'll be strong, and I'm going to dance every dance."

As the evening progressed, more and more women stopped Kristi to thank her for creating the ball. Josh stood by her side, pleased by the admiration they showed.

"It's getting embarrassing," she told him. "I'm going to take a break. I hope the ladies' room isn't crowded."

"Take your time," he said.

She walked into the lounge, surprised to hear someone crying. She stepped around to the seating area, where a woman in a bridesmaid's dress, was wiping her eyes.

"Can I help?" Kristi asked, switching into work mode.

The girl looked up, startled.

"Lexi? Oh, my gosh, I had no idea you were here. What's wrong?" She sat beside her.

"It's nothing. I'm fine."

"It's obviously something. Please say it isn't Tori."

"It isn't Tori."

But, Kristi heard a strangeness in Lexi's voice that said otherwise.

A bride in a spectacular, designer gown peered around the corner. "Are you coming, Lex? David's waiting."

"In a minute," Lexi said.

"I'll give you five. If you're not back, I'm coming after you."

"Fine."

After the woman left, Kristi asked, "Who's David?"

Lexi took a breath that dragged nearly all the air from the room. "David is a mistake I made six years ago." She looked up at the ceiling as if the answer to a problem were hidden there. "This isn't the time for a discussion. Go back to the party. It's a lovely ball, Kristi. You did a fabulous job."

"Alright, I won't bug you. But, I'm going to call you next week. We're going to get together, okay?"

"Okay."

Kristi walked back to the table, wondering what kind of mistake Lexi had made six years before. She'd never heard

Lexi mention David, or any guy, for that matter. Lexi had been a single mom forever—well, for five years, anyway.

She found Josh talking to JT and Rose, and put Lexi out of her thoughts.

"It's time for me to call it a night," Rose said.

"Afraid you'll turn into a pumpkin, Gran?"

"I'm the one who's beat," JT said. "She could go on till dawn."

"True," Rose said. "Besides, I'm so excited about our trip, that I won't be able to sleep."

"Trip? What trip?" Josh asked.

"Your father is taking me on a round the world cruise." She smiled at JT. "It's something I've wanted to do for as long as I can remember. It was all those years on the docks, I think. Your dad has agreed to go with me."

Josh drew back, looking at his father in surprise. "Around the world?"

"Yes. I'm ready for a break. The Princess is in good hands. You don't need me hanging around anymore, Josh. It's time for you to take charge."

"But, I thought," Josh began.

Rose interrupted him. "Don't argue with your father, Josh."

Josh looked from Rose to JT. "I hardly know what to say."

"I thought I'd taught you better than that." Rose sounded like she was talking to a boy instead of the man who towered over her. "You say 'thank you,' and 'bon voyage'."

Josh put his arm around his father. "Thank you, Dad. I mean it. I hope you know that I'll do my best to make you proud."

"You already have, son."

As JT and Rose walked toward the door, the band started their final set. Josh stood stock still, and silent.

"Are you okay?" Kristi asked.

"I'm fine. I'm...shocked. This is so unexpected, particularly since the ball is obviously a success."

"I told you he was going to retire."

"You did. I seriously didn't believe it."

"Sort of like me doubting the ball would happen?"

"Yes, sort of like that."

"It's a huge thing, Josh. It's what you wanted. I'm happy for you. Congratulations."

He looked down at her, and Kristi could sense the depth of his happiness. "It's a brilliant night for both of us."

Georgia and Wyatt paused as they danced nearby. "Last set, you two. Don't waste the moment."

"She's right," Josh said. He put his arm around Kristi and they moved to the floor. It looked like a kaleidoscope in black and white, the dancers twirling like a ballet troupe.

Kristi closed her eyes as they danced, joy bubbling up inside, threatening to spill on to her cheeks. She swallowed the tears before she said, "This has been the most perfect night of my life. Nothing will ever compare."

"It fulfilled both of our dreams. But, it's set a standard, not exceeded every possibility. Let's leave a little hope for the future."

*

Kristi felt as though every light in the city lit their way home; everything sparkled, or glowed, or shone with a particular brightness she'd never noticed before.

Josh walked her up to her door. "Will you come in?"

"Yes. I'd like to talk for a minute."

"Okay."

Once in the living room, he lit the fire. "You don't mind, do you?"

"Of course not."

He took both her hands in his. "There's something I'd like to share with you."

His serious tone gave her a start. "What?"

"My life," he said tenderly. "In the short time we've known each other, you've made me happier than I ever could have imagined. I've laughed more—lived more—loved more—than I ever thought possible." His grip tightened. "I love you, Kristi. Will you marry me?"

There was no room left in her heart for any more joy; it burst with happiness. "Oh Josh, I love you too." Tears stopped her words. "Yes." she said. "Yes. Yes. Yes!"

He kissed her, his tears mingling with hers. "Next year, I want you to dance at the Bridal Ball in your wedding gown."

At the second Bridal Ball. "This night really is perfect."

"What about a glass of champagne?"

"Oh, Josh...I don't have any."

"Actually, you might. I asked your mom to put a bottle in the fridge."

"Mom?"

"Yes. I met her for lunch last Tuesday."

Kristi couldn't figure out why he looked so sad.

"If your father had been here, I would have asked his permission to marry you. Since he isn't, I wanted your mother's blessing."

Her heart filled with equal measures of joy and sorrow. Her father had missed so many events in her life. Josh had honored him, even in his absence.

"Did Mom give you her blessing?"

"I don't know. We'll have to check the fridge."

THE END

Also by Linda McGinnis

Sweet Refrain series: Six young women become roommates at Willette College in the late fifties, and spend the next four years learning about friendship, life, tragedy, and love.

Till I Kissed You
Devoted to You
Let It Be Me
Love Of My Life

Cloud Dancer series: A California girl spends three summers on a Pueblo and falls in love with a handsome, enigmatic young Pueblo Indian.

Pueblo Summer
Second Summer
Summer Ghost
Summer Vows

Dreams of Home
Chronicles the struggles of two Japanese families in Hawaii during World War II.

The Bridal Ball series: Love, friendship, and a dream come true.

The Bridal Ball

Coming soon

The Bridesmaid's Waltz (The Bridal Ball 2)
The Best Man's Two-Step (The Bridal Ball 3)

When not writing,
Linda enjoys traveling, photography,
and quilting.

Visit her on the web at:
LindaMcGinnis.com

Made in the USA
Las Vegas, NV
19 December 2022